W9-BEF-138

THE MARLENE DIETRICH MURDER CASE

Previous Novels by George Baxt:

The Noel Coward Murder Case

The Greta Garbo Murder Case

The Talking Pictures Murder Case

Who's Next?

The Tallulah Bankhead Murder Case

Satan Is a Woman

The Alfred Hitchcock Murder Case

The Dorothy Parker Murder Case

Process of Elimination

The Neon Graveyard

Burning Sappho

The Affair at Royalties

"I!" Said the Demon

Topsy and Evil

A Parade of Cockeyed Creatures

Swing Low, Sweet Harriet

A Queer Kind of Death

THE MARLENE DIETRICH MURDER CASE

BY GEORGE BAXT

St. Martin's Press
New York

THE MARLENE DIETRICH MURDER CASE Copyright © 1993 by George Baxt. All rights reserved. Printed in the United States of America. No part of this book may be used or reproduced in any manner whatsoever without written permission except in the case of brief quotations embodied in critical articles or reviews. For information, address St. Martin's Press, 175 Fifth Avenue, New York, N.Y. 10010.

Design by Basha Zapatka

Library of Congress Cataloging-in-Publication Data

Baxt, George.
    The Marlene Dietrich murder case / George Baxt.
        p.   cm.
    ISBN 0-312-09334-9
    1. Dietrich, Marlene—Fiction. 2. Women detectives—Califor-
nia—Los Angeles—Fiction. 3. Hollywood (Los Angeles, Calif.)—
Fiction. I. Title.
PS3552.A8478M37   1993
813'.54—dc20   93-21737
                                                              CIP

First edition: May 1993

10 9 8 7 6 5 4 3 2 1

for
Robert Fletcher
and
Jack Kauflin

we remember the same things

⦇ ONE ⦈

MARLENE DIETRICH'S KITCHEN in her rented Beverly Hills mansion was a masterpiece of modern design. It was the kitchen that cemented her decision to rent the house. She had left Germany for the United States a month earlier and arrived in New York on April 9, 1930. After a whirlwind week of newspaper interviews, newsreel interviews, radio interviews, and being wined and dined by Adolph Zukor, who ruled Paramount Pictures (Marlene's new employers), with an iron fist, she had settled with a sigh of exhaustion and a sigh of relief into her first-class compartment on the Twentieth Century Limited.

A Hollywood star. The fantasy a reality. The dream come true. The script of her first American film, *Morocco*, on the seat next to her. Costarring with Gary Cooper and Adolphe Menjou. Gary Cooper. How she longed to sleep with Gary Cooper. Rudy wouldn't mind. Her husband, Rudolf Sieber wouldn't mind at all. He was content living with his mistress, Tamara Matul. Marlene was glad he was content. She was glad he had Tamara to love and amuse him. Marlene and Rudy had married six years earlier, and a year later she gave birth to her adored daughter, Heidede, more frequently called Maria.

This magnificent kitchen. For five days after arriving in Hollywood, accompanied by a Paramount representative, she had hunted for an appropriate house. Josef von Sternberg cautioned her, "Don't rent too expensive a place. Don't sign a long lease. If *Morocco* fails and you fail with it, they'll send you back to Germany."

Fat chance, she said to herself. She was a European smash in von Sternberg's *The Blue Angel*. She could act, she could sing in a voice husky with the seductiveness of the sirens of the Rhine. She projected a subtle eroticism and an exotic sexiness that appealed to both men and women. Fail? Me? Marlene? Lucie Mannheim and Brigitte Helm were two of Germany's biggest stars, but they lost Lola-Lola in *The Blue Angel* to me. Von Sternberg favored me over them, even though I was too heavy and needed to lose twenty pounds. But the way I looked at him at our first meeting, the look that promised everything but didn't deliver anything until I had a signed contract. Fail? Me? *Morocco* was a smash hit, a sensation. Dressed in a tuxedo in a nightclub in North Africa, I dared wrap my hands around a woman's face and kiss her full on the lips. I could hear the rest of the company on the soundstage gasp. Those sharp intakes of breath. The dark look on von Sternberg's face as he lit a cigarette. And my audacious query, "Didn't you like it? Shall I do it again? I can make it more suggestive." He kept the scene in the film. He knew it would give Marlene her much sought after celebrity, and it did.

And then *The Blue Angel* was rushed into American release and Frederick Hollander's "Falling in Love Again," which she sang with a contemptuous cynicism that would become her trademark, became her signature. And now she had her magnificent kitchen. What the world did not yet know was that this glamorous mother preferred to cook and bake and concoct exquisite soups, stirring the pot with the enthusiasm of one of the three witches in *Macbeth*. Marlene reigned in the kitchen, and today, so did chaos.

"I smell something burning," said Anna May Wong, who was noshing on a plate of pickled herring.

Marlene hurried to one of her four stoves while brandishing a pot holder. She moved a pan of codfish balls from the flame and stirred the contents with a large spoon.

"They're fine, they'll be okay," she said with a small smile. There were five other cooks in the kitchen and all exchanged knowing glances. Had one of them come close to burning something, he or she would have been banished into culinary exile. Tonight was Marlene's big night. Over one hundred people invited to join her in welcoming the New Year, 1932. Nineteen thirty-one had been a glorious year. *Morocco*, *The Blue Angel*, and *Dishonored*, in which she again scored as a German spy based on the exploits of the notorious, albeit somewhat dumpy, Mata Hari. And now, with von Sternberg directing her for the fourth time in succession, she had completed her most erotic and suggestive film to date, *Shanghai Express*, in which she and Anna May Wong were a pair of extraordinarily unusual prostitutes who murder a Chinese warlord.

Anna May said, "Why don't you let these professionals do the cooking," gesturing to the five cooks, who awaited an explosion from Dietrich.

Marlene abandoned the codfish balls and pushed an errant strand of hair back into place. "Who said they're not cooking? There's plenty for them to do." She faced them with hands on hips. "Don't you have plenty to do?" The five busied themselves while Marlene continued, striving hard to overcome her tendency to supplant *r*'s with *w*'s. "Now really! All I'm cooking are my specialties. I am famous for my specialties." Anna May nodded in silent agreement. "Everybody in Hollywood looks forward to my specialties." And again Anna May nodded in tacit agreement. Specialties were indeed Dietrich's specialty. "Those codfish balls are a Scandinavian delicacy. A recipe handed down from the Vikings."

Anna May stuffed a cigarette into a holder decorated with jade chips. "I didn't know the Vikings were famous for their cuisine. I thought all they did was pillage and rape women."

"In between they ate," said Marlene with her usual logic. She pulled a chair to Anna May's side and sat. "Why don't you finish the herring?" Marlene chewed on a radish. Anna May blew a smoke ring. "What's bothering you?"

"Not working is what's bothering me. How many parts are there for Chinese women? And when there is one, it's played by Myrna Loy, who is from Helena, Montana, which is hardly a Chinese province.

"Nineteen thirty-two will be better. Mercury is leaving retrograde and the New Moon will bring a series of offers for you to work. Jupiter will be entering your house."

"He doesn't have a key. I'm thinking of going back to Europe. I was doing great in films and the theater until Paramount sent for me for *Daughter of the Dragon*." She added morosely, "That and *Shanghai Express* is all I've done in almost two years, besides redecorating my apartment house."

"Don't you own that apartment house?"

"Yes, but it's not a very big one."

"It's not the size that counts."

"All the apartments are occupied by friends and relatives, so I can't charge too much rent."

"Why not? Don't be victimized by parasites! Anyway, Carroll Richter predicts a wonderful 1932." Carroll Richter was making a fortune as astrologer to the stars and much of that fortune came from Dietrich. "You mark his words. Next year your ship will come in."

"I'm beginning to think my ship did come in but forgot to unload its cargo."

"What you really need is a love affair."

"That's all you seem to think about."

"It's such pleasant thinking. Now I shall prepare my Bavar-

4

ian meatballs à la Schumann-Heink. I got the recipe from the great soprano. I've improved on it. I use chopped sirloin, not cheap chuck." A thought struck her. "Anna May, last April, when I came back from Germany with Rudolf and little Maria, we met this French actor on the train."

"I think you told me about him."

"Maybe I did. His name is Raymond Souvir."

"That doesn't sound familiar."

"Very handsome. Very charming. He must be very rich, I think. He lives very lavishly. He's coming to the party."

"And you plan to introduce us."

"Of course I do, but I have no ulterior motive, I assure you." She was quartering a sirloin steak and then subdividing the quartered sections. "He travels with a very select group, all European for the most part except for Dorothy di Frasso."

"I should have guessed the Countess di Frasso would have gotten her claws into him."

"Oh, Dorothy's not so bad. She's just pushy. Just a clever American girl who managed to marry into Italian nobility and walk off with a lot of her husband's wealth after she divorced him."

"She still doing it with Gary Cooper?"

Marlene shrugged. "It's too exhausting trying to guess who Gary's doing it to these days. Di Frasso or Lupe Velez, or this society girl he's been squiring, Sandra something." She was dropping chunks of sirloin into a grinder and pulverizing them. She resembled a cameraman the way she diligently ground away, and Anna May marveled at the contented expression on Marlene's face. Here was a true *Hausfrau*, if only she weren't so eaten up by ambition. "Anyway, Raymond is bringing a Chinese musician, a violinist. Now let me see, his name is Ding Dong something."

"Dong See," corrected Anna May.

"You know him?"

"Marlene," Anna May underlined her name with exaggerated patience, "Dong See is internationally famous."

"Well I never heard of him."

"I can't understand how come! He's appeared to great acclaim in all the capitals of the world."

"If he played in Berlin, then it had to be after I left. Anyway, he'll be here tonight; maybe you'll like each other."

"You mean because we're both Chinese?"

"Oh, for crying out loud, Anna May, from the time we met and became friends, I haven't been able to fathom your taste in anybody. You think Clive Brook is a bore."

"He is. Don't you agree? Those few love scenes you did with him in *Shanghai Express*, I expected icicles to form on your lips."

"You're right. He's a cold fish. But very charming. And what about Herbert Marshall? I saw him flirt with you at Ronald Colman's party. Does the fact that he only has one leg put you off?"

"Not at all. I think he'd be nice to have around if I needed to touch wood."

"What are you looking for in a man?" asked Dietrich with exasperation.

"I'm not looking for a man!"

"Then what *are* you looking for?"

"A job!"

Police Inspector Herbert Villon sat at his desk flipping through the pages of *Picture Play* magazine. Seated in a chair opposite him, Hazel Dickson, who enjoyed the dubious profession of selling gossip to newspapers, magazines, and their columnists, attacked a fingernail with an emery board. She heard Villon saying, "Oooh, what I'd like to do to Helen Twelvetrees."

"That's one of the things I like about you, Herb. You know, like the way you suck your teeth and clean your nails with toothpicks. I'm the lady who's generous with her favors, in return for which I get the occasional dinner, a couple of drinks, an invitation to the Policeman's Ball, and 'Ooooh, what I'd like to do to Helen Twelvetrees or Barbara Stanwyck or Ginger Rogers or Ruth Chatterton. . . ."

"Not Ruth Chatterton," said Villon, now ogling a photograph of Sally Eilers, "too old."

"I wish Chatterton could hear you say that so I could hear her sigh of relief. Will you put that damn magazine down and answer the question?"

"What question?"

"The one I asked you before you zeroed in on Twelvetrees. Are you wearing a tuxedo tonight?"

"Why?"

"What do you mean 'Why'? I'm taking you to Dietrich's big bash tonight. It's the most sought after invitation in town! Two dozen parties were canceled when Marlene announced she was giving hers."

Villon lowered the magazine. "You're chummy enough to call her Marlene?"

Hazel moved on to another nail, another enemy she assailed with vigor. "The last time I interviewed her she cooked me a Wiener schnitzel."

"Do tell."

"Don't be so snotty."

"I'm not being snotty. I'm being impressed. I'm even jealous. I'd like Marlene to cook something special for me too."

"Wear your tuxedo and make a good impression tonight and maybe she will."

"Do you think Helen Twelvetrees will be there?"

"How do I know?"

"Did Dietrich really invite you or are we crashing as usual?"

"Personal invitation by phone." She shifted in her chair. "She likes me. I don't peddle gossip about her."

"And how come you don't?"

"Because I genuinely like her. She's a great gal. With her, all that glamour stuff is a put-on. She thinks it's a big nothing. The only thing she likes about it is the money. She pulls down a hundred and fifty thousand a picture; where does that hit you?''

"If she wasn't already married I'd propose. And what about him living in Switzerland with a mistress?''

"It don't bother Dietrich, it don't bother me. Let me put it to you this way. I know plenty of dirt about her. Plenty of *real* dirt. But I ain't selling it to nobody. Let the others trade in on her. I value her liking me. She got me in good with Claudette Colbert where before Claudette would never talk to me, only to Florabel Muir of the Daily News Syndicate.''

"So now it's Claudette.''

"Well, you don't expect me to call her Shirley, do you?'' She placed the emery board into her handbag, placed the handbag on his desk, folded her arms, which meant she meant business, fixed him with a firm look, and asked, "What about the tuxedo?''

"I'm a cop, honey. Cops don't wear tuxedos.''

"What do they wear besides a sneer on their lips or a coffin?''

Villon lowered the magazine. He favored her with a sweet smile. "Hazel, why'd I ever get mixed up with you?''

"I'm not sure, Herb. I thought it was my mother you were after.''

"She's got great gams for an old broad.''

"The tuxedo, Herb. I blew a month's salary on a Coco Chanel.''

"Maybe after the party you can hock it.''

"Go to hell.''

"I can't. We're going to Dietrich's party. And stop looking daggers at me. I'm wearing the tuxedo, okay?'' She favored him with a look of contentment. "What real dirt you got on Marlene?''

"That's for me to know and you to never find out.''

"What about her astrologer, Carroll Richter?''

"What about him?''

"He must have plenty on her.''

"What makes you think that?''

"His crystal balls!''

* * *

In Marlene's kitchen, where she was now preparing several baking pans of apple strudel, Anna May was sipping a cup of tea and marveling at Dietrich's industry. It was a warm day outside and the kitchen was overheated. One of the butlers had opened all the windows and another had set up floor fans, which gave some relief to everyone working in the rooms. But the ovens were ablaze and would stay ablaze to keep the food warm through the party. Marlene was telling Anna May how an astrologer in Berlin, an Egyptian, had predicted she would have to cross a vast expanse of water before achieving true fame and fortune. And here she was.

"It's amazing."

"His prediction?"

"The way you believe in astrology."

"Don't you? The Chinese and the Egyptians were the first great practitioners of astrology."

"My grandfather was an astrologer, as a matter of fact. And he was pretty damn good at it. When Doug Fairbanks was looking for a girl to play the treacherous Chinese maid in his *Thief of Bagdad*, I was dying for a chance to audition but I thought he'd think I was too young. I was only fourteen. But my grandfather had my chart done for me and he said, 'You will play that part.' And I did."

"There, you see?" She shouted to no one in particular, "I need more white raisins!" and very quickly they materialized on the table where she was working. Anna May was deep in thought. Marlene caught her look and offered her a penny for her thoughts.

Anna May said, "My very good friend Mai Mai Chu. She's the astrologer who did my chart. Shall I ask her to the party? She's very very good. All the bankers and investment brokers swear by her. She predicted the '29 market crash."

"Oh yes?"

"My mother and her mother were great friends. Mai Mai lived in Paris for a decade or more. She knew the literary set. Hemingway, Fitzgerald, Sylvia Beach, all that gang. My mother suspected she might have been a spy for the Allies during the war."

"I wish I'd known that. She could have given me some tips for my part in *Dishonored*."

"She's been asked to work with Garbo."

"On what? Greta's doing a spy movie?"

"Don't you read the trades? She's doing *Mata Hari*."

Dietrich smiled and winked. "I got there first."

Anna May was crossing the kitchen to a wall phone. "I'm going to call Mai Mai now. If she's free, I'm sure she'll agree to come."

Mai Mai Chu was a petite woman of an unguessable age and delicately pretty features who lived in an elegantly furnished loft apartment on the perimeter of Chinatown. She was lighting incense in a little glass tumbler before a statue of Buddha. As smoke started curling out from the incense, Mai Mai said to Buddha, "Anna May Wong is phoning me." The phone rang. Mai Mai smiled. She said into the mouthpiece, "Hello, Anna May. So nice to hear from you."

"You're putting me on!"

"You know better than that. I sensed you and that's that. I've also been sensing Eleanor Roosevelt. I sent her a note assuring her her husband would win the Democratic nomination for president. And he's going to win. Actually, if they ran Rex the Wonder Horse opposite Herbert Hoover he'd also win. Nice people, the Roosevelts, but his mother's a harridan. I visited them at her Hyde Park estate this past September. Tastelessly furnished. What time is the party?"

"I don't believe this!" Anna May said to Dietrich, "She answered the phone with 'Hello, Anna May; so nice to hear from you' and now she asks, 'What time is the party'!"

Marlene was fascinated. "I'll have my car pick you both up."

"Wonderful. I hate driving on New Year's Eve." Anna May and Mai Mai agreed that the car would first pick up Anna May and then come for Mai Mai at her building on the outskirts of Chinatown. After a moment's silence, Mai Mai said, "There could be danger."

Anna May paled. "What kind of danger?" This drew Dietrich to Anna May's side, holding a glass of champagne and puffing anxiously on a cigarette. Anna May's hold on the telephone had tightened.

Mai Mai said, "The instruments of danger are a group of Miss Dietrich's guests."

Anna May repeated this to Marlene, who gave no reaction.

"Just a minute," said Mai Mai. She placed the receiver down on the table and pressed her delicate fingertips against her temples.

Marlene was disquieted. "What's wrong? Why aren't you talking? Has she hung up?"

"No no. She's done this before. She's probably placed the receiver on the table while she presses her fingertips against her temples. She does this when she needs to release tension."

Mai Mai returned. "It is nothing. Anna May, shall I expect you around nine?"

"Yes, I'll be there promptly at nine."

After she replaced the receiver, with delicate mincing steps, Mai Mai Chu wafted to her crystal ball, which rested on a purple velvet–covered cushion on a small table handcarved from ivory. She looked into the crystal ball and asked, "What shall I wear tonight?"

"Danger," whispered Marlene. And then her face was aglow, "How exciting!"

"Danger from some of your guests." Anna May's eyes were dark with foreboding.

"That is quite possible," said Marlene as she refilled her glass with champagne and filled another for Anna May, "I've invited the Marx Brothers."

⟪ TWO ⟫

IVAR TENSHA'S CUSTOM-BUILT orange Rolls-Royce smoothly made its way toward Marlene Dietrich's New Year's Eve party. To Tensha, it was like floating on a magic carpet to the palace of an Oriental potentate. He knew a lot of Oriental potentates, but he couldn't think of one as exotic and as glamorous as the glorious Marlene. He sat in the back of the magnificent machine with Countess Dorothy di Frasso and Monte Trevor, a self-styled film producer from Great Britain. The portable bar was well stocked with champagne, a brand bottled in France exclusively for Ivar Tensha. His signature was on the label. Nothing was too good or too expensive for Ivar Tensha, the Romanian munitions czar.

"Ivar, you have a very silly expression on your face," said di Frasso. Trevor was refilling their glasses. He didn't spill a drop, so smooth was the drive.

"I was thinking of Marlene," he said with a heavily accented voice.

"Marlene deserves better than a silly expression. Don't you agree, Monte?"

"I wish I could get her for a movie," said Trevor, "I dream of casting her as *Salome*."

"*Salome,*" whispered Tensha, "the dance of the seven veils." Di Frasso expected drool to seep from his mouth, but none was forthcoming.

"And as Herod," continued Trevor, "I see this young actor Paramount has brought over from London, Charles Laughton."

Di Frasso agreed. "That would be very interesting. You'll need someone sexy for John the Baptist. How about Gable?"

"Dietrich and Gable. Now wouldn't that be a fascinating combination." Tensha licked his lips. If he wasn't so damned rich, thought di Frasso, he'd be repulsive. She wondered if there was a Mrs. Tensha, and if so, how to get rid of her.

Said Monte Trevor, "Louis B. Mayer doesn't lend his stars without driving a hard bargain."

"Whatever the money," said di Frasso, "it would be worth it for Gable. He's hot box office."

Tensha spoke softly. "I can get anything I want from Louis B. Mayer." Di Frasso thought she detected menace in that simple statement. Monte Trevor thought, here I am in the backseat of a Rolls-Royce owned by one of the world's wealthiest men, a man who seems to be actually buying my bullshit of producing a film about Salome. Maybe he's interested in putting up the money. I could budget it for two million and walk away with half a million for myself. That's how Alexander Korda operates in England, that shrewd Hungarian.

Trevor heard di Frasso saying, "Monte, your lips are moving but no sounds emerge. Are you all right?"

"Oh quite, quite my dear. I was just formulating a budget for *Salome* off the top of my head."

"Is that where you keep your money?"

Trevor laughed, but not heartily. This woman is dangerous, he thought, I wouldn't want her for an enemy. "I think *Salome* needs to be done on a lavish scale. The way Cecil B. DeMille would do it."

"How lavish?" asked Tensha.

"Roughly I'd say two million."

"Dollars?"

"He doesn't mean dinars," said di Frasso flatly.

"Even if it was dinars, it would be too much," said Tensha, who proceeded to light a cigar that to di Frasso resembled a miniature torpedo. Tensha's cigars were made especially for him in Cuba from tobacco grown on his own subsidized farm fifty miles outside Havana. The cigar bands of course carried Tensha's signature.

Trevor felt himself deflating, but he persisted as any good con artist would. "Don't you find the prospect of being involved with motion pictures exciting?"

"War pictures. I like war pictures!" Tensha's eyes were ablaze with fervor. "Bombs. Bullets. All calibers. Blood. Lots of blood. Maimed and mangled bodies. Explosions. Soldiers trembling and quivering on barbed wire. Women sobbing and screaming as their children are swept with machine-gun fire."

Di Frasso commented dryly, "I'm sure Monte plans on some spears and a few flaming arrows and perhaps a catapult or two hurling rocks onto parapets."

Tensha made a vulgar noise. "Too tame. By me, *Salome* is salami."

Trevor said in a tiny voice he didn't recognize as his own, "But what about the dance of the seven veils?"

Di Frasso interrupted. "Perhaps she could do it during the Battle of the Marne?"

"That," said Tensha, "could be very interesting."

"Yes!" said Trevor enthusiastically, "for each veil she sheds, she shoots an officer."

"From the hip?" asked di Frasso.

Trevor glared at her. She was busy renewing her face. They were almost at their destination. The cigar smoke was causing her eyes to tear. She asked Trevor to lower a window. While carefully rouging her lips, she eyed the chauffeur, who was staring at her in the rearview mirror. Not that young, thought the chauffeur, but what the hell. If she could be a ticket to a screen test. Gable got to where he is by using older women,

14

Pauline Frederick, Alice Brady, Jane Cowl. His first wife who taught him all he'd ever know about acting, Josephine Dillon, was twenty years older. And his current wife, Rhea, she's at least fifteen years older and rich to boot. His eyes sent di Frasso an unsubtle signal. She rewarded him with a raised eyebrow, which she hoped he recognized meant she was lowering her guard.

"My dear," she heard Tensha saying, "never with the hired help. It is so bourgeois."

She replied with a smile, "And where did you get the impression I'm descended from landed gentry?"

"My guests will be arriving any minute now!" shouted Marlene in her magnificent ballroom. "You must hurry!" She was yelling at a workman atop a ladder fixing clusters of balloons to the ceiling. His was the last to be set in place. At a signal, all the clusters of balloons affixed to the ceiling would fall at midnight. She had borrowed technicians from the studio to set up the electrical system that would release the balloons at the touch of a button. Her maid Gloria was urging her to return to her suite and finish dressing. Marlene waved her away impatiently as she spoke to the orchestra leader. "Not too many waltzes! Waltzes are for Marie Dressler's parties. And when I make my entrance down the stairs . . ."

"I have a magnificent arrangement of 'Falling in Love Again,' " said Gus Arnheim, the orchestra leader whose usually hefty fee she had beaten down to scale for him and his musicians. After all, wasn't it a privilege to play at Dietrich's party?

"No!" she boomed. "For my entrance you will play 'There'll Be a Hot Time in the Old Town Tonight'!"

Arnheim blanched. "We don't have the sheet music."

Dietrich bristled. "You're musicians, aren't you? You're professionals, aren't you? You can improvise! Improvise! Start rehearsing!" She hurried away to check the trays of hot and cold hors d'oeuvres stacked in the pantry.

Arnheim commanded, "Okay, boys, let's give the lady

what she wants." The drummer made a nasty noise, to which Arnheim said, "You'll never give her that."

Somewhere on a bumpy road in Benedict Canyon, a tired Hispano-Suiza dreaming of an imminent retirement after too many years of service coughed and chugged its way to Dietrich's party. The chauffeur prayed the old veteran would make it back to the Russian Embassy before breaking down. In the backseat, Gregory Ivanov, one of Russia's most skillful diplomats, held his wife's calloused hand. Natalia Ivanov had worked on a collective farm outside Minsk, where she guided tractors and maneuvered ploughshares and hoed and raked and seeded until her arm muscles were the envy of every male comrade she had bedded with unrestrained alacrity. The Russian word for 'nymphomaniac' is much too complicated, but Natalia was too simpleminded to be bothered by complications. On an official visit to her collective while Gregory Ivanov was still a small cog in the vast Bolshevik wheel, Ivanov took one look at her tensors and her threatening breasts and it was love at first sight. With the not-so-little woman behind him and pushing, he soon made his way into the diplomatic corps and rose rapidly to the top, like cream in a bottle of unpasteurized milk. There was no end to his ambitions, and wangling his post in Los Angeles by betraying three of his closest friends and his mother, who wrote odes to wheat and scythes, was just the beginning of the progression of his own five-year plan.

Natalia grunted.

"What bothers you?" asked Gregory Ivanov.

"I will look like a gnarled oak tree in a room full of movie stars."

"If so, Natalia Ivanova, then you will be an original. Movie stars! Poo! With their perfect bodies and their lacquered nails and their coiffured hair, can they compare to you?"

"No," she said darkly, "because I'm a mess."

"I love you the way you are, my beloved. Warts and all."

"I'm homesick."

"I know. But we can't leave until I have finished . . . you know."

She nodded. Although they spoke in Russian and the chauffeur was a college student who was hired because he claimed he didn't understand Russian, they trusted no one. But soon, if all went according to plan, he whispered to her, "We will rule the world."

She snuggled against his chest and smiled, revealing a row of brown stumps that passed for teeth. The chauffeur wondered as he stared at her in the rearview mirror if she enjoying gnawing tree bark.

Dietrich stood in front of a floor-length mirror, admiring the silver lamé dress designed for her for this occasion by Paramount's Travis Banton. Its line was simple and majestic. The neckline was trimmed with mink. Gloria, the maid, adjusted the mirror and Marlene admired the back of the dress. It was cut to the base of her spine, daringly sexy. She didn't need a brassiere. Her breasts were arrogantly firm. It would be years before they'd need an adjustment. She would wear no jewelry. She had no need to. She was a sun that had no need of satellites.

"Madam, you are exquisite," said Gloria.

"I know." Gloria was in her midtwenties and said she aspired to nothing but a husband, children, and a small house at the beach, any beach. She had been an extra in the nightclub scene in *Morocco* and caught Dietrich's attention when the star saw Gloria move another extra out of the way of an arc light that made Dietrich look five years younger. Dietrich was impressed, struck up a conversation with the girl, and offered her the job as her maid. Gloria was thrilled and accepted at once. Although she tended to shout a lot and raise her voice and demand perfection in everything, underneath it all Marlene was Mother Earth. She was kind to the people who served her and her daughter, and her generosity was legend. It was predicted by her advisers she would die a pauper, a prediction she responded to with a shrug. She believed in herself. She would always overcome adversity. After all, wasn't she the only movie star in the world who could play a musical saw? Darling Igo Sym, he said she was his best pupil. She toyed with the idea of regaling her guests with a few selections tonight, but then tabled the idea as they might find it unsophisticated.

"Gloria . . ."

"Yes, Miss Dietrich?"

"Pour two glasses of champagne." She indicated the cooler that contained a chilled bottle of Dom Perignon of a vintage year. "I want us to greet the New Year now, alone. Go on. Pour them."

"Oh, Miss Dietrich!"

"Don't be silly, Gloria. I am a mere mortal, but don't you ever tell Garbo."

"You're driving too fast!" yelled Dong See. "Slow down, for crying out loud, you'll kill us!"

Raymond Souvir maneuvered the white Cadillac through the tricky and threatening curves of Malibu Canyon Road with the skill and dexterity of a professional competing in the *Grand Prix*. "I've never had an accident in my life, so relax."

"There's a first time for everything."

"Don't be frightened, be excited. Tonight you're going to meet the crème de la crème of motion pictures. I had tea with Marlene on Sunday and she let me see the guest list. There'll be everybody but Rin Tin Tin. Marlene doesn't approve of animals at large gatherings. Anyway, the dog's a has-been."

Dong See's fists were clenched, knuckle-white. There were tiny beads of perspiration on his forehead; he seemed paralyzed. He prayed in Chinese, English, and French, this an affectation. The speedometer continued to read eighty. He knew the car could do over one hundred. He prayed it wouldn't. "Please Raymond . . ."

"Oh shut up and think about sex. Marlene's arranging a test for me. She's going to do it with me, and von Sternberg's directing. What a terrific woman. She's nothing like what you see on the screen. Do you know when I was first brought to her house by Claudette Colbert, she was in the kitchen . . ."

"I know she's devoted to cooking . . ."

"She was on her knees scrubbing the floor! Can you imagine? Dietrich scrubbing her kitchen floor! Unbelievable!"

"Look out for that truck!"

"Why? Is it doing something unusual?"

The limousine transporting Anna May Wong and Mai Mai Chu to the party was upholstered with zebra skin. A closed window separated the passengers from the chauffeur, and Anna May was glad the man couldn't hear their conversation. Mai Mai was all doom and gloom. "There is no hope for our China," she said sadly.

"I'm a native American, Mai Mai. I was born here."

"Nevertheless, China is a lost cause. First overrun by the Japanese, who will torture the people and pillage the cities, and then the Communists will take command. A very grim scenario, very grim. I suppose Carroll Richter will be at the party?"

"And you will be very nice to him."

Mai Mai smiled her charming, delicate smile. "I am always nice to everyone. I was even nice to Gertrude Stein and Alice B. Toklas, and it is not very easy to be nice to them, although Gertrude is nicer than Alice, who is very possessive and very sharp-tongued and should either wax her mustache or shave it. Did you meet them when you were in Paris?"

"They were out of town looking for truffles."

"Of course, Carroll Richter is a fraud. He despises me."

"How do you know that?"

"I have done his chart. A mutual friend gave me his date and hour of birth. Actually, he doesn't make the most of himself. He should be writing a syndicated newspaper column."

"Perhaps one day he will. What's wrong?"

Mai Mai's eyes were closed, her tiny hands covering her tiny mouth. Then her eyes flew open and her hands dropped slowly to her lap. "It's here again. The warning. Danger, Anna May, danger."

"Do you see Marlene threatened?"

Mai Mai's voice was sepulchral. "I see all of us threatened. All of us." She reached over and took Anna May's hand. "I have had this premonition before. In Paris, at a ball given by Ivar Kreuger, the match king. Of course you've heard of him."

"Of course. He had a scheme to rule the world. . . ."

"It seemed silly to a lot of people, but Ivar was a genius. And a group of very powerful people believed in his scheme and joined him in implementing it. But Ivar was a madman. He went out of control and had to be destroyed. Very little has been heard of the scheme since. But those people still exist. And my charts tell me they have reactivated. They are on the move again. Our very being is threatened, Anna May, the sword of Damocles hangs over our heads, waiting to fall and destroy."

Then she fell silent. Anna May said nothing. She looked out the window at peaceful Beverly Hills, at houses still illuminated with Christmas decorations, some of them sweetly simple, such as a creche with the Virgin Mother cradling the infant Jesus. Some of them vulgarly garish such as an expensive electrical depiction of the first Christmas supper with waiters dispensing separate checks.

Anna May's heartbeat was unusually rapid. By nature she was a calm and unflappable woman. Now there was heat in her cheeks and moisture on her upper lip and she dabbed at it with a lace-trimmed handkerchief. What Mai Mai had told her disturbed her. Mai Mai was a genius; her father had told her this and she had great respect for his judgment. If there was an opportunity later, she would share what she had heard with Marlene. Marlene was a practical woman, a very intelligent and a very clever one. Look at how she manipulated her husband and von Sternberg and Adolph Zukor and Ben Schulberg, who was the West Coast head of Paramount Pictures, but, according to rumor, not for much longer. People seemed to like to be manipulated by her, she did it with such grace and subtlety. The way she loved her daughter, but didn't dote on her or indulge her. The way she defied the studio when they insisted she keep Maria sequestered from the public eye, as the presence of a daughter might damage Dietrich's glamorous image. So Dietrich was the bellwether, and other actresses revealed they were mothers. Gloria Swanson, Miriam Hopkins, Constance Bennett, even when the legitimacy of their children was in question. Lots of actresses went to the desert for their health and returned many months later with "adopted" babies. Some could even name the father.

Yes, she would share this knowledge with Marlene, and the sooner the better, although she'd be hard put to explain what she thought Marlene could do about it.

Marlene was in her daughter's bedroom, where Maria's nurse sat in an easy chair reading Tiffany Thayer's racy version of *The Three Musketeers*. Maria was a beautiful child, and now, fast asleep, her mother thought she resembled an angel in repose.

"Did she enjoy her dinner?"

"Oh, yes. She's like her mother. She loves her food."

"She mustn't like her food too much. I have a fat problem and I don't want her to have one too. Now listen, if the party gets too noisy and awakens Maria, come and tell me and I'll send them all home."

"Nothing awakens Maria. She sleeps like a log."

"I wish I could say the same for me. Well dear, Happy New Year."

"And to you, Miss Dietrich." God, but she's gorgeous in that slinky, shimmery gown. And me, me in this damned uniform, alone on New Year's Eve reading Tiffany Thayer. Oh, what the hell, D'Artagnan's banging Milady deWinter. Some girls have all the luck.

Marlene went swiftly down the hall to a room at the rear of the house. She knocked lightly on the door and entered. An actor dressed as Father Time and a midget dressed as the New Year's baby sat playing cards and drinking gin.

"Everything all right, boys?"

"Everything's fine, Miss Dietrich. Dinner was great." Father Time was a once popular silent screen actor down on his luck. Von Sternberg had asked her to hire him.

"How's the diaper, Ambrose?"

The midget chuckled and said, "A perfect fit. The gin's great too."

"Go easy on it. I don't want the old year reeling out and the New Year staggering in."

"Don't you worry about us," said Father Time. "We're pros."

"Happy New Year." Marlene shut the door behind her. Father Time. Once he'd been the king of the mountain, and now he was at the bottom of the heap. What a cruel profession, what a cruel town. Well, they'll never do it to me. She moved to a balcony hidden by drapes that overlooked the ballroom. The guests were arriving. Soon she'd make her entrance. She would time it very carefully even if she had to wait for the very last star to arrive, and that would undoubtedly be Constance Bennett. Well, thought Dietrich, Connie darling, no bitch upstages Dietrich, especially in her own home. The orchestra was playing "Sonny Boy." Al Jolson must have entered with his wife, Ruby Keeler. Marlene returned to her suite for another glass of champagne. She found Anna May Wong waiting for her.

"Darling! Why didn't you send Gloria to fetch me?" Gloria was pouring champagne for them.

"I only just got here. I'm glad I got to you before you joined your guests."

"You're frightened. What's wrong?" Gloria distributed the glasses and then discreetly disappeared.

"You'll probably think I'm foolish. But you've got to hear what Mai Mai Chu told me in the car."

"Where is she?"

"She's downstairs studying the guests."

"What do you mean 'studying' them?"

Anna May took Marlene's hand and led her to a settee. "You've got to hear this. And when I'm finished you can tell me I'm either a damn fool or that you're as disturbed as I am. But Marlene, Mai Mai is no damn fool and she's very disturbed. And Mai Mai doesn't disturb easily. You remember what she said on the phone this afternoon, there will be danger in this house tonight. Well, it came to her again on the drive here, but Marlene, this time Mai Mai was truly frightened. . . ."

"Tell me," said Marlene, "tell me everything. And I mean *everything*." She took a heavy swig of champagne.

⟪ THREE ⟫

HAZEL DICKSON'S ROADSTER was old but proud. For the past five years it had served her well, transporting her over many thousands of miles on the trail of a lead or nosing out the tidbits she would sell to the newspaper columnists who hoped to titillate their hungry and faithful readers. Although Hazel was carefully steering up the long driveway where stately rows of cedars of Lebanon formed an arboreal honor guard, the roadster seemed to know its own way to the stately front door. One of a dozen parking attendants replaced Hazel at the wheel, eyeing Hazel and Herb Villon with suspicion. Surely they were meant to use the servant's entrance. Herb was not at home in a tuxedo and Hazel was wearing her Coco Chanel, the latest in evening pajamas. It was a daring new style that Dietrich had introduced to America when she returned from Paris the previous April.

They could hear the orchestra treating Cole Porter's "You Do Something to Me" with reverence and respect as they passed through the entrance. The butler on guard at the doors recognized Hazel and wished her a Happy New Year. She would have preferred hearing him tell her how ravishing she looked, but a girl can't have everything. Herb was impressed by the huge foyer with its grand staircase leading up to the ballroom. Maids and butlers were flying up and down bearing trays of food and party favors. "There are four bars upstairs," Hazel advised Herb, who had muttered something about being thirsty.

"If Helen Twelvetrees is here, introduce me to her."

"And then what?"

"And then I shall ravish her on the dance floor in full view of everyone."

"And what will her husband be doing?"

"Keeping score, if he's a good sport."

Entering the ballroom, Herb had the good manners not to yell "Wow!" Instead he said to Hazel, "If they drop a bomb on this place, the only thing left of Hollywood will be walk-ons and extras." He recognized Maurice Chevalier. He assumed the woman with the French heartthrob was his wife, Yvonne. There was Fredric March with his wife, Florence Eldredge, looking as though he wished he were with somebody else's wife. March's lechery was a Hollywood legend. John Gilbert, holding what was probably a tumbler of whisky, had arrived with his young bride, actress Virginia Bruce, but Hazel spotted her dancing with a French actor recently arrived in Hollywood, Charles Boyer. John Gilbert was trying to act gay and insouciant, as though his star was not descending, the talkies being unkind to him and his once huge horde of fans dwindling as rapidly as sand falling through a sieve. Gloria Swanson, albeit only five feet tall, looked majestic in a black gown studded with multicolored paillettes, and artfully wielded a black ostrich fan that managed to sidesweep anyone in her immediate vicinity. Hazel heard a woman commenting on Swanson, "She has a classic profile. Very old."

Jules Furthman, the highly respected writer who had scripted *Shanghai Express*, was talking to columnist Sidney Skolsky, a diminutive man whose forte was telling his readers what the stars wore in bed, if they wore anything. Furthman was expounding on another writer, who was accused of stealing his latest plot from de Maupassant: "He'd plagiarize an obituary." Skolsky reminded Furthman that he'd lifted *Shanghai Express* from de Maupassant's *Boule de Suif*, to which Furthman responded swiftly, "Not all of it!"

An ardent young man reciting a Browning love poem to lovely actress Dorothy Jordan was overheard by the impeccable but drunk John Barrymore, who cackled to his stunning wife, Dolores Costello, "My dear, methinks I am hearing verses."

Herb, holding his second gin and tonic, was having a wonderful time eavesdropping on the stars and delighting in their uninhibited bitchery. Hazel had left him and was off in search of salable items. Herb heard director George Cukor, a recent arrival from New York with the sharp tongue of an avenging serpent, say of an actress long on ambition and short on talent, "She's ferociously fought and clawed her way to the bottom."

Dong See had downed several brandies, neat, to calm his shattered nerves. Raymond Souvir was anxiously looking for Dietrich, and a maid told him she had not yet made an appearance. The former silent screen star Pola Negri, who after a three-year absence was back in Hollywood to make her first talking film for Radio Pictures, *A Woman Commands*, had much of the room buzzing with surprise as she engaged in what seemed to be a very warm and friendly chat with her once arch rival at Paramount, Gloria Swanson. A lip-reader might have been delighted at what Negri was telling Swanson. "I roll the batter very very thin until you can almost see through it. Then I mash cooked prunes into the cottage cheese and spread a good layer on each individual square of batter. After I roll them and place them in a pan of lightly melted butter, I put them in the oven and *bake* them."

"Bake? Not fry?" Swanson looked so astonished, one might have thought she'd heard an option drop.

"Bake, my darling, bake. Believe me, are those yummy blintzes!"

Bela Lugosi of *Dracula* fame was apparently bemoaning his

fate to Hazel Dickson. "So what is fame, what is success, what is money without someone to love?"

Hazel was pragmatic. "Have you considered taking up a hobby?"

"What kind of a hobby?" asked Lugosi in world-weary tones.

"Of course, something that would interest you. Something you could sink your teeth into."

Countess Dorothy di Frasso swept into the room with Ivar Tensha and Monte Trevor in her wake. She accepted champagne from a waiter and an hors d'oeuvre from another and to her horror realized she was chewing on a disguised anchovy, and she despised anchovies.

"Is there anything else I can get you?" asked a waiter.

"A stomach pump." She grabbed a napkin from the waiter's tray and rid herself of the anchovy. A gulp of the bubbly had a needed cleansing effect, and then with an infectious joie de vivre she took to the task of introducing the munitions king and the British producer to all her friends and acquaintances, and they were legion. Within minutes Tensha and Trevor were swimming frantically in a sea of celebrity names and celebrity faces. From Edward G. Robinson to Evelyn Brent to Louise Brooks to Paul and Bella Muni. Soon they were hanging on for dear life to such familiar names and faces as Lilyan Tashman and Edmund Lowe and Victor McLaglen and then onward to Jackie Cooper and his mother and Mitzi Green and *her* mother and then to a sad young thing whose husband had run off to Mexico with her wealthy mother, di Frasso commenting sotto voce to her escorts, "The brute married her for her mummy."

Then di Frasso took egotistical delight in pointing out the many men who'd been to bed with her. Tensha asked with a rare twinkle in his eye, "Tell me, my dear, were you ever a virgin?"

Di Frasso laughed. "Ivor, I was a virgin way back when virginity was an asset." They were joined by Raymond Souvir and Dong See. Souvir commented on the presence of Gregory and Natalia Ivanov. Di Frasso explained, "Marlene specializes in eclectic guest lists. Actually, I suspect the Ivanovs are here because Marlene and Joseph von Sternberg have been haunting the Russian Embassy for research on the life of Catherine the Great. They want to do a film of her life with, of course, Marlene portraying the empress."

"I thought the Communists despised royalty," commented Dong See.

"Not when it could turn a profit," said di Frasso. "They certainly treasure the treasures they confiscated from the deposed peerage. They've been selling them throughout the world to finance their five-year plan." She addressed Tensha. "I'm told you've acquired some priceless religious articles."

"Oh, yes. I have a taste for icons studded with precious jewels."

Di Frasso said wearily, "While I have a taste for precious studs."

A buzz went up in the room. Constance Bennett was making her entrance, a dazzling creature in one of Gilbert Adrian's more unique designs, the dress daringly slit from ankle to thigh, and wearing jewels that were assuredly worth a movie star's ransom. Gloria Swanson, who loathed Constance Bennett, asked the star's sister Joan, "What will she do with all the wealth she flaunts? She certainly can't take it with her."

"If she can't take it with her," replied Joan Bennett, "she won't go."

Hazel Dickson said to Herb Villon, "Oh, thank God."

"For what?"

"Now that the Bennett bitch is here, Marlene will make *her* entrance."

In her suite, Marlene was pacing and digesting what Anna May Wong had told her. Mai Mai's premonitions were certainly disturbing. The delicate Chinese woman was not your ordinary, run-of-the-mill astrologer predicting that you will meet a tall dark stranger who will rape you; she was a psychic, a genuine psychic, a woman possessed of powers Marlene found both awesome and frightening. Marlene thought these were terrible burdens for a woman she knew to be small and seemingly defenseless. When a young actress in Berlin appearing with Max Reinhardt's celebrated and respected Theater Ensemble, she now remembered she had heard of the amazing Mai Mai Chu almost a decade before Anna May mentioned knowing her. Now she was here, under Dietrich's roof, suffering a premonition or premonitions she couldn't clearly decipher.

Danger.

"I see danger!"

Gloria, the maid, hurried into the room. "Miss Dietrich, Constance Bennett has arrived and Gloria Swanson is saying terrible things about her!"

"As well she should. Connie is a terrible woman. Come, Anna May, let's go downstairs."

Anna May was wise in the ways of Dietrich. "I'll go first. Give me a few minutes and then make your entrance."

She was out of the room before Marlene could politely demur and hurried down the stairs into the overpopulated ballroom. Dorothy di Frasso spotted her, "There's Anna May Wong coming down the stairs. She'll probably know the identity of the strange little Oriental woman wandering the room and staring at everyone. God knows what she's looking for."

"Perhaps an honest man," suggested Monte Trevor, not knowing any himself.

"There, look at her," cautioned di Frasso, "now she's staring at our group. Do any of you know her?"

No one replied.

The orchestra was spiritedly rendering "There'll Be a Hot Time in the Old Town Tonight" and the ballroom erupted into thunderous applause. Slowly, sensually, sinuously, a wicked and very worldly-wise smile on her face, Marlene Dietrich triumphantly descended the staircase into the ballroom.

Joseph von Sternberg sipped his drink. *You are my creation.*

I made you. I discovered you and taught you to be Marlene Die-trich, the magnificent star, not the fat little frump I auditioned in Berlin. I recognized that under those twenty pounds of fat there was screaming for release the stunning creature descending the stair-case. I too am that creature. Marlene, you are my doppelgänger. The *doppelgänger*, the occult creature Germans believed was a person's other self. Von Sternberg signaled a waiter for a fresh drink.

Hazel Dickson said to Herb Villon, "She makes every woman in this room look like Baron Frankenstein's cre-ation."

"Oh, I wouldn't go that far," replied Herb, adding with disappointment, "I guess there's going to be no Helen Twelve-trees."

"There's a Helen Twelvetrees," Hazel assured him, "but not here tonight."

Hands on hips, Jean Harlow said to Joan Crawford, who clung to the arm of a new boy in town, Franchot Tone: "Can you beat that broad?"

To which Crawford responded, "The point is, Baby"—everyone at MGM called Harlow 'Baby'—"you *can't* beat that broad. My hat's off to her."

Natalia Ivanov was crying softly into a handkerchief. There was no consoling her, and her husband refrained from trying. Unlike Dietrich, Natalia could never ask the mirror on her wall, "Who's the fairest one of all?" They would have been surprised to learn that Dietrich never questioned her mirror. She didn't have to. She knew the answer.

Kay Francis embraced Dietrich. "It's a tewwific pahty, dahl-ing. And yaw so democwatic. Evewy stah from evewy studio is hewe. But how did you dawe ask Connie Bennett and Lilyan Tashman to the same pahty?"

"Why not? They're both friends of mine." She almost said 'fwiends' but she had greater control over her impediment. Kay Francis didn't give a damn, not when they were paying her seven thousand dollars a week.

"Didn't you know?"

"Know what?"

"Lilyan caught Connie in bed with her husband, Eddie Lowe. She beat the stuffing out of Connie!"

"That's all right. Connie has stuffing to spare. Forgive me, darling, I have so many guests to greet."

"Go wight ahead, sweetie. I want to meet Anna May's astwologuh fwiend. I think she's so fascinating." She wafted away on a cloud of Russian Leather.

Hazel waved at Marlene. Marlene wondered if the formidable-looking gentleman stifling a yawn was Hazel's policeman boyfriend. If there was truly danger tonight, she would find the presence of an officer of the law very comforting. Marlene and Hazel embraced. Hazel introduced Herb Villon, and Marlene recognized his name and said warmly and sincerely, "I'm so glad Hazel brought you." Villon felt good all over and was deeply in love with Dietrich. Hazel would be relieved to learn Helen Twelvetrees had been overthrown. Marlene swiftly and lucidly told them about Mai Mai Chu's dire prediction, and Villon, who had in the past resorted to psychics when at an impasse in a particularly puzzling murder case, was openly sympathetic to Dietrich.

"Perhaps it would be wise for you to send for reinforcements, Mr. Villon."

"Call me Herb. Why do I need reinforcements?"

"The danger!" exclaimed Dietrich.

"What danger?"

"The danger I just told you about! Mai Mai Chu's premonition." Hazel shifted from one foot to another while Villon explained to Marlene, "I can't call for reinforcements because of a psychic's premonition."

"Why not?"

"My chief would think I'm nuts."

"You can't be nuts. I can see for myself you're a highly intelligent person."

"Marlene, this is New Year's Eve. The entire police force is out keeping law and order. People go wild on New Year's Eve. They might send for me to go out there and help."

Marlene stared into his big brown eyes and at his craggy good looks and respected the intensity with which he spoke to her. "But supposing something terrible happens?"

"*Then* I request a backup and we pray there's a backup available."

Anna May Wong joined them. She knew Hazel well and was happy to meet Villon. She told Marlene, "Mai Mai is creating quite a stir. She either amuses people or makes them uncomfortable. She's foreseeing things and I think she's in a mood to perform. Would you like her to?"

Dietrich gave the offer some thought and then smiled. "Will she be outrageous?"

"She will be whatever she will want to be. I've seen Mai Mai in situations like this before, and I can assure you, she's never boring."

"I'm a bit of a psychic myself," said Dietrich, "and I have a feeling this will be a night to remember. Come. Let's get her started."

The ballroom was hushed. Mai Mai Chu sat on a plush chair on the orchestra platform. She looked like a porcelain statuette come to life. She spoke softly but clearly, and everyone in the room could hear her. Anna May Wong stood next to her. She addressed the guests.

"With Marlene's kind permission, I have asked my dear friend Madam Mai Mai Chu to perform for us tonight. Actually, Madam Chu volunteered. She has much on her mind that she wishes to share with all of us. Madam Chu is a world-renowned and respected astrologer . . ."—Carroll Richter stood stiffly at a bar clenching a highball and choking on the scream welling up in his throat—". . . and equally of importance, she is a psychic possessed of the most amazing, and perhaps to some of us, very frightening powers."

There was a buzz humming in the ballroom. It was a buzz familiar to veteran Hollywood party-goers. It consisted of amusement mingled with expectation peppered with cynicism and a dollop of incredulity. Hazel heard a dimwitted starlet ask her escort, "I thought a psychic was something you took when you have an upset stomach."

Anna May continued. "This afternoon, when I phoned from this house to invite Mai Mai to join the celebration tonight, she told me she sensed danger here."

Again the buzz, but this time one of increasing interest and curiosity. Dorothy di Frasso exchanged looks with Ivar Tensha and Monte Trevor. The Ivanovs had joined them and Gregory squeezed Natalia's hand. Dong See stole a look at Raymond Souvir, who was hypnotized by the look of anxiety on Marlene Dietrich's face. Out of curiosity, Herb Villon's eyes were two spotlights sweeping the room studying the reactions of various guests. Hazel knew she was on to a potentially great story and was glad Louella Parsons, the queen of Hollywood gossip for the Hearst newspaper syndicate, was ill with the flu and couldn't attend. More likely she and her physician husband had polished off one too many bottles of bootleg rye and were too sick to make it. Lolly Parsons paid handsomely for hot items.

"This evening, on our way here together," Anna May continued while wondering if a lecture tour with Mai Mai might prove handsomely profitable, "Madam Chu again was struck by the premonition of danger cloaking this house tonight. Since our arrival, she has been moving among you, studying your faces, and from some of you she has been getting what she refers to as interesting vibrations. She will also share with you some of what she has learned the past few days from her charts. And speaking from experience, when I despaired of being hired by Doug Fairbanks for *The Thief of Bagdad* when I just an inexperienced youngster, she told me I'd get the part, and bless her heart, I did. Madam Chu has spent many years abroad in Paris, in Berlin, in Moscow, you name it, she's been there; in other words, she knows international acclaim and respect. My dear friend, Madam Mai Mai Chu."

Anna May accepted Dong See's arm as he assisted her from the platform. They had been introduced earlier and took an instant liking to each other. Madam Chu smiled at her audience and spoke reassuringly. "Do not be frightened by what I say. What I say to you is a guide, a warning, the opportunity to avert what is inevitable. There are those who scoff at astrology, yet there are those who live by it and thrive by it and learn from it. My psychic powers are true powers. I can no sooner deny them as I cannot deny the inevitability of death. And none of us can deny the inevitability of death."

She knew she had them; some were fascinated, some restrained an urge to scoff vocally, some believed, and some wanted to believe, anything to ease the misery of living.

Mai Mai said, "My charts tell me there are several disasters impending. Perhaps this New Year, perhaps the following year, an ocean liner will catch fire and sink off the Atlantic Coast. Many lives will be lost. A pleasure cruise that will turn into a horrifying nightmare. And also in the same vicinity, which is in the area of the state of New Jersey and the Atlantic Ocean, an airship will explode and burn and again many lives will be lost. This airship will be of foreign origin and the suspicion will be that the cause of the explosion will be the sabotage of a terrorist organization."

What she was saying was incredible to many, amusing to others, and to some, absolute hogwash. Groucho Marx had arrived with his wife when Mai Mai began speaking and asked Marlene, "Where's the other three jugglers?" Marlene gently put a finger on his lips and he just as gently kissed it as his wife pulled him away.

Now Mai Mai really disturbed the guests. "My charts tell me there will be a terrible second world war. There is a dangerous cancer growing in Europe in the form of a little man with horrifying ambitions to rule the world." Marlene clasped her hands tightly together. She knew this man. She had heard him speak at a street rally. He had seen her perform on stage opposite Hans Albers in the musical *Two Bow-Ties*. He had sent her flowers and invited her to dine with him but she rejected him; he frightened her. And his vast army of followers was increasing at an alarming rate. She had heard and seen this for herself on her trip abroad the previous April.

Mai Mai was saying, "I tell you this because it is possible to avert these disasters, this European holocaust. I am giving you knowledge, and knowledge is power when used correctly." She coughed a very tiny and modest cough and cleared her throat. "A national tragedy is imminent. My charts are very powerful where this is concerned. The child of an American hero is under the threat of kidnapping. The child will be murdered."

Director William Wellman shouted, "Do you mean Lindbergh?"

"The charts do not give names."

"Well, hell," said Wellman to actor Richard Barthelmess, "I know Lindy. Maybe I ought to tip him off."

"I wouldn't worry," said Barthelmess. "She's just a pretty good lounge act."

Anna May could see Mai Mai was thirsty and chose to send her a glass of champagne. Mai Mai was standing. "What I tell you now I did not read in my charts. It is what I sensed and felt as I walked among you this evening." Her eyes pierced ahead. "There is here tonight an actress who is marked for murder. Her killer will escape detection."

"That could be any one of us," Thelma Todd whispered to Nancy Carroll, who merely shrugged.

Mai Mai said, "There are several suicides in this room, and I say to these people, do not despair, there is always hope and friends to sustain you and—" She stopped dramatically. "*Danger!*" she howled, "*Danger!* It is right here with us, terrible *danger!*"

Marlene shivered, and Herb Villon put a protective arm around Hazel Dickson's shoulders. Mai Mai's eyes moved from one person to another but Marlene could not tell whom she was particularly looking at. When she returned her glance to Mai Mai, the petite woman was drinking from a glass of champagne.

Then from the rear of the ballroom, someone shouted "Happy New Year!" Mai Mai stared ahead into space as the glass slipped from her fingers. She heard the orchestra blasting "Auld Lang Syne" and in a misty haze saw multicolored balloons wafting down from the ceiling and then she heard Marlene shrieking "Catch her! Catch her!"

Mai Mai fell from the platform into Herb Villon's strong arms. He gently lowered her to the floor as Marlene and Anna May ran to Mai Mai. Mai Mai stared up at them, but she saw nothing. Marlene said, "God in heaven, she is dead." She did not realize she was speaking her native German.

Herb Villon said to Hazel, "Get the pieces of her champagne glass. Wrap them in a handkerchief. Don't let anybody step on them. And if somebody does, tell me who it is." But Hazel was quick. She had the pieces of glass carefully placed in her handkerchief and then safely placed the folded handkerchief into her evening bag.

Herb said to Dietrich, "*Now* Marlene. *Now* I call for an ambulance, the coroner, and backup."

The tableau that Herb and Marlene and Hazel and Anna May and the unfortunate Mai Mai formed went unnoticed by most of the revelers. The New Year had begun! Nineteen thirty-two was here! Everyone blew horns and wore funny hats and drank more bootleg booze and champagne, and the morning would provide one gigantic hangover.

Only the group surrounding the corpse stayed sober. Villon was led to a phone and he called headquarters. Anna May Wong and Marlene Dietrich stood with their arms around each other. They heard the Countess Dorothy di Frasso saying to her friends, "Why the poor dear! I guess the excitement was much too much for her! She's fainted!"

◖◗ FOUR ◗◗

THE NEW YEAR had aged thirty minutes before Herb Villon's backup arrived. His assistant, Jim Mallory, arrived in an unmarked car followed by two squad cars of detectives, sirens blaring, scaring the hell out of rabbits and coyotes and several of Dietrich's guests who had reason to fear the police. The coroner had preceded them, and Mai Mai's body was placed on a couch in the library across from the ballroom. Two butlers carried the corpse, Anna May accompanying them.

"What happened?" asked Miriam Hopkins. "Is she sick?"

"She's dead," said Anna May.

"How awful!" said Miriam Hopkins. "It must have been her heart. The excitement. Oh, the poor little thing."

Villon and Mallory were conferring after Herb had dispatched the other detectives to keep an eye on the exits and make sure no one left. "It's going to be hopeless questioning all these people." Dietrich had joined them. "The best we can do is get their phone numbers."

"My secretary can provide those," volunteered Dietrich. "I think it is pointless to detain anyone who wants to leave." She looked around the room. "Though it doesn't look as though anyone has any intention of leaving. Quite a successful party." They didn't miss the irony in her voice. "I never saw anyone give Madam Chu the glass of champagne."

"I thought it was Anna May," said Hazel Dickson.

"No," said Villon. "I saw her talk to a butler. She was probably telling him to get some champagne for Madam Chu. She was standing near Countess di Frasso and her entourage. They must have heard Miss Wong ask for the champagne."

"Strange," said Marlene, "it was like an optical illusion." Jim Mallory couldn't believe he was standing next to this great celebrity. He was mesmerized by her beauty, overpowered by her perfume, and hypnotized by her commanding tone of voice. Villon was puzzled by Marlene's statement, and Marlene was quick to explain. "I was fascinated, of course, by Madam Chu's predictions. But at the same time, I noticed she was always directing her eyes back to one group of my guests. I couldn't be sure which and I tried to follow her gaze. When I turned my eyes away from Madam Chu she was empty-handed; a few seconds later, she was holding the glass of champagne."

"Which group of guests do you think particularly interested Madam Chu?"

"Frankly, Herb, I think it was the Countess di Frasso and her entourage. Ivar Tensha, the British film producer. . . ."

"Monte Trevor," contributed Hazel.

"Yes. Him. Raymond Souvir, the young French actor. That's him talking to Nancy Carroll." Anna May had returned from the library. "The Ivanovs were standing near them and, oh yes, the violinist, Dong See. Anna May, are you all right?"

"I could be better. I phoned my father and told him what happened. He's contacting her family. They're in San Francisco. The coroner is examining the bod . . ."—she hesitated for a second—"is examining Mai Mai. I heard him say he suspected *nux vomica*. Herb, do you know what it is?"

Jim Mallory spoke up. "*Nux vomica* is the seed from which strychnine is extracted."

"Strychnine." Marlene's voice was ghostly. "How terrible."

Villon asked Hazel for the handkerchief with the champagne glass shards. He instructed Jim to get it to the police lab and have it tested immediately. Jim collared another detective and transferred the errand to him. He didn't want to miss a moment of Marlene Dietrich. He would treasure the memory and dine out on the story for the rest of his life.

"Di Frasso's friends, Herb. I have a feeling Mai Mai Chu might have met some of them before. Probably abroad when she lived there." Marlene had his undivided attention. "Perhaps they are the danger that terrified her. And she was truly terrified those last moments before she collapsed. I saw her face. I'll never forget the look. I've seen nothing like it before in my life. It was so awful."

"I saw it too," said Anna May. "And I think what it signified was the terror of her realization that the danger was to herself and to no one else. I think she recognized then that it was she, Mai Mai, who was marked for murder. And by then it was too late to protect herself; she had sipped some champagne."

Jim Mallory said, "All it takes is a sip of strychnine and whammo."

"Jim, spare us." Mallory blushed. Villon said to Marlene, "Is there somewhere I can question these people?"

"Yes, there's a study next to the library. Would it bother you if Anna May and I sat in on your inquiries?"

"Not at all. Listening to them might jog a memory. There was a hell of a lot going on in this ballroom tonight and I'll be damned if I can remember a fraction of what I saw or heard."

"I can," said Hazel, who had already phoned Louella Parsons's assistant, Dorothy Manners, to give her the scoop on Mai Mai Chu's murder. Hazel was promised a fat fee, to which Hazel said to herself, "A very happy New Year, Hazel darling."

Herb shot Hazel a look and then addressed Anna May. "Miss Wong, this is my assistant, Jim Mallory. Would you accompany him and point out the Countess, the Ivanovs, Tensha, Mr. Trevor, Raymond Souvir, and Dong See?"

"Of course," said Anna May.

"And Jim," Villon's voice was cautionary, "just say they're wanted for some routine questions; don't frighten the hell out of them or they'll clam up."

Marlene smiled at Anna May and then at Villon. "Don't worry, Mr. Detective, we'll help loosen their tongues. Between us, Anna May and I speak a lot of languages. We especially talk turkey." She led the way to the study. The orchestra was torturing "The Sheik of Araby" while a nasal tenor bleated the lyrics into a megaphone, a bad imitation of the popular crooner Rudy Vallee. Blissfully, no one paid any attention to him. Several guests watched with curiosity and suspicion as Marlene led the way to the study. The butlers who had carried the body into the library had spread the word that it was suspected Mai Mai Chu had been poisoned.

"*Champagne!*"

"*But how?*"

"*Was there poison in the bottle?*"

"*My God! Supposing there's a madman loose at the party!*"

"*I don't think so. Chaplin's at home with Paulette Goddard.*"

William Wellman, the director, said to Gary Cooper, "I phoned Lindbergh ostensibly to wish him and his wife a happy New Year. I sort of matter-of-factly let drop Madam Chu's premonition about the possible kidnapping of a national hero's baby, and you know what that modest bastard said?"

"Nope."

"There are a lot of other national heroes around. Can you believe that?"

"Yup." Monosyllables were about as articulate as Gary Cooper ever got.

Seated on chairs arranged in the hallway outside the study, Monte Trevor asked Ivar Tensha, "Why do you suppose our group was singled out for questioning?"

"Possibly the police have recognized us as the privileged

class. Why does it worry you? Have you never been questioned by the police before?"

Trevor's face reddened. "Not seriously."

Natalia Ivanov clutched the crucifix she always carried in her purse, mouthing pleas for help to Saint Olga while under his breath her husband reminded her they were supposed to be antireligious.

"Not positively," said Natalia.

Dong See puffed on a scented cigarette while Raymond Souvir wondered if the body had yet been removed from the premises. Souvir had an abnormal fear of dying, having survived a train crash in Switzerland. His face paled as he saw the library door opening, and a few moments later two police attendants wheeled the body out and into the house elevator, where they were a tight squeeze.

"Oh, God," said Souvir while Dong See chuckled and thought, How anyone who drives a car as wildly as he does could be afraid of death is beyond me. Orientals were taught not to fear death but to welcome it as an adventure in a new dimension. On the other hand, he himself was in no hurry to cross the Great Divide and planned on a long and profitable life.

Inside the study, the Countess Dorothy di Frasso was a charming study of poise and cooperation. She sat in a comfortable chair facing Herb Villon, who sat behind a small desk that seemed much too delicate in construction for his large frame, while at his left sat Jim Mallory recording the interrogation. He was never without a looseleaf pad, and only he could translate his own peculiar scrawl of shorthand. Marlene and Anna May were on a love seat to the right of the desk, and Hazel Dickson perched on a window seat, which also afforded her an excellent view of the comings and goings in the driveway below.

Villon had asked the Countess if she had met Mai Mai Chu before tonight.

The Countess said, "I didn't even meet her tonight! No one introduced us. Every so often I did find her staring at us and

I was wondering at first if she disapproved of our not mingling with some of the other guests. But I'm sure you understand, Mr. Villain. . . ."

"Villon."

"Oh, do forgive me. Villon. Anyway, you know Hollywood and understand the pecking order. It's all so cliquey. I mean the Constance Bennett bunch doesn't mingle with the Norma Shearer bunch, and even at parties they tend to keep themselves apart from each other. It's really terribly tiresome. By the way, darling, where were Norma and Irving tonight? Surely you invited them."

"They had a previous engagement and Irving Thalberg tires so easily. They're with Helen Hayes and Charlie MacArthur."

"Oh, really?" The Countess looked chagrined. "And they didn't invite me?"

Marlene decided the question didn't deserve an answer. She couldn't understand why she had invited the woman to her own party. She wasn't particularly fond of her; in fact she felt sorry for her. Other than Gary Cooper, Dietrich thought her taste in men was execrable, especially her fondness for Italian gangsters.

Villon was talking to di Frasso. "Were you bothered by Madam Chu's rudeness in staring at you?"

"No, because I didn't believe she'd singled me out. She was giving equal time to other members of my group."

"You said your escorts tonight were Mr. Tensha and Mr. Trevor. Have you known them long?"

"I met Mr. Tensha in Rome a few years ago. It was at a state dinner given by Mussolini. Dear Benny, he's such a sweetie. And he's made the trains run on time, can you imagine that?"

"I suppose so. I'm not big with trains. You were living in Italy at the time?"

Her voice darkened. "I was married to the Count. We weren't in Italy all that much. I'm the restless type. I like to move around a lot."

"But you didn't move around a lot tonight."

"Tonight I was in a ballroom. Outside there's the whole world for me to play in."

"Did any of your group acknowledge having seen Madam Chu before?"

"Well, frankly, and I hope I'm not casting undue suspicion, but I had the feeling she knew or recognized several of my bunch. On the other hand, they've all had their pictures in newspapers and magazines. I mean, for instance, there have been the stories that Raymond Souvir is to be screen-tested with Marlene. And Ivar Tensha! My dear, he certainly is celebrated as the munitions czar. Dong See is a celebrated musician. I mean, the only frumps in the group are the Ivanovs, but I seem to remember even they had their pictures in the papers when they joined their embassy here. And as for myself, well," she flicked imaginary lint from her dress, "I'm always news."

"Did you by any chance see who gave Madam Chu her glass of champagne?"

"I don't remember that at all. I assumed it was Anna May because I heard her say to someone she thought Madam Chu was getting hoarse and could use a drink, something like that. Frankly, it seems rather ridiculous to me that anyone would choose to murder the woman. Her predictions were harmless. I mean, a madman who wants to rule the world! That's grade-B movie stuff. And as for World War Two . . . oh dear. I don't buy that at all. And then, to suggest someone in the room will be murdered and someone else will commit suicide, my dear Mr. Vill . . . on, anyone in this room could make those generalizations and sound mysterious and ominous. Everybody knows the two Johns, Gilbert and Barrymore, are drinking themselves to death. And I could think of several ladies out there I'd be only too happy to accommodate with assassination. "She smiled in the direction of Dietrich and Anna May. "Present company excepted, of course."

"Why?" asked Marlene.

"Oh, darling, you know we've never competed for any-one."

Dietrich wore an enigmatic smile. Everybody in the ball-room knew she and Gary Cooper had a red hot affair during the making of *Morocco*, which crazed von Sternberg and di Frasso, who had succeeded in stealing Cooper from the vola-tile Lupe Velez.

"What about Monte Trevor?"

"What about him?"

"Where'd you meet him?"

"Oh. Let me think. Oh, of course. In London. If I recall correctly, it was a party Gertie Lawrence was giving for the Prince of Wales and I recall Monte had the audacity to try to convince the Prince to star in a film of *Ivanhoe*. Well, he is terribly photogenic, don't you think, Marlene?"

"I've never met him."

"Oh, haven't you? He's a bit of a bore. Come to think of it, all the royals are bores. It's all that incest and intermarriage. I like Monte Trevor. He's an honest fraud. And he does manage to get a film made every now and then. Why Marlene, tonight he was trying to convince Ivar on the drive here to back a production of *Salome* to star you!"

"How flattering," responded Marlene, "and how apropos; like John the Baptist, many a man has lost his head over me."

Jim Mallory was salivating. If only to be given a chance to lose his head over Marlene Dietrich.

"Monte dangled the bait, but Ivar didn't bite. Anything else?"

"Did you know Raymond Souvir in Paris?"

"He insists we met at a dinner party at Feodor Chalia-pin's, but I don't remember the occasion at all. And as for Dong See, we were introduced at a reception for him in Shanghai after one of his recitals, and I remembered because he was so charming and attentive. He's changed some since then, but then I suppose we all change over the years." There was a pause and she asked, "Am I sitting in what they call the hot seat?"

"Actually Dorothy," said Marlene, "you're sitting in an Adam original. I bought it at an auction for a very fancy price."

Hazel Dickson was starving. She wondered if she dared ask Marlene to send to the ballroom for some food. She knew Herb Villon was not thrilled about her sitting in on the interrogations and she was sure that by now the mansion was being besieged by reporters and photographers. She looked out the window and decided she too was psychic. There they were in the driveway, milling about anxiously, being held back by some of Herb's minions. Well, she'd beaten them all to it and knew that Herb would suffer some flak because of it. He was often being accused of favoring Hazel on a murder case.

"How else can I assist you?" asked di Frasso with exaggerated graciousness.

"You've been very helpful. Thank you. Would you ask Mr. Tensha to come in?"

"I'd be delighted."

Hazel wondered if she could ask the Countess to get her a plate of turkey and ham, but by the time she got up her courage, di Frasso was out and Tensha was in.

"Cigar?" asked Tensha of Villon, indicating a row of his brown torpedos in his inside jacket pocket.

"No, thank you," declined Villon. "I don't smoke them."

"And if you don't mind, Mr. Tensha," interjected Marlene, "I'd be grateful if you didn't either. The room is small and it's already quite close in here."

"Hazel," ordered Villon of his girlfriend on the window seat, "open the window." She did as requested.

Despite being deprived of a cigar as a prop, Tensha was quite composed. He said to Marlene, "This is a terrible thing to have happen in your home. And Miss Wong, we have not been introduced, but I know the deceased was your good friend and I offer my condolences."

"Thank you," responded Anna May softly. Such ye olde worlde courtliness, thought Anna May, such an anachronism coming from a man who profits from death and destruction.

Hazel could tell Herb didn't like Tensha. Offering the cigar was a mistake. Now if he could only produce a ham and cheese on rye she might fall madly in love with him. She heard Herb ask Tensha, somewhat facetiously, she thought, "You deal in munitions?"

"Indeed."

"Are you in this city for business or for pleasure?"

"Both."

"Have you ever met Madam Chu before tonight?"

"In passing and very briefly, I recall social occasions in Berlin and Paris and perhaps also in Rome when we were both under the same roof."

"You were not ever friends?"

"Oh, no. Madam Chu I understood to favor bohemian circles where I am very uncomfortable."

"You don't consider tonight a bohemian occasion?"

"No, tonight was quite delightful until Madam Chu's unfortunate murder. In fact, she fascinated me. The thought of a second world war! You can imagine how a prospect like that appeals to me."

Herb Villon positively hated him. Herb had served in the recent war in the infantry and had suffered a chest wound. He had seen his buddies dropping around him like ninepins in a bowling alley. There was many a night he awakened to the imagined screams of a comrade begging God to give him another chance at life. And this son of a bitch sitting on an antique chair with a pocket load of hundred-dollar cigars slavers at the possibility of a frightening premonition becoming a reality. Don't these people ever get struck by lightning?

"I can tell you that Madam Chu had won the respect and admiration of many dignitaries the world over. Albert Einstein adored her. I was told she warned the Romanovs to get out of Russia as the revolution was imminent, but I don't think that was a premonition. I think she got it firsthand from Leon Trotsky, with whom it was rumored she had an affair."

Both Marlene and Anna May arched an eyebrow upon

hearing this delightful gossip. Anna May whispered to Marlene, "I'm so glad for Mai Mai. I always had the feeling she wasn't getting much."

"But Trotsky!" Marlene suppressed a shudder.

Villon continued, "The others? Mr. Trevor, Dong See, Raymond Souvir, the Ivanovs?"

"The Ivanovs I met here at a reception at the Russian Embassy. He's a simpleton. She is very deceptive."

"How so?"

"I think she is a very clever woman. She professes to peasant origins and has the calloused hands to prove it, but she was smart enough to manipulate her husband into his present position in the embassy. I don't like the man. I think he's a pacifist and they are no use to me." He longed for a puff of a cigar. "As for Trevor, I met him in London. He's always out to separate me from some of my fortune. He's not smart enough. Otherwise, I find him quite harmless. Souvir I do not know. As far as I'm concerned, he's just another pretty face. Dong See is a gifted musician, but I do not travel in musical circles."

You don't travel in circles at all, thought Marlene; you are a smooth, calculating monster. Which is why you are a billionaire and I am not and never will be.

Villon said to Tensha, "I read in the papers you are negotiating to buy an estate here."

"I've bought it. I do a lot of business in the Near East and the Far East and I decided it would be less tiring to break the long journey with a place of my own in Hollywood. I have purchased the estate of a silent film star who apparently has been silenced forever by the talkies. Perhaps you have heard of Clara Kimball Young?" They had. "She was heavily in debt and I came to her rescue. The place needs a lot of work."

"Your group was standing near Madam Chu before her death. Did you see the person who gave her the glass of champagne?"

"I really don't remember. Wasn't it you, Miss Wong?"

"No, it wasn't."

Tensha said to Villon, "Perhaps it was a butler. I remember one passing among us with a single glass on the tray."

Marlene filed that statement away. *I remember one passing among us with a single glass on the tray.* And with all eyes focused on Mai Mai Chu, how easy it would have been for someone to drop a poisoned tablet into the glass. Her eyes met Villon's briefly. She sensed he too harbored a similar suspicion. She liked him. Hazel's a lucky girl. He's a good detective and he's a good man, and baby, let me tell you, a good man nowadays is hard to find. She surfaced from her reverie and realized Tensha had been dismissed.

"You didn't ask him to send in one of the others?" said Marlene, somewhat surprised.

"After him, I need a breather," said Herb.

"I need food and I'm going to get some. If I miss anything, you can tell me later." Hazel hurried out of the room and Marlene began pacing.

"Very interesting, Mr. Tensha," said Marlene.

"I loathe him," Villon stated flatly. "I expected dollar signs to flash in his eyes at the prospect of another world war."

"Don't be foolish," said Marlene, "we'll never see another one in our time. The world is too poor. This Depression won't disappear in the near future. But Herb, a few interesting things he said. A butler passed among them with a single glass." Herb smiled. The lady was smart. "The old trick of concealing a pill in the palm of the hand and passing it over the glass."

"That's probably the way it happened," Villon concurred. "But from whose palm did the pill drop?"

"You can discount Dorothy di Frasso," said Dietrich.

"Why?" asked Villon, as Jim Mallory feasted on Dietrich with feverish eyes.

"The only poison she dispenses is with her tongue. And besides, what would her motive have been?"

"Dorothy didn't murder Mai Mai," Anna May agreed. "But I feel certain it was one of the others."

"Mr. Tensha is so smooth. As for Dong See, he says he does not travel in musical circles. And I'm sure Dong See does not travel exclusively in musical circles. He's certainly not traveling in one tonight, unless you consider Gus Arnheim's cacaphony musical. Oh God, what a night!" She was at the door and opened it a crack. The noise from the ballroom was obscenely deafening. "Can you beat that! They have to know by now Mai Mai was murdered, but they go on celebrating as though murder among them is a common occurrence." She shut the door and faced Villon.

Villon said, "You look like a tiger about to pounce."

"Do I? All I want to know, Herb, is who's next?"

"You mean who's next to be murdered?"

"No, who's next to be questioned. There won't be another murder tonight. You know as well as I do Mai Mai was murdered because she knew too much about the backgrounds of some of the suspects. And it goes back to Europe where they first met. I think Mai Mai knew something terrible. I think Mai Mai, had she not been poisoned, would have revealed something very, very sinister. And how convenient of the murderer to have some *nux vomica* in his possession."

Herb asked winsomely, "Why, my dear Marlene, doesn't everyone carry some poison on them for an emergency? Well, let me tell you from a lot of past experience, professional killers are always well prepared. And one of this bunch I'm questioning tonight is a professional killer. And damned clever too. Jim, I want to see Monte Trevor next." As Jim went to get Trevor, Herb said to Marlene, "Marlene, you've got the makings of a good detective."

"I agree with you. It's a necessary talent when you deal with the kind of men I come up against. And let me tell you, Herb, you're pretty darned good yourself."

Monte Trevor preceded Jim Mallory into the room. He hesitated for a few moments, and Villon said, "Come in, Mr. Trevor and sit right there. There's no need to be afraid."

Or is there, wondered Marlene.

◖ FIVE ◗

MARLENE THOUGHT MONTE Trevor looked more like a greengrocer than a film producer. On the other hand, what was a film producer supposed to look like? Sam Goldwyn had been a glove salesman. Jesse Lasky had played a saxaphone in vaudeville. D. W. Griffith was both a failed actor and a failed playwright. Looks are deceiving, she reminded herself, and not only Trevor's looks are deceiving. There is someone here who is dangerously deceptive, who should look like a murderer, but again, what should a murderer look like? Tensha profits from death and should be the most obvious choice to be a murderer. But with his power and money, wouldn't he arrange for someone else to do his dirty work? He didn't look like a munitions maker, he looked like a puppeteer behind a Punch-and-Judy show in a Paris park. Could Raymond Souvir be a murderer? Why not? And why not Dong See? A hand that delicately wields a violin bow could just as delicately pop a death pill into a glass of champagne. And there's the Ivanovs. The Communists thrive on purges. They murder in job lots, hundreds at a time if the stories coming out of Russia can be believed. Natalia Ivanov is an ambitious woman, but what could there have been in this peasant's past that would have triggered Mai Mai's suspicion? Likewise her husband, an oaf in sheep's clothing. This is too exhausting, and she wasn't paying attention to Villon's questioning of Monte Trevor. She caught a glimpse of Jim Mallory's face and from his strange look wondered if he was suffering from an upset stomach.

"Madam Chu is not unfamiliar to me," Trevor was telling Herb. "I read an interview with her in the London *Times* . . . ooh, let me think . . . um . . . yes . . . some ten or more years ago . . . and I thought at the time she had possibilities as the subject of a feature film. But who to play her other than Miss Wong here, and she was not yet on the threshhold of her present celebrity. It would have meant casting an Occidental actress and expecting the makeup department to work a miracle."

"Did you make contact with Madam Chu?" Herb was toying with a pencil while staring at Anna May. He couldn't read a thing in her face. Truly inscrutable.

"As a matter of fact, we had tea at the Savoy. I think it was the Savoy. Maybe the Mayfair Club? The Dorchester?"

"The setting is of no importance, Mr. Trevor, only the cast of characters."

"Yes, of course, ha ha. You Americans do insist on cutting away the fat and the gristle. Well, as I said, we met and I broached the subject of filming her story. It seems I wasn't alone with the idea. A French director approached her in Paris, I think it was René Clair, and another had met with her in Berlin. But she said something quite sensible. I can't quote her accurately, it was so many years ago, but she said something like this. 'There is no story, Mr. Trevor, there are only my gifts, and how do you dramatize gifts?' Quite an intelligent woman, I'm happy to say. Anyway, truth to tell, a few years later I did a movie about a clairvoyant and it was a terrible flop."

"Has making films been your only interest, Mr. Trevor?"

"What do you mean?"

"Have you been involved in other schemes, something that might pique Madam Chu's interest in you?"

"I don't understand. Filmmaking is my life."

"Possibly not always all that profitable. I'm a Hollywood baby. Born and brought up here. I have met lots of film producers, and except for a chosen few, most of them are usually hard up for some green paper."

"Too true, oh yes, too too true."

Marlene whispered to Anna May, "The more nervous he gets, the thicker his accent."

Villon spoke. "So it stands to reason to get your hands on some eating money you from time to time dabbled in some extracurricular activities."

His face was red and the veins stood out on his neck. "I don't deny there have been some very ugly rumors about me in Europe. I have enemies. Doesn't everyone?"

"Can you repeat some of those ugly rumors?"

"They're too ugly to repeat!"

"You're among friends, Mr. Trevor."

"Friends don't cross-examine people without any provocation."

"You're not being cross-examined, Mr. Trevor. You're being questioned. No one forced you into this room. You could have refused to cooperate."

"Oh, ho ho ho!" There was no mistaking the sneer in his voice. "Haven't I heard *that* before."

"Then you've been questioned by the police before."

He leaned forward, angry. "Thanks to those bleeding ugly rumors spread by a jealous rival who thought I was having it off with his wife!"

Marlene laughed and couldn't resist asking, "And were you having it off with his wife?"

"I never denied it! But those rumors were inexcusable! And I'm so angry I'll tell you what those rumors were and possibly still exist." He crossed one leg over the other and clasped his knee with his hands. Marlene felt sorry for him now. Only too well did she understand what it was like to be victimized by ugly rumors. "Word was spread that I was financing a prostitution ring. Then there was a story circulating that I was profiting from an organization specializing in illegal adoptions. It was said I traveled the Continent and Asia setting up a ring to steal infants and then offer them up for adoption at very fancy prices."

"Dreadful," said Marlene.

"Dreadful indeed! Who has the time and the money for that kind of an operation? And then the rumors that I was an extortionist, that's how I supposedly largely financed the production of my films. Would you like to hear more, Mr. Villon? Can you digest some additional sordid details?"

Villon said with a small, not unfriendly smile. "You should write your autobiography."

"I am," he said. "I call it *So Help Me God!*"

"Madam Chu was particularly interested in your group. I'm sure you were aware of this."

"I most certainly was. I thought it was me who was the reason for her attention, so I introduced myself and reminded her of the time we took tea at the Sav . . . maybe it was the Grosvenor House?" He could see Villon was growing impatient. "Anyway, she remembered me and then absolutely floored me when she said, 'But do not plan on the realization of a film about Salome'! How about that. I'd been discussing that very idea with Mr. Tensha and the Countess di Frasso on the drive here, and Madam Chu sensed it just by looking at me. That's what she told me. She sensed it just by looking at me. I say, do you suppose she knew she would die tonight?"

No one responded.

"Oh, dear. It is a terrible thought, isn't it?"

"After that tea with her, you had no further dealings with Madam Chu?"

"None." He said it so softly, Villon and Marlene were sure he was lying.

"Tensha says he knew you in Europe. Likewise the Countess. What about the others?"

"I never met any of them until tonight." He had uncrossed

53

his legs, and the palms of his hands rested on his lap. Then he whipped a handkerchief out of his pocket and dabbed at his face. "That's all I can tell you."

Villon dismissed him and Trevor almost leaped out of the room, missing crashing into Hazel Dickson by inches. "If ever anyone looked like a fox being chased by the hounds. Did I miss much?"

"You missed the fox," said Marlene. And what a fox. She knew he spilled the ugly rumors about himself to show he had nothing to fear from them or from Villon's questions. She said to the others, "I think he was fun. Didn't you, Herb?"

"I wouldn't want him to marry my sister."

"Don't be mean, Herb," said Hazel. "You know she's desperate for anyone to pop the question. While I'm on my feet, can I page any of the remaining suspects for you?"

He asked for Dong See, who attacked upon entering with a volley of indignation about being kept waiting and how dare he be subjected to such treatment and how dare anyone think him capable of murder. He might louse up Paganini or Kreisler, but poisoning Mai Mai Chu was so unthinkable, so awful. He paused for breath and Herb jumped in.

"Am I correct in assuming, since both you and the deceased were celebrities on the international circuits, that your paths have crossed before?"

"Mai Mai was a fan of mine and I a great fan of hers."

"But you didn't have much conversation with her tonight, did you?"

"You are quite correct. When I first saw her I waved at her, but she looked right through me, or so I thought. Then I realized she was very preoccupied and probably having one of her visions. I decided I would wait until after her . . . contribution to the evening, when conversation would be easier. A tragic decision on my part. I never dreamt tonight was the last we would see of each other." He turned in his seat to Anna May. "At least we're the better for having known her." Anna May nodded in agreement, and Marlene put her hand over Anna May's.

Responding to other questions, Dong See said that on various occasions he had met Tensha, Trevor, and di Frasso abroad, but had never become intimate with them. To him, the Ivanovs were ciphers, and he totally disapproved of Communists; they didn't pay well. Raymond Souvir was something else. "We were good chums in Paris, good pals. He's a dangerous driver" was added as an afterthought.

"Is there anything else dangerous about him?" Villon asked.

"I think a woman is better qualified to answer that question." Jim Mallory thought his smirk most unbecoming.

"I hope you have no immediate plans to leave the city."

"I shall be around for several months. I'm composing a concerto and have rented a secluded house in the hills." Mallory recorded his address and phone number.

Dong See composing a concerto, Hazel was thinking. Not the greatest item in the world, but still, it might be worth something to *Etude*, the foremost musical magazine.

Raymond Souvir was a much more affable subject of interrogation. He bubbled with enthusiasm at the prospect of his screen test with Marlene, he adored Hollywood and wasn't the climate magnificent, not like the damp and wetness of Paris except in the spring when Paris was glorious and so conducive to romance. And so many beautiful women, how clever of you Marlene and also how brave to invite so many gorgeous creatures into your home to greet the New Year, oblivious of the fact that Marlene liked women and many women were her friends and she didn't give a damn if they were more beautiful and more glamorous than she, because they weren't and that's that. In little over a year she'd become an icon of the silver screen, rivaled only by the enigmatic Garbo, whom many predicted she would soon topple from her pedestal, a prospect that held little interest for Dietrich.

Right now she was wishing he'd shut up and let Villon get on with the questioning. She'd ignored her guests much too long, and by this time she was sure many wanted to go home. Happily, a detective entered with a note for Villon from the coroner and Villon instructed him to lift the embargo on the mansion and let the guests come and go as they pleased. He was pretty damn sure his killer was one of the favored seven suspects.

"How's my party going?" Dietrich asked him.

"Great! Nobody's leaving. And the food's terrific. Boy, those potato latkes!"

"The secret is to keep them thin, very finely grate the onions, and fry them only in Crisco."

With a bewildered look on his face, the detective departed while wondering if she was intimating that she herself had made the potato pancakes.

"Excuse me," Villon said to the actor, who realized he'd been talking too much and now sat placidly awaiting Villon's attention. Villon read the coroner's note, showed it to Mallory, and asked him to pass it on to Marlene. All outward symptoms of the victim pointed to strychnine and he was sure the autopsy would confirm it. Marlene shared the note with Anna May.

Villon studied Raymond Souvir's face briefly before starting his questioning. Dark, suave good looks, typical of a professional model, but he suspected a trace of fear in the eyes. Perhaps it was just nerves; probably Souvir had never been questioned by authority in his past, but who could be sure. Baby-faced killers were epidemic in America. He started the questions. Yes, Souvir had met Mai Mai in Paris several years ago when he was just starting out in show business and occasionaly sang at *Le Boeuf Sur Le Toit* and other popular clubs. Singing was his first profession after a brief career as a photographer's model, and it was Mai Mai who advised him he had latent acting gifts. So he studied with a succession of teachers and then won a lead in the Paris production of Elmer Rice's *Street Scene*, playing the naive son of a Jewish radical. This brought him a few screen offers, and he made three, which brought him to the attention of a Paramount talent scout who suggested that von Sternberg test him for the part of Dietrich's suave and wealthy protector in her next movie, *Blonde Venus*.

"Over the years," asked Villon, "have you kept in touch with Madam Chu?"

"No, not really. But Dong See might have told you, he and I became very good friends in Paris. He would tell me what Madam Chu was up to, and how frequently some of her premonitions displeased people. You know, like tonight, who wants to know there'll be another world war?"

"Tensha." It was Marlene who literally spat the name.

"Of course," agreed Souvir, "munitions." In response to Villon's question as to whether he had ever met any of the others previous to tonight, Souvir said, "I was once interviewed by Mr. Trevor for a film he was planning to do in Paris, but I don't think he remembers me. I met the Countess di Frasso at some parties, but I don't think she likes me." He looked embarrassed. "I once turned down an amorous advance she'd made." He laughed and it was a very nervous laugh. No, he did not see who gave Mai Mai Chu the glass of champagne, because at the time he was trying to signal a waiter to get a glass for himself. As to the Ivanovs, he shrugged and said, "They do not interest me. They are, well, they are peasants."

And where did you spring from, Marlene wondered, from what countryside and from what poor little village where papa probably had a small farm from which he scraped a meager living, where mama was an exhausted wife who had birthed half a dozen brats, most of them unwanted, and milked the cow and sowed the seeds and baked the bread and darned and mended the threadbare rags they wore the year round. Don't be so mean, Marlene admonished herself. He might also be the son of a wealthy manufacturer whose doting father had financed his career.

"Have you any idea which of you might benefit from Madam Chu's death?"

"*Monsieur?*" Souvir looked like a startled faun. Had he

only just realized that he was being questioned because he was a suspected murderer? "Are you thinking that I put the pill in Madam Chu's champagne?"

Villon leaned forward. "How did you know anyone put a poisoned pill in her champagne?"

"Why, why, it was discussed while we were waiting to be questioned. I, I . . . I think it was the Countess di Frasso who said if the champagne was poisoned it could only be with a pill because it would be impossible to pour a liquid into the glass even if the waiter was walking very slowly. As it is, I cannot imagine how one places a pill in a glass when there's danger of being seen by so many people. Oh . . ." There was a strange expression on his face. Villon waited. He knew he was about to hear something important. "Mr. Villon," he pronounced it *Vee-yon* and Hazel thought Herb's name was certainly sexier when spoken with a French accent, "you remember I told you I didn't see who gave Mai Mai Chu the glass of champagne because I was trying to signal a waiter for a glass of my own. But now I remember how it really was. I stopped the waiter who was carrying the champagne to Madam Chu and asked him to please bring me one too. He only stopped for a few seconds."

"More than enough time for someone to seal Madam Chu's doom." Maybe even you, Mr. Frenchman.

"Yes. I'm sorry. I didn't realize. How terrible. In a room so crowded, so noisy, so many of us pushed against each other, it is difficult to remember what one has seen or heard or said."

Villon said to Mallory, "See if di Frasso is still here. If she is, I want to talk to her again."

Souvir turned in his chair to Marlene and Anna May Wong. "I am *distressed!* That I might have been the instrument . . . it is too terrible for me to contemplate!"

Hazel was curious about Mallory's hasty departure. She caught Villon's eye and he signaled her to be patient.

"We all inadvertently make mistakes, Raymond." He wasn't reassured. Anna May was thinking, he stopped the waiter, he could have dropped the pill himself. That was exactly what Marlene, Villon, and Hazel Dickson were thinking. But soon the three would wonder what motive he could possibly have. Unless, as he himself said, he was the instrument. The person instructed to poison the champagne.

"Too ridiculous," said Marlene aloud.

"What's too ridiculous?" asked Villon.

"I'll tell you later."

"Tell me now."

"Later." Her tone of voice said, Don't mess with a Teuton.

"I'm so sorry," Raymond Souvir said in a sad, tired voice.

Nice delivery, thought Marlene. Even the way he's slumped in the chair, he has possibilities. Even if he is almost as pretty as I am. If he gets the part, the women might spend more time looking at him rather than looking at me, which is where they're supposed to be looking. But then, this is moviemaking. Von Sternberg will edit the picture to make sure they mostly look at me. Hell, they won't take their eyes off me after that number where the gorilla enters, makes threatening and subtly obscene gestures at the chorus girls, and then unscrews its head revealing its *me*, *Marlene*, wearing the gorilla suit. God it'll be hot under those lights.

Villon thanked Souvir. Marlene said to the actor, "Stick around for a while, darling, and we'll have a drink. I'll be finished here soon."

"Yes. I'd like that." He hurried out.

The Ivanovs as a replacement for the handsome, gentle young Frenchman were a culture shock. They entered with Jim Mallory, who told Villon he had found the Countess and she was damned annoyed at being recalled but was sitting outside smoking a cigarette and tapping a foot, but he didn't specify which. He brought a second chair to accommodate Gregory Ivanov, Marlene having winced with apprehension when Natalia settled onto the Adam, like a dirigible docking into port.

Hazel thought the Ivanovs were a great double act. If they could master a soft-shoe routine and a couple of choruses of "Dark Eyes" they might be a cinch playing specialty houses.

No, they didn't know Madam Chu personally but had seen her once at a reception in Moscow. They had heard she had once been a mistress of Trotsky's, but Trotsky was now in disfavor and living in exile in Mexico. Gregory asked if they knew that years ago he had been an extra in Hollywood films, and only Jim Mallory was amused by the non sequitur. Neither one of them saw Madam Chu accept the glass of champagne from the waiter, not that this information was necessary any longer, but it did elicit from Natalia that she remembered the waiter pausing briefly next to Raymond Souvir, as she also wanted another glass of champagne. No, they didn't know if Madam Chu had any enemies in Russia, but Gregory had sat behind her at a screening of *Thunder Over China* and she voiced disapproval of the treatment of Orientals in that film. Anna May told Dietrich that they should have heard what she thought of Warner Oland's portrayal of the evil Dr. Fu Man Chu and that Mai Mai was even sorrier that they shared the same surname.

When Villon told them they could go, they quickly thanked Marlene for her hospitality and for a most unusual evening and promised they'd soon be inviting her around for a bowl of borscht with a boiled potato and a dollop of sour cream.

"Yogurt is healthier," said Marlene, having the final word, as usual. Mallory fetched the Countess di Frasso, who was thoroughly annoyed at being brought back for further questioning and said so in no uncertain or polite terms.

"And really Marlene, a lot of your guests are wondering why you're ignoring them!"

Marlene replied, "I will apologize when I return to the ballroom."

"And I certainly don't understand why you and Anna May are privy to these questionings."

"Because I asked them to," said Villon. "I admire their minds and they're being very helpful."

And very decorative, thought Jim Mallory.

"How did you know a strychnine pill was dropped into Madam Chu's champagne?"

"I didn't know; I deduced. The whole party is buzzing that she was poisoned, and I heard one of your detectives mention *nux vomica* and I happen to know the seed of that plant is poisonous, so I had to figure out, and I gather quite correctly, that the pill was an abstract of strychnine. So I shared my knowledge with the others. I must say it didn't seem all that surprising a bit of information to any of them except the two Russian peasants, and I think they're still astonished by indoor plumbing. Is that all?"

"It'll have to be."

"What do you mean by that?"

"It means I got the information I wanted."

She stormed out of the room. Hazel asked, "Aren't any of you hungry? Marlene, the food is absolutely sensational. Your guests attacked everything as though they'd been victims of a famine. Well, Herb, what did you learn tonight that I might use?"

He said matter-of-factly, "One of them is a murderer."

Marlene was lighting a cigarette and Jim Mallory cursed himself for not having leapt in with his lighter. "I'm sure I'm not the only one who had a bit of trouble with some of Raymond Souvir's testimony. If he stopped the waiter, he had the best opportunity to doctor the champagne."

"You're not the only one," said Villon, "but there's no reason why he wanted to murder the woman, unless he, like all the others, is pulling off a pretty good masquerade. I've a theory, but if you're in a hurry to get back to your guests, Marlene, it can wait until tomorrow."

"I'm a firm believer in the present, Herb, such as there's no time like, etc."

"What kind of a threat Madam Chu posed, I do not know. But somehow, somewhere, she stumbled on information that put her life in danger."

Danger! There is danger!

"I think in the past she had small inklings of a plot that in some way links our suspects, and when she saw them together, she had a pretty good idea what was afoot. And someone knew she knew something, and she posed a threat. I think what she knew had been brewing in her mind for several years. She knew these people before at some point or another, and she served them premonitions, her kind of information. Probably seemingly harmless at first, but then as the scenario began taking shape and lengthening, she realized she was onto something more or less of a powder keg."

Hazel asked facetiously, "Sort of like an international plot of some kind? Something linked to that madman she predicted would one day try to take over the world?"

"He's very real, Hazel. He exists. His name is Adolph Hitler. And he is extremely dangerous." Marlene had Hazel convinced.

"Well, my dears," continued Hazel, "I didn't detect any Germans among tonight's septet of suspects."

"There's me," said Marlene. "I'm a kraut, and I can be pretty damned dangerous. And on the other hand, I've also been threatened. When Emil Jannings began to realize I was walking away with *The Blue Angel*, he tried to kill me. I can still feel those brutal hands around my neck. Fortunately, von Sternberg swatted him with a riding crop."

"Anna May, Mai Mai didn't manufacture some of these premonitions, did she?"

"Never. She sometimes misread the charts, but she never tried to marry her astrology to her psychic powers. Very often when she did a chart a premonition flowered, but that was the extent of it. Mai Mai didn't have a dishonest bone in her body."

"But Herb, nobody knew Mai Mai was to be here tonight. Only Anna May and I knew."

"Isn't it possible she spoke to someone on the phone who said they were coming here tonight, and she said, 'Oh, I'll be there too,'" asked Herb.

"Very possible," agreed Marlene, "and whoever it was

came prepared to kill her. Now, who among them did she know so intimately that she'd phone and say, 'What are you doing tonight'?"

"No one," said Anna May. "If I hadn't ask her to join me tonight, she would have spent the evening with herself and her charts. No Marlene. No Herb. Someone phoned her. It had to be someone who was desperate to see her and quiet her."

"How I adore puzzles!" exclaimed Marlene. "Let's keep thinking, and now I must return to my party. Young man!" Jim Mallory realized he meant her. His knees were turning to jelly. "Would you be a darling and escort me back to the ballroom? She put her arm in his and thought she heard him say *Ideedoonerd*. What he had said was, "I'd be honored."

Of course, the first step he took, he tripped.

⟪ SIX ⟫

BEDLAM REIGNED IN the ballroom. The reporters and photographers had invaded the premises once Villon ordered the security laxed, and most of Marlene's guests were cooperating with the gentlemen of the press. Marlene was immediately surrounded like a wagon train besieged by Commanches and as usual handled the reporters with tact, savoir faire, and good humor. Villon admired the way she fielded their questions while making sure the photographers were favoring her best angles. Hazel Dickson turned the other cheek to the sniping of her envious colleagues, the least nasty comment being called "Teacher's pet." Anna May bore the brunt of the inquiries into the personal and private life of Mai Mai Chu while Herb Villon told the press he had some good leads and hoped to have a more concrete story for them within the next few days.

Anna May and Marlene posed for the photographers in a variety of groupings, none of them particularly original. Marlene posed with Raymond Souvir and Joseph von Sternberg, and then Marlene was grouped with Anna May and Dong See. Ben Schulberg, the West Coast head of Paramount Pictures, managed to corner Marlene privately for a few seconds.

"What's going on? Are you in the clear? There must be no scandal!" Scandal, thought Marlene, what about you and Sylvia Sidney. What she said was, "Murder is always a scandal, Ben, and it's unfortunate it happened in my house, but since it did, there's nothing we can do about it. Make the most of it! *Shanghai Express* will soon be going into release and here are Anna May and I, both in the picture and both the center of a murder mystery. That should prove profitable publicity."

His eyes lit up. "You've got something there. I'll remind the press you're both in *Shanghai Express*. You're not under suspicion, are you?"

Said Dietrich wearily, "No, Ben, The detective in charge is a friend of a friend and I'm being cooperative. Actually, I'm enjoying the experience tremendously. I'm learning a lot about police work. Maybe we could do a movie with me as a detective."

"There's nothing glamorous about you as a detective."

"Why not? I could wear a low-cut holster." She saw Villon having a private conversation with Anna May and wondered what was going on.

Anna May was telling Villon about Mai Mai's loft downtown on the outskirts of Chinatown. "The keys must be in her handbag." Villon told her the handbag accompanied the body to the morgue. He signaled Jim Mallory to his side and told him to call the morgue and have them deliver the handbag to his office. He was looking forward to several hours in Mai Mai's loft.

Marlene's eyes caught Raymond Souvir deep in a discussion with Dong See. Souvir seemed agitated. Marlene longed to have a talk with the actor. She found Hazel Dickson and asked her to separate the two men. "I want a little time alone with Raymond," she explained.

"Who wouldn't?" asked Hazel as she set off to accomplish her mission. A moment later, Marlene had her arm through one of Souvir's and walked him to an isolated spot near the bandstand. A downbeat orchestration of "With a Song in My Heart" served as a background.

Souvir said, "I saw Mr. Schulberg talking to you. Does he know I'm a suspect?"

"Don't let it bother you, Raymond. Ben Schulberg has more serious problems at the studio. He may soon be out of a job."

"Oh my God, supposing his replacement doesn't like me? Ben Schulberg likes me. He told someone he did."

"Stop fretting, Raymond. The studio spent a great deal of money importing you for this test, and they will make the test. Von Sternberg wants the test and I want the test, and whatever Marlene wants, Marlene gets. Now tell me, before we're interrupted, have you ever had an astrological chart done for you?"

He said quickly, "No."

"Now, Raymond," she bore down heavily on his name, "Mai Mai Chu didn't forecast your stars in Paris?"

"I . . . I . . ."

"Raymond, this is Marlene. Never lie to Marlene. Marlene is a great believer in and respecter of the truth. The truth will out. Am I right in saying that in Paris, thanks to Dong See's friendship with Mai Mai Chu, she did your chart?"

He was deflated. "Yes. It was a birthday present from Dong. But that was two or three years ago. I haven't seen Mai Mai since, that is until tonight."

"Why did you try to hedge?"

"Because I'm afraid. I want nothing to do with this case. I didn't kill her. I swear on my mother's life."

"What was going on just now between you and Dong."

"Nothing was going on."

"I saw you, and my eyes are very good. You were upset about something. Did it have something to do with Dong's friendship with Mai Mai?"

"No! I told him how upset I was at being questioned by the detective. It could be bad publicity, and Marlene, I need to succeed in Hollywood."

"And if you don't?" His shoulders slumped. Marlene was sympathetic. "You'll always have a career on the Continent. And you're still young. If you fail this time, there's the chance of another try for the brass ring. Now tell me the truth, did you know there was a plot to kill Mai Mai?"

"No! I knew nothing about Mai Mai. I just happened to be here, that's all."

Dietrich decided on another tack. "When Mai Mai read your chart, did she reveal anything startling or unusual that the future held for you?"

"I don't believe in the stars, Marlene, I believe in myself."

"You don't believe in the stars and yet you want to be one."

"Please don't put me on."

"Raymond, I have had myself charted many times. I'm a Capricorn. What's your sign?"

"Taurus."

"Of course. The bull. Very stubborn. You must have had some prognostication from Mai Mai that you've never forgotten."

"Yes. She predicted that my success in France would continue. But that . . ."—he hesitated. She waited. ". . . that it would be interrupted. There would be a scandal."

"Wouldn't it be ironic that it might be Mai Mai's murder?"

"Yes, that's what I was telling Dong."

"Really? But you seemed so upset. If you don't believe in the stars, why be upset? Shrug it off and get on with your life."

"I had forgotten it until Dong reminded me. He thought he was being funny."

"I have learned from experience that humor wears many faces. Some cheerful, some nasty. You mustn't let it upset you. You mustn't let the fear of failure hang around your neck like a dead albatross. You live extravagantly, I assume you have a great deal of money."

"That won't last."

Marlene arched an eyebrow. "Oh?"

"What I mean is, I have to continue earning to live on the scale that I do."

"Don't we all, darling? They pay me one hundred and fifty thousand dollars per picture and I haven't a nickel saved. But my charts tell me my star will shine for many many years to come, so I don't worry." She smiled and said, "Dong See has found us. Don't look so upset. Laugh. Go ahead. Laugh." He laughed, a laugh that had the strength of an infant's burp. Dong See joined them. "Well Dong, I was hoping to ask you to play for us tonight, but I suppose now it's too late unless you chose to do 'Danse Macabre.' "

"Anything at this point would be an anticlimax," said Dong. "I'm tired, Raymond. Much though I'm not looking forward to it, please drive me home."

Marlene took each man by an arm and said forcefully, "Not until we've had a drink to the New Year. I think it's going to be a fascinating and exciting year. In fact, I don't have to think, the charts assure me that's how it will be." She was steering them to the nearest bar. "By the way, Raymond, by any chance was your father a farmer?"

"My father? My father owned a draper's shop in Rouen. That's where I was born." And he refrained from adding, And I wish I was there now.

No farmer, thought Marlene. Wrong again. At the bar, a young actor was wiping liquid from his shirt front with a bar towel.

"What happened?" asked Marlene.

"I tried to drink champagne from Carole Lombard's slipper. It was open-toed."

Jim Mallory watched the bartender pouring three glasses of champagne for Marlene, Souvir, and Dong See. How fickle she is, he thought sadly. She asks me to escort her into the ballroom, I trip and fall flat on my face, everybody laughs, and I look and feel like a damned fool. He felt an arm around his shoulders and looked into Herb Villon's sympathetic face. Villon said, "Don't ask for a star, Jim. You have the moon." And indeed, looking out a window, Mallory could see a full moon in the sky.

"That explains it," said Jim.

"Explains what?"

"Tonight. The edginess. The uneasiness. The murder. Full moon. Nothing goes right when there's a full moon. Madam Chu's handbag is on its way to your office."

"Good boy. How's for some champagne?" He led Mallory to the bar, where Marlene greeted them, raising her glass high and offering a toast. "To Mai Mai's murderer! May you catch him before he strikes again!"

Dong See asked, "You think there'll be another murder?"

"There has to be. One is never enough, isn't that so . . ." —she imitated Souvir—". . . m'sieu Vee-yon?"

"Not necessarily."

"If you catch the killer within the next ten minutes, then you're right. But you won't because he or she isn't about to confess or give themselves away, and you don't have enough evidence to pin it on anyone, so by the law of averages, the killer will strike again."

Villon laughed. "You've seen too many movies."

"I rarely go to the movies, Herbert Villon. The killer will strike again because he has to." She held center stage and showed she intended to make the most of the spotlight. "He's afraid that either he's been seen spiking Mai Mai's drink or there's someone who's a party to his crime and can't be trusted and must therefore be silenced. Right, Herb Villon?"

"I hope you're wrong." The bartender had poured drinks for him and Mallory, and Herb lifted his. "I can't stand a case cluttered with too many corpses."

"Can't you handle the traffic?" She was enjoying baiting him. She'd bet her bottom dollar that she and Villon were on the same wavelength. She hadn't told anyone yet, and she soon intended to tell Villon, but she was convinced that Mai Mai's murder was a conspiracy and she was convinced Villon had come to the same conclusion. "It stands to reason there has to be another victim, what with so many suspects involved. Oh Raymond, you're perspiring. You mustn't take me so seriously. It's the New Year and I haven't eaten and I'm feeling a bit light-headed, and look at Dong See, a masterpiece of composure. Where are the others? Let me see, the Ivanovs I'm sure have gone home. Too bad there's no snow; she could have whipped the horses mercilessly as their sleigh headed back to the embassy, fearful of being pursued by a pack of wolves with red-rimmed eyes. But no fear, Natalia Ivanov would wring their necks and skin them and stitch together their hides into a very handsome lap robe.

"Ah! Monte Trevor! He has trapped the luscious Miriam Hopkins and is probably offering *her* Salome. Look how eager she looks. Miriam is a true daughter of the south, all corn pone and hominy grits and thick slices of ham drowning in a sea of pineapple juice laced with brown sugar. Our Miriam sure does know how to play the coquette. *Gott im Himmel!* She slapped his face and there she goes flouncing off in a rage. He didn't offer her Salome, he offered her his very own extraordinarily revolting self for a romp in her boudoir. Good for you, Miriam, I see you in a refreshing new light, no longer the loud-mouthed, demanding, and insulting boor that we all know you to be.

"Who's missing? Let me think. Of course. Ivar Tensha and Dorothy di Frasso. And here's Hazel to claim her detective. Hazel? Have you seen the munitions maker and the gossip maker? Wait! There's the Countess worrying Gary Cooper! Oh, poor Gary, his vocabulary is as limited as his self-restraint. Unless my instincts betray me, he'll be her late snack and her breakfast. But wait, wait, who is the patrician beauty coming to claim him?" She sipped her drink. She was enjoying herself enormously. "I remember, the Sandra something to whom we are told he has offered matrimony. Don't hesitate, young woman, grab him. He is very very eloquent when horizontal. Aha! The Countess retreats! She's studying the stag line. The one at the end, darling, the handsome creature with the cleft in his chin. Cary Grant. Tallulah's already made a bid, but I don't think he's listening to offers. The Countess sees him. She is sashaying towards him. But wait. There's Groucho! He's loping towards her with his gorgeous leer."

Groucho pounced on Dorothy di Frasso, took her in his arms, and asked, "May I have this dance? You can lead, but let me guess where. Please dance with me. I'm a terminal case. I'm not sure which terminal. Union Station or Grand Central." The Countess tore away from him and with a shrug Groucho went in search of a fresh victim.

Marlene laughed and continued. "But where is Tensha? Could he have left without saying goodnight to his hostess, who admits that for a while she was a bit derelict in her duties. But it isn't every hostess who has the good luck to have a murder committed under her very roof and under her very nose. Surely Tensha would have sought me out to thank me for a perfectly wonderful evening despite a fatal flaw. Ah! As they say in very bad operettas, Here he comes now."

Ivar Tensha had the Countess on his arm, an obscene cigar in his mouth, and an anxious look on his face. The Countess di Frasso looked none too happy. Monte Trevor was coming up behind them with the kind of look that made Dietrich wonder if he was planning to make off with the silver. Tensha took Marlene's hand and kissed it. She planned to scrub the hand with a strong disinfectant. "Thank you for such a wonderful evening. Despite the unpleasantness, I had a very lovely time. Good night to all of you."

"I'm sure we'll be meeting again," said Villon.

Marlene cried out in despair, beautifully timed and beautifully acted, "But you can't leave so soon? It's the shank of the evening." It was one in the morning, but to Marlene any hour of the night was the shank. "There is still so much for us to talk about. I insist you have one more drink with me. I insist! Do not demur! Bartender?"

"Yes, Miss Dietrich?"

"Fresh drinks all around. In fact, there's something missing from the champagne!" She diplomatically refrained from suggesting that what was missing was strychnine. "A few drops of green mint in each drink. It does wonders for your sinuses. Will any of us ever forget this night? Will you, Dorothy? Or you, Mr. Trevor?" She smiled at Villon, who could tell she was up to no good, and whatever it was he hoped it would take effect.

"May I join the party?" Anna May Wong looked wan and unhappy.

"Of course, darling. How terrible this has been for you. Anna May knew Mai Mai Chu since she was a child. Anna May, do you think Mai Mai read in her chart that tonight foretold tragedy for her?"

"She might have," said Anna May. They'd discuss the possibility earlier. What is Marlene up to, she wondered.

Marlene's eyes were like the beacon atop a lighthouse as they swept from face to face. "Have any of you who knew Mai Mai before tonight had their charts done by her? I know Monsieur Souvir had his read several years ago, a birthday gift from Dong See. Raymond is a Taurus. Taurus the bull. Very stubborn. He does not tell much. Dong, did Mai Mai read you?"

"I think so. I don't recall."

Anna May stared at him. Obviously she has read you and you remember what was important to remember.

"You, Mr. Trevor. You tried to get Mai Mai to star in a film about herself. I'll bet you dollars to doughnuts before rejecting your offer she did a chart and was guided by it."

"By Jove, come to think of it, she did do a chart and the bloody thing did work against me."

Anna May said, "Then she also did your personal chart."

"Actually, she did. But I couldn't remember the time of my birth, I was so young then. She chose the neutral hour of twelve noon."

"That's a common practice among astrologers when the subject doesn't know the actual time of birth. It doesn't make for too accurate a chart, but the approximation is serviceable." Anna May wondered if Raymond Souvir was feeling ill.

Marlene wasn't satisfied with Trevor's response and beamed her eyes at Tensha. "Mr. Tensha, why do I have a

hunch Mai Mai once did your chart? I think tonight was not
the first time you heard her predict another world war."

He took the cigar out of his mouth and stared at the ash. He
knew better than to flick it on the floor. He couldn't stand the
thought of Marlene ordering him on his knees and commanding him to wipe up the mess with a handkerchief. Though had
he had a better view of the rest of the ballroom, he would have
seen a vast expanse of untidiness that did not speak well for
the community of Hollywood luminaries. "Marlene, you
make me think of Cassandra. She was also a bit of a witch.
Madam Chu did indeed read my chart several years ago and
headed me off from what she predicted would have been a
disastrous marriage. I was smitten with a German actress
named Lya dePutti."

"It was *you*!" gasped Marlene.

"I gather you knew Lya," said the munitions czar.

"I adored her. She committed suicide. Was it because of
you?"

"I choose to think not. I gave her a handsome settlement to
release me from our marriage contract."

Hazel Dickson was telling Herb and Mallory that Lya
dePutti had been Emil Jannings's leading woman in a brilliant
German film, *Variety*, six years earlier.

The bartender had freshened Marlene's glass. "Tell me,
Mr. Tensha, did she put you off anything else?"

"No. She did predict I would have a long and unhappy life.
Does that answer you satisfactorily?"

"Not really. But it will serve for now. Dorothy? What
about you? It seems to me there would have been at least one
occasion when you might have looked for Madam Chu's
services."

"I find your smugness most unbecoming, Marlene. I don't
see at all what horoscopes have to do with Mai Mai's murder."

"Horoscopes, my dear Countess di Frasso, have everything
to do with Mai Mai's murder. May I tell her why, detective
Villon?"

Hazel stared at Villon with a quizzical expression. *The son of a bitch has been holding out on me. He's told Marlene something but he hasn't told me. He'll sleep alone tonight.*

Herb Villon's expression was neutral. He was like a car idling at a traffic light, waiting to shift gears. He didn't know whether to consider hugging Marlene or strangling her. At the same time, he knew there was no stopping her. She'd had a lot to drink, although he didn't know this didn't matter, as she could drink almost a case of champagne a day, and frequently did, without any telling effect. He said, "By all means tell her whatever you plan to tell her, but I don't remember telling you anything."

"That's quite right, Herbert, so stop staring daggers at him Hazel, he's perfectly innocent of whatever you think he's guilty of. So what I'm telling you, my dear Dorothy, is a deduction of my own, and I think it's a damned good one." She paused for dramatic effect, took a deep swig of the bubbly, let her eyes slowly travel from face to anxious face, wishing en route she could pat Raymond Souvir on the head to assuage his apparent anxieties, winning Anna May's admiration for the way she had the circle of people hanging on her every movement, her every word, and finally came back to Dorothy di Frasso. "In all these charts, I think Mai Mai predicted something involving the seven people she saw tonight before she was murdered. What she predicted was too terrible for her to try to handle. And I don't think she realized the enormity of the prognostication until she saw all of you together. She suddenly realized that on separate occasions she had made this same terrible prediction about all of you. But someone knew this could happen, especially when told that Mai Mai was being brought to my party by Anna May, and so it was necessary to plot to kill Mai Mai. And it didn't matter if she proved to be an immediate threat or not. She simply had to be eliminated as a precaution."

"Absolutely, utterly ridiculous!" said Dorothy di Frasso.

"That's what some nasty critic wrote about me in my first

film, *The Little Napoleon*. I don't know what's become of the critic, but I'm sure doing fine."

You sure are, thought Herb Villon, and whether you know it or not, you've just set yourself up as a target. He decided to try to take the curse off it. "Marlene, where do you get such outrageous theories?"

Marlene feigned sadness. "Ah, Herbert. Is it so outrageous? Is it any more outrageous then the Teapot Dome? The Boston Red Sox scandal? Your Jim Fiske's plot to destroy the American economy in 1879 or whatever the hell the date was?"

Ivar Tensha offered Dorothy di Frasso his arm, which she took willingly. There was obviously no Mrs. Tensha, and she was in need of a healthy bankroll. The crash of '29 had hurt her more than she thought. Marlene kissed Souvir goodnight and then made a swipe at Dong See's cheek but didn't quite connect. She shook Monte Trevor's hand and decided there was more strength in a filleted codfish. She caught the odd look with which Tensha favored her as he looked over his shoulder on his way toward the staircase. Dorothy di Frasso waved goodnight to several people as she passed them on the way out, and then she too took a last look at Marlene. Marlene raised her glass of champagne to her and then downed the contents.

Herb Villon said to her, "If you're looking for trouble, I think you've found it."

She looked coy. "Are you mad at me?"

Marlene Dietrich or no Marlene Dietrich, I'll slap her silly if she's after Herb, thought Hazel.

"You went a little too far, I think."

"I don't think so. I also don't think I know what I'm talking about, but the theory just came to me in a champagne flash and I just couldn't stop myself. Anyway, it made a lot of people uncomfortable. Maybe not all of them, but a lot of them. Now, whose got the keys to Mai Mai's place. It's somewhere near Chinatown, right Anna May?"

"She's amazing," Herb said to Jim Mallory.

Mallory said, "I'd go through fire for her without wearing asbestos."

"Herbert," commanded Marlene, "we must go to her apartment and search her files. I'm sure she keeps files. We must search her files for horoscopes, copies of horoscopes, and then we'll find out for sure if I'm crazy or not. Mr. Mallory, you don't have a drink! Quick bartender, champagne for the adorable Mr. Mallory and his adorable dimples. Quick, Herb, catch him. I think he's fainting!"

◖◗ SEVEN ◗◗

THE ORCHESTRA WAS playing "Good Night, Ladies" without much energy and even less enthusiasm. The few remaining guests who were still ambulatory took the hint and made their departures without so much as a 'good night' or a 'thank you' to their generous hostess. Marlene had indeed set a magnificent table, and never again would her guests witness the Niagara of bootleg booze and champagne she had provided.

What a waste of time, Gus Arnheim, the orchestra leader, was thinking. She could have thrown this bash at the Cocoanut Grove, one of the industry's most popular night spots, which was his steady venue, and there wouldn't be this mess to clean up. Not so much a waste of time as a waste of money. The party must have cost many thousands; what profligate spending in these financially depressed times. Then he reminded himself, Miss Dietrich is a queen, and queens are only happiest reigning in their own palaces.

Marlene urged Anna May Wong to spend the night in a guest room, and the emotionally exhausted actress was more than grateful for the offer. A butler escorted Anna May to the room.

Herb Villon stood in the hallway that separated the ballroom from the den and the library, obviously loath to leave. He'd sent Hazel home with Jim Mallory, Hazel trying her best not to be suspicious of why Villon was remaining behind.

From inside the ballroom, where she was pacing about in a wide circle, very deep in serious thought, Marlene saw Villon from a corner of her eye. She went to a bar, grabbed a bottle of champagne by the neck, dexterously maneuvered a grip on two glasses, and slunk her way toward the waiting detective with an exaggerated gyration of her hips. "I had an idea you'd hang around after the others left." She led the way to the library. "It's more comfortable in the library," she said, "unless Mai Mai's ghost is in there trying to make contact with you to name her killer."

"I don't think she knew who her killer was. In fact, I don't think she had much time to do much thinking. Strychnine works faster then a whore on the make."

Marlene handed him the bottle. "Here, darling, put your thumbs to work."

"You sure you want more of this stuff?"

"Darling," she said wearily, "let me hear the cork pop." She took a cigarette from a Tiffany box on a table, lit it, and then sank into an overstuffed easy chair. She heard the pop and was at peace. She watched him pour through smoke-fogged eyes. She accepted her glass and he sat opposite her in a Morris chair. They toasted the New Year for the umpteenth time, and Marlene kicked off her shoes. "Imagine being a wallflower at my own party. I didn't dance one dance tonight." She laughed. "Wait till I tell Maria in the morning. Anyway, Herbert Villon detective first class par excellence, you stayed because you don't think my conspiracy theory is all that farfetched."

"No more farfetched than the one I'm kicking around. My big problem is picturing these seven suspects as conspirators. I can't see them working in concert. Some of them don't seem to know each other that well."

"M'sieu Vee-yone," and she thought of Raymond Souvir's

moments of stress, "when I walk on the set of a movie the first day of shooting, I might have met some of the other actors at some time or other, but mostly, I haven't. In no time, in a few days or so, it's as though we've known each other for years. Shooting a movie is a form of conspiracy. We actors are working in concert under a director we hopefully respect and with technicians who we know will do their damndest to make us look good, and if the Gods are smiling on us, our conspiracy will result in nine to twelve reels of a very entertaining movie. When we're finished, we move on to the next conspiracy, probably never to see each other again, though in this town that's hardly avoidable. I hope I'm making sense."

"You're doing great."

"Let me continue. As to seeing these seven as conspirators, let's begin with the two who have come to us already professing great affection for each other as bosom buddies, though neither one of them has much of a bosom to speak off. Raymond Souvir and Dong See."

"Souvir's a frightened rabbit."

"And rabbits are great survivors. That's why they have so much time to multiply. Souvir is frightened, perhaps, yet according to Dong See he drives like a devil pursued. Reckless drivers have a very macho image of themselves, and I believe Raymond Souvir is mucho macho. He's also very ambitious. And I suspect he's also very ruthless. The French are usually very ruthless, which is why I adore them and plan to spend my fading years in one of the better *arrondissements* of Paris. Souvir is driven by ambition. His only real worry tonight was whether the powers-that-be at the studio would cancel his test if he were implicated in Mai Mai's murder." She took a deep drag on the cigarette. "I don't think you are reading Raymond's fear correctly. There are lots of kinds of fear. I think Raymond, like all the others, has been very glibly lying. Let's begin with his life-style.

"He rents a very expensive, furnished house on Doheny. He's at one club or another every night of the week except Sunday, I've been told, squiring a variety of beauties who have expensive tastes. Where does the money come from? His career in Europe? Let's examine that. He's had some success as a singer and made three films. I know the kind of salaries they pay in Europe. Nothing to compare to what we're paid here. Raymond hasn't been on the scene long enough to amass any impressive bank account or assets. The road to success is paved with parasites with their hands outstretched. So I suspect Raymond is being financed."

Herb was sponging up her information. "You mean somewhere in the background there's a rich sponsor."

"It's certainly not his family. They're middle class and like all good French people live strictly within their means. The only French person I know who's heavily in debt is Mistinguett, and that lady is famous for her legs, not her business acumen. My theory is that Raymond is financed by a group, a company, a corporation."

"Why?"

"How the hell do I know? We're only talking theory, right? Why is that bottle so far away. Put it on the table between us." Chore finished, Herb settled back in his chair. "Raymond and Dong See profess a great bonding between them. This is not unusual between men without the specter of sex rearing its delicious head. How this came about I can only speculate. The usual deduction, if they're not lovers, is they were introduced at some point, liked each other, and nursed the friendship along. But from the dark side of my speculations I see them assigned to like each other."

"They're good friends, strangers in a strange city, and yet they're not living together."

"Exactly, darling. Musical professionals are a drearily demanding and temperamental species. Living with them can be hell. And in Dong See I detect a very selfish, very single-minded young man who is terrified in Souvir's passenger seat. Musicians are very disciplined; they have to be or they're second-rate. Dong See is very disciplined. I'm sure he does as he's told."

"Meaning he knows how to take orders and follow through."

"That's my theory, mind you. I don't want to be charged with slander should you one day turn on me."

"I don't turn that easily."

"That's what I thought. Now the Ivanovs. They are Bolsheviks, not the best example of Bolsheviks, but they'll do until something more dangerous comes along. They are underlings and will go through life as underlings. They were born to obey orders, although I suspect Natalia, behind all those phony tears, is a very determined woman. If this conspiracy is international, then of course the Ivanovs are the cubs of the Russian bear. Actually, I'm rather amazed the Russians are participating in a conspiracy with members of the outside world, because the Bolshies are so isolated and so insular. They are very suspicious people, and trust my words, their isolation and suspicion will be their undoing. Maybe not in our time, but in time. Let's set them aside and save them for future reference."

"I hope for their sakes they turn out to be priceless treasures. They're both so nondescript I almost feel sorry for them."

"They should do something about their teeth." She paused, sipped some champagne, took another drag on the cigarette, and then, stifling a yawn, said, "Monte Trevor. Is he or isn't he?"

"Is he or isn't he what?" We know he's produced movies."

"Is he or isn't he a conspirator. And if he is, why?"

"Do you suppose it takes special credentials to be a conspirator?"

"I don't know. I've never been one, except as a member of an acting company." She laughed. "Come on, Herb. We're both thinking conspiracies are secret meetings in sinister old mansions with hidden wall panels leading to secret passageways that end in a heavily draped room with a solitary lamp in the middle of a round table, and sitting around the table a mysterious assemblage of people with black hoods masking their faces."

"I saw that movie and I hated it."

"I didn't see any movie. I made it all up. I don't think Monte Trevor could conspire to form a poker game. But here he is, arriving at the party in the company of the very socially prominent Dorothy di Frasso and the very powerful and fearsome Ivar Tensha. I don't see Tensha as a man who suffers fools easily, so Monte Trevor must have some kind of a certain something to attract Tensha to him."

"I should think Tensha's the type who needs a lot of errand boys, a master at demanding servility. I'm sure he has his henchmen deployed all over the world."

"Henchmen, hmm. Monte Trevor could be an ideal henchman, couldn't he?"

"Especially if it could mean raising the financing for a movie."

Marlene gestured at the bottle and Villon refilled her glass. "Dorothy di Frasso is a very shrewd, very calculating woman. She's been welcomed in international circles for years. She has a charming façade and is very democratic. She entertains royalty and commoners alike. Of course, she adores Mussolini, which makes her suspect in my book. Could she be a conspirator? And if so, to what purpose?"

"She has useful contacts, you say." Marlene nodded. "That's very important to a conspiracy."

"So we mustn't dismiss Dorothy too easily. Although I also suspect she has designs on Tensha."

"Why not?"

"She hasn't a hope in hell. Men like Tensha never marry, and if they do, they sequester the little woman in a villa in some forest or another where she takes up with her chauffeur or else spends most of her time developing housemaid's knee from all that genuflecting in church."

Villon said, "Tensha would have to be playing a very important, very powerful role. I don't see him taking a backseat or playing a secondary role."

82

Marlene was staring into her drink. Herb exaggerated clearing his throat and Marlene looked up. "I was thinking of Raymond Souvir stopping the waiter who was bringing Mai Mai her drink."

"Butler," Villon corrected her.

"Butler, waiter, they're all the same damn thing. Wait a minute!" She was on her feet. "He wasn't one in my regular employ. He was hired for the party along with several others. I got them all from an agency. My butlers weren't circulating serving drinks. I placed them in doorways so they could guide people to the bathrooms or whatever, take coats, keep out the uninvited."

"You think this man might have doctored Mai Mai's drink?"

"Why not?"

"Why yes? Could he have known Mai Mai? Highly unlikely."

"But he could have been paid to drop the pill. Isn't that possible?"

"In a case of murder, anything's possible." Villon's back ached, and he was beginning to long to get home and postpone further speculation to a time later in the day, but Marlene was just warming up and not about to let him escape.

"You need food. Let's go to the kitchen and scramble some eggs." She put on her shoes. He dutifully made his way with her to the kitchen, where the hired help were still cleaning up. Marlene grabbed Herb's wrist. "That's him. The butler. The one drying the pans."

The man looked tired but smiled affably when Marlene put her hand on his shoulder. "You did a very good job tonight. You all did." Her voice encompassed all the help, who managed to look pleased by the compliment. "Of course," she said to the man, whose name was Morton Duncan, "it was terrible that Madam Chu was murdered."

"It must be awful for you," commiserated Duncan, "having her done in right here on the premises. Being such a good friend of yours."

"Yes, it was sad she was 'done in,' as you so quaintly put it, but she was not a good friend; tonight's the first I laid eyes on her."

"Oh. I was under the impression she was an old friend."

Herb took over. "You brought the drink to Madam Chu, didn't you?"

Duncan looked uncomfortable. "Sir, I didn't know it was poisoned."

"I'm not saying you did. Who asked you to bring the drink to her?"

"Miss Wong. She took it from the bartender and placed it on my tray and asked me to take it to Madam Chu, but to use discretion when interrupting her dissertation."

Marlene said, "Anna May most certainly did not poison the drink. You couldn't possibly suspect her."

"I could suspect anybody. It's a free country." He asked Duncan, "And Mr. Souvir stopped and asked you to bring him a glass too, didn't he?"

"If you mean the Frenchman, he did that."

"You didn't see someone's hand passing over the glass?" continued Villon.

"Well, sir, in the moment or so that the Frenchman distracted me, that could have happened, but I didn't see it. There was such a crush of people around me, I was having difficulty getting through to Madam Chu. Believe me if I had seen anything that seemed out of sorts I would say so, Miss Dietrich. It pains me to know that I was the bearer of death."

Bearer of death. Marlene stifled a laugh. The ancients killed the messenger who brought bad news. They should kill critics who write bad reviews. She said to Duncan, "I'm sure it's a very painful memory. But you were just an instrument, don't blame yourself."

They left the man and Dietrich was soon busy scrambling eggs. Marlene asked Villon, "What do you think? Do you believe him?"

"I have to believe him. I'll do a check on him. See if he has any record."

"I hope he doesn't. I think he might be a poet. 'Bearer of death.' Wasn't that sweet? Can you imagine those words spoken by Erich von Stroheim? He'd really make you tremble at the sound of them." With a cigarette dangling from her mouth, she continued scrambling the eggs, into which she poured some cream, then added a dash of cinnamon and just a drop of curry powder. Villon heated ham, which he cut from the bone, a remnant of the party's buffet.

"You know something, Herb? I just had a terrible thought. There were so many people at the party tonight, maybe we're barking up the wrong conspiracy. Maybe one of the other guests is the guilty party."

"They weren't clustered around a waiter carrying a tray that held a poisoned glass of champagne. Believe me, Marlene, the killer is one of my seven suspects. . . ."

"*Our* seven suspects, Mr. Villon. I'm in on this with you, and don't you dare try to cut me out! Don't slice so much ham; we'll have to eat it all or it dries out. And there's nothing so appalling as dried out ham. Take it from me, I've worked with enough of them. Now, before I forget, what time tomorrow are we going to Mai Mai's loft? Not too early, we both need some sleep. Of course, Anna May must be there with us, in case there are things written in Chinese, and she can translate for us. And, of course, that darling assistant of yours, Jim Mallory. Now wasn't that strange, fainting the way he did."

"He was overcome with love."

"Love? Nobody has fainted because of love since the middle of the last century, and even then, I suspect it was all feigned. Who's he in love with?"

"You."

"Really? How adorable. But in a very nice way, you must tell him he'll have to step to the rear of the line. Herb, if only you knew what I have to put up with. Get the plates. The eggs are ready."

In the guest room, Anna May Wong was pacing the floor. She couldn't sleep what with Mai Mai's face contorted in the agony of her death throes reflected everywhere she looked. She could still hear her father's cry when she told him Mai Mai was dead, murdered.

"How often I warned her, how often I pleaded with her to exercise greater discretion with her premonitions. Why didn't she listen? She was always so headstrong, so foolhardy. She was not a true Chinese woman."

Poor father. A true Chinese woman. And what is that? Subservient, obedient, with bound feet. Thank God I never had to undergo that agony of the primitive custom of the binding of women's feet.

Always so headstrong, always so foolhardy.

Stubborn. Like Taurus the bull. Stubborn, like Dong See, a Taurus. Why think of him now? Strange, his friendship with Raymond Souvir. Such an unlikely pairing. But still, why not?

She found a negligee in the closet and put it on. She recognized it as one Marlene had worn in *Dishonored*. She left the room quietly in search of the kitchen to warm up some milk. When she reached the kitchen, there were Marlene and Villon eating ham and eggs.

"Oh good!" cried Marlene.

"What's good about not being able to sleep? I'm going to warm up some milk."

"Warm up some red wine. *That'll* make you sleep."

"No, thank you, I've drunk enough tonight."

"Tomorrow, Anna May, we go to Mai Mai's apartment. We need you there in case there's any Chinese that needs translating."

"Marlene, it's all in Chinese. She always did her charts in Chinese." They now had the kitchen to themselves. Anna May stirred the milk with a spoon. "My father said on the phone tonight, Mai Mai was always so headstrong, so foolhardy. If she knew something of such great importance, why didn't she take it to the proper authorities?"

Marlene placed her fork on her plate. "Maybe she did. And whatever authority she went to was the wrong authority. Isn't that a possibility, Herb? And of course it's a probability the wrong authority was a guest at my party tonight." Herb chewed thoughtfully. "Anna May, the milk's boiling over."

"So are all of our conjectures," said Herb. "We've got an awful lot on the plate. Now to sift what we've got and sort it out and then put it back together again in a different shape, which will show us the face of the killer."

Marlene looked at her wristwatch. "It's 4 A.M. If we meet again at two this afternoon, that ought to give us plenty of time to sleep. I've got several New Year's Day invitations, but the hell with them. Finding Mai Mai's killer takes top priority." She rubbed her hands together at the prospect of unmasking a murderer. "I wonder which of our suspects are boiling some milk to help them get some sleep."

◖◗ EIGHT ◖◗

SLEEP ELUDED DOROTHY di Frasso. She was annoyed when Ivar Tensha refused her offer of a nightcap. They had dropped off Monte Trevor at his hotel, the Beverly Wilshire, the producer accepting his dismissal reluctantly. Thankfully the bar was still open and catering to some noisy revelers. Monte had a horn blown in his ear and confetti flung in his face and tried to look good-natured about it, but barely succeeded. He ordered a highball with a double shot of scotch and settled onto a stool to rerun in his mind the reel of film whose subject was Dietrich's party and Mai Mai Chu's murder. *Dangerous. Very dangerous.*

Dangerous. Very dangerous. Di Frasso wore her most diaphanous negligee as she reclined on the chaise longue in her bedroom. She puffed on a Sweet Caporal and watched the smoke rising to the ceiling, which was decorated with several seraphs in various suggestive poses. She wasn't thinking of a least likely suspect, although a voracious reader of murder mysteries; she was thinking of a least likely victim. Mai Mai Chu. Strychnine. Dear God. She, di Frasso, came close to being the victim. Her throat was parched and she considered swiping the champagne from the tray while there was the opportunity when Raymond had the butler's ear for a few moments. Thank God she hadn't. Whoever dropped that pill was good, very damned good. She considered herself a highly observant person—one had to be to survive in the circles in which she traveled—yet she had not seen the hand that presumably passed over the glass, dropping its lethal potion like a bomb over enemy territory. To do that required nerves of steel and a deadly variety of chutzpah.

Chutzpah was a popular word in Monte Trevor's vocabulary. The definition of *chutzpah* was a man who murders his parents and then throws himself at the mercy of the court as an orphan. Monte was feeling like an orphan. He was always wallowing in loneliness and self-pity on holidays. He was a bachelor, and what little family he had were scattered to the four winds and did not keep in touch with each other. He had hoped the night would continue with Tensha and di Frasso; there was much to discuss and disseminate about the party and the murder. He recognized that di Frasso's priority was getting a romantic stranglehold on Tensha, and he also recognized that Tensha was not interested in falling under whatever spell she was hoping to cast. A more important thought possessed him: Why kill Mai Mai Chu in full view of Marlene's guests? From his point of view it was a foolish move, but he had to admit it took the courage of an egomaniac to kill her there. The bartender placed a bowl of peanuts in front of Monte, and the producer gratefully helped himself. He'd eaten nothing at the party. Villon's questioning had erased his appetite. Why didn't di Frasso find him appealing?

The Countess had poured herself a glass of chardonnay and was chain-smoking. How did Monte Trevor weasel his way into Tensha's good graces? She was surprised to find him in the car when Tensha came to pick her up. She'd known him in London and once almost succumbed to his entreaty for her to do a screen test for a movie he was planning about Lucrezia

Borgia, *With This Ring I Thee Kill*. That was another of his projects that never came to fruition. Had I done the role, would I be in a different position today? Would my star be shining as lustrously as Marlene's? I would have made it in talkies, I'm sure; I have a lovely voice and my speech is without impediments like the 'r' problem Marlene and Kay Francis have in common. Marlene does a pretty good job of masking hers, while Kay doesn't give a damn and knows her fans find it adorable when she calls to her beloved Wichard or Wobert or Wonald. Oh, to hell with those clever females. What have I gotten myself into? Oh Christ, it'll be headlines today. My face will be plastered on every front page of every newspaper across the country and probably most of the rest of the world. Those reporters and photographers were positively ruthless in pursuit of their stories.

Dottie! That news hen called her Dottie! How dare she! I am the Countess Dorothy di Frasso! Not Dottie! "Hey Dottie! Poison is a woman's weapon! Did you have it in for Chu?"

Rude guttersnipe. What desperation, what fear, what awesome fear did it take to compel Mai Mai's elimination in full view of all those people? I must say Marlene handled the incident magnificently. That crude detective person letting her and Anna May sit in on the interrogations, how irregular! Hmmm. I wonder if there's something going on between Marlene and that Herbert Villon. I gathered they only just met tonight, or last night as it's now five in the morning; could Marlene have operated that quickly?

Now who the hell is phoning me at this hour? The hell with them. I won't answer. They'll go away. They'll assume I have the phone turned off. How dare they have the *chutzpah* to call me at this hour of the morning and on New Year's Day of all things! Oh, but supposing it's Tensha. He can't sleep either and he's wondering if he might drop by for a spot of breakfast. She hurried to the phone.

"Hello?" Disappointment. "Monte, you're drunk. Sleep it off. *What?* How dare you make such a suggestion! *I could kill you!*"

* * *

Gregory Ivanov sat on a kitchen chair holding a glass of hot tea into which Natalia had dropped his usual four lumps of sugar plus a soupçon of slivovitz. Natalia shuffled about the room, which was as shabby and worn as the bathrobe she was wearing. The two-story house that claimed to be the Russian Embassy was equally shabby and worn, but the rent was gratefully cheap. The owner had reclaimed it from a prostitute whose specialty was bondage, and the basement was a wreck what with the all the chains that had to be pried loose from the walls, all the bloodstains that had to be scrubbed clean with a powerful detergent, and the cloying scent of lilac toilet water, which the prostitute had favored. Natalia was sipping from a snifter of brandy and smoking a cheap Mexican-made cigarillo, listening to her husband shlurping his tea.

Her voice was dark with foreboding. "It was wrong to murder Mai Mai at the party."

Gregory said with irritation, "What difference does it make where she was killed as long as the deed is done."

"Not there. Not in full view of all those people. That detective is no fool, he's not your typical dumb officer of the law we have seen in so many American films played by Tom Kennedy. Ha ha. Very funny."

"What's very funny?"

"Tom Kennedy."

"He's an oaf. We will be hearing from this Villon again, you know."

"You fool. We have diplomatic immunity. We could have refused to be questioned."

Gregory snorted and almost spilled some tea. "Wouldn't that have been clever. Then one or the other of us would surely be suspected as the guilty party. Poisoned pill! *Borshamoy!*" He knew his addressing God was pointless, as He had turned a deaf ear long ago to the revolutionaries who had overthrown and assassinated the Romanoffs. He was in the basement where the czar and his family had been herded together on that last day of their lives. He was recruited to be

91

one of the killers. The little czarevitch was so brave, so hope-lessly brave as he stared at the soldiers who were about to pull the triggers. It mattered not to the boy, he was doomed to die soon of the deadly hemophelia with which he had been cursed at birth. And Anastasia, the beautiful child with her sweet, little puppy eyes. Was it possible the rumor was true that she had survived that massacre? But how? Gregory was, like Nim-rod, a deadly shot. He was positive he'd gotten her between the eyes, and what came dripping down her face was not mascara as he knew the czarina forbade her daughters the use of cosmetics.

Natalia now sat at the kitchen table, which was covered with a piece of peeling oilcloth; she said firmly, "Gregory, we must rise above this. We must prevail. We are here for a purpose that could make us both very powerful, and power is a tool which we can use to turn some formidable profits."

"You are talking capitalism!" he thundered.

"Gregory," she spoke his name with a caress, "if Madam Dietrich's life-style is capitalism, then I am more than willing to be seduced. Which of those two do you think dropped the pill?"

"Why so modest? Two? There are seven of us."

She favored him with a knowing look. He sipped his tea. She sipped her brandy. Both wished aloud there would be no suspenseful delay of further instructions.

The drive back from Marlene's was even more harrowing than the drive getting there. Raymond Souvir was like a ma-niac possessed as he took the hairpin curves on two wheels. Dong See shrieked and cried and pummeled the actor's shoul-der, but Souvir was impervious to his entreaties or the pain he was inflicting. When at last Souvir pulled up in front of Dong See's secluded lair in the Hollywood hills, Dong See surprisingly didn't fling open the door and make his escape. Instead, he said in threatening and measured words, "You have a suicide wish."

"I have a wish to get home in a hurry and think."

"You have a psychological desire to die. If the automobile doesn't kill you, fear will."

"I wish I hadn't come to this damn place."

"You wanted to be a star in this country. An international celebrity."

"The newspapers today will make me an international celebrity. Sooner than I expected. Oh Christ, there's no turning back. There's no getting out of it. Unless it's canceled, I have to do the screen test with Marlene. Even if it's just a screen test, she'll wipe me off the screen. I'll never get that part. It's so hopeless. It's no use. Mai Mai's chart said I wouldn't get the part."

"Mai Mai was always so right. Her charts don't lie."

"There's another reason I'll never get the part."

"What's that?" asked Dong See through a stifled yawn.

"I can't act."

"I thought you were rather nice in your last film."

"It was wrong to kill Mai Mai at Marlene's."

Dong See erupted. "I'm so goddamn tired of hearing that name! Mai Mai this! Mai Mai that! She shouldn't have been killed at the party! What would have made more sense? The Brown Derby? The balcony of Grauman's Chinese? The opportunity to kill her obviously presented itself, and so it was done. Now go home and drink a glass of wine and get some sleep, if you don't kill yourself en route!"

Very greedy woman, thought Ivar Tensha as he soaked in his bathtub scented with salts. The perennial cigar was jammed in his mouth and one could well wonder what Sigmund Freud might make of Tensha's passion for oversized cigars. On a stool next to the tub, there rested a glass filled with chopped ice and the Italian liqueur, *Strega*. *Strega*. The Witch. The Countess di Frasso. Indeed a witch, a very bewitching witch. He'd been tempted to catch the bait she'd dangled in front of him earlier. "Darling, wouldn't you like to come in for a nightcap?" But the nightcap she offered wasn't quite the right size. He never dared spend the night with women. Screw them and send them home in his car with perhaps a monetary token of both his esteem and his generosity. But spend the night with one? Heaven forbid. Tensha talked in his sleep and that could prove dangerous. One unfortunate young lady back in Bucharest had to be quietly eliminated because he'd made the mistake of falling drunkenly asleep before he could send her on her way, and did she get an earful. Very tragic. So young. So beautiful. She ached to enter a beauty contest. She might have been a contender. Now she was just a memory.

Monte Trevor is getting wearisome. He sticks to me like a barnacle on the hull of a ship. He does come in handy to run my errands, but sooner or later I might have to succumb to his entreaties to finance a film for him. Who knows? If I finally yield, the damn thing might show a profit. I suppose I could be interested if it's a movie about Jesse James or the Dalton Boys or any one of those western outlaws. I dote on the stories of their lives, even if they are vastly overexaggerated. After all, I have so much in common with those outlaws. I'm probably the biggest thief in the world. I have billions. Why do I want more? What can I do with more power? Could I finance a search for a cure for cancer? Would I finance such medical research? I hate doctors; I hate doctors as much as I hate chess and lawyers. What do I like? Who do I like? Who did I ever like?

Mai Mai Chu.

There'll never be another like her. Never. Impossible. After they made her, they shattered the mold. How well she understood me, she and those dreadful charts. How much I once loved her. The infatuation was brief but memorable. April in Paris with Mai Mai. She was not impressed by my vast wealth or my position in the world of finance. She liked me for myself. She made no demands. She was never jealous. She was too proud of her own niche, which she had carved for herself with her unusual gifts. Presentiments. Predictions. The stars. Charts. He was a Gemini. Gemini the twins. Two people. Mai Mai told him she usually liked Geminis, mostly preferring them over those born under the other signs. But reading his chart doomed his presence in her life and she quickly brought to a close their brief liaison. They remained friendly, but try as he may to revive the spark, there was no hope of renewing their romance.

Mai Mai was dead. Mai Mai was poisoned. That is not the way she should have died. Mai Mai was a delicate creature and she should have had a delicate death. A heart attack in her sleep perhaps. Or if it had to be by poison, then a poison less powerful than strychnine. But the opportunity fortuitously presented itself and had to be taken. Like the opportunity to foment the rattling of sabers. War is hell. War is highly profitable. Highly profitable? Don't be so modest. Immensely profitable. War in the Far East. War in the Near East. War in South America and Central America and in Mexico, where there was always some peasant with the ambition to be another Pancho Villa. Bring on another Armageddon! How he loved the sound of it. Armageddon. He would be forever grateful to Mai Mai for her prediction of a second world war. Had she known the plot was under way to make a deadly reality of her very accurate prediction, would it have provided her a measure of happiness as death quickly overtook her? Another major conflagration. To paraphrase a quotation from the Bible, his treasury would runneth over.

The cigar was dead and there was no match or lighter at hand with which to revive it. He placed the remaining half cigar on the stool, to be smoked later. Waste not, want not. The first light of dawn appeared. Another day in lotus land. This detective. This Villon. He will continue to be a nuisance. The investigation might prove very troublesome. It might be advisable to lead a lamb to the slaughter. Perhaps award a murderer to the eager Villon and have done with it.

Lazily, he added more hot water to his tub. He added more salts and savored the odor. He scrubbed his back with a brush while wishing there was a beauty sharing his tub who would lower her head and pleasure him erotically. Not like that starlet he had entertained several nights earlier, who rebuffed his request because she was a vegetarian.

*   *   *

Marlene slept fitfully. Twice she looked in on Maria, and the second time her daughter was smiling. *Liebchen* is having a sweet dream, how nice. Marlene quietly looked in on Anna May. Happily, she was asleep. Unhappily, there were signs on her cheeks that she had been crying. Tears for Mai Mai. A damp memorial. Marlene returned to her room. She went out on the balcony and watched a lovely sunrise. There was a balmy breeze and there was a busy afternoon awaiting her. She also had to learn her lines for Souvir's screen test, which was scheduled for the next day. Did Souvir have the stuff for stardom? Did Souvir have the stuff to commit a murder? Did Monte Trevor or Dong See? The Ivanovs? Natalia could commit murder, especially if there was a hammer or a sickle handy, but what would compel her? What motive? The seven suspects danced in Marlene's head and she knew they'd be performing there until the murderer was found. She wanted a bath. It was too early to disturb her maid. She could run her own and be at peace with her own thoughts.

Peace? Would she ever know peace again? A murderer at large. Mai Mai in a refrigerator in the morgue awaiting an autopsy. She wished they had known each other; they might have been good friends. Peace, hah! Von Sternberg's wife on the warpath threatening to sue Marlene for alienation of affections. What affections? Joe told her he had ceased loving his wife, Riza Royce, at least a year before discovering Marlene. Riza had begged for the lead in *The Blue Angel*, but she was a mediocre actress. Now she contented herself appearing in foreign-language versions of American films while contemplating separating von Sternberg from a large chunk of cash. The bathroom was steaming up and Marlene poured her special brand of bath salts imported from Italy into the tub. The hot water would relax her, invigorate her. She bunched her hair together and tied it with a ribbon. She lowered herself into the water. She admired her reflection in the mirror. But why was she frowning?

*   *   *

Morton Duncan's visitor to his apartment was displeased. "More money? We agreed on one hundred dollars."

"I didn't know the pill was poisonous. I didn't know it would kill her. You said it was a practical joke. It would make her uncomfortable, gassy, something like that. But it killed her. And I had a close call with Dietrich and the detective in the kitchen. I talked my way out of that one all right, but pretty soon they'll cotton to the fact that I was the only one who could have poisoned the drink. For crying out loud, man. Now I'm a murderer. Indirectly sure, but I could cop a stretch for it! That Villon is no fool. And Dietrich's a hell of a lot smarter than I thought. I've got a brother in San Juan Capistrano. I'm going there until this thing cools down. I want five hundred dollars. Not a penny less."

"Or else?"

"I'm making no threats. But I agreed to help with a joke, not a murder. Damn you, five hundred dollars!"

"I don't have that much on me. I have about two hundred. I'll get the rest to you tomorrow."

"It's tomorrow already."

"You're a pain in the ass. Can I have a glass of water?"

"In the kitchen."

"Show me."

Duncan led the way into the kitchen. He was filling a glass of water as his visitor found a carving knife and plunged it with ferocity into Duncan's back. The glass fell and shattered in the sink. Duncan clawed at his back with what little strength was left in him. He felt his knees giving way as his visitor stepped back out of the way as Duncan fell forward and lay spread-eagle. His visitor heard Duncan's death rattle and was satisfied. With a dish towel, he wiped the hilt clean. He tossed the dish towel aside and went back into the combination living room and bedroom. Why, he wondered, was Los Angeles squalor so much more squalid then any other city's squalor? He had traveled the world and seen slums too awful to describe. He'd seen rats the size of dogs chasing and attacking children. Not that the room wasn't tidy. There was neatness in its shabbiness. Duncan's murderer left the building cautiously. It was quiet in the streets. Dawn was just breaking, but the only activity he could see was a milkman with his horse and wagon farther down the street making deliveries. Duncan's murderer hurried around the corner, where he had parked his sports car, got behind the wheel, and leisurely drove away.

Wearing a terry-cloth robe, Marlene hurried downstairs to the ballroom. She continued down the hall to the room at the end. She had forgotten them in the confusion of the murder. She opened the door to the room and there they were. Fast asleep in easy chairs, Father Time and the New Year's Baby. Deep in alcoholic stupors. Marlene smiled. They had probably wiped themselves out with gin long before midnight. She went in search of her butler, found him tidying up in the study, and told him to pay them double the promised ten dollars and send them home in a car.

"Don't wake them up. Let them sleep it off. Give them another couple of hours." She continued on to the kitchen, eager for breakfast. Anna May Wong had preceded her there and was enjoying a cup of steaming hot coffee and a cigarette.

"Well, good morning early bird. Less than an hour ago I looked in on you and you were fast asleep."

"A very troubled sleep, let me tell you. Nightmares. Awful."

"Villon is meeting us here at two," Marlene reminded her.

"That'll give me plenty of time to go home, bathe, and change. Is your driver available?"

"He'd better be." She crossed to the intercom on the wall and buzzed the chauffeur's quarters above the garage. The voice that finally replied was heavy with sleep. He heard his instructions, and Marlene asked the cook for some whole-wheat toast and jam. She said to Anna May, "He's getting himself together." The cook brought her a mug of coffee into which Marlene spooned some honey.

Anna May sat back and commented. "How do you do it?

You've had almost no rest and you're as fresh as the morning dew."

"It's my Italian bath salts. Very restorative. I'll give you some to take home with you."

"I have restoratives of my own. My mother has them sent from China."

"Oh, yes? Maybe I should try some of those. Us girls can't have too many restoratives. Try some of this honey. It's local. I buy from a man who claims his bees are oversexed, which is why his honey is richer."

Anna May shuddered. "What won't they think of next."

The butler entered. "Miss Dietrich. You have a visitor."

"I do? I'm not expecting anyone."

"She apologized for dropping in unexpectedly. She says you were old friends in Berlin."

Marlene shot a 'heaven help me' look at Anna May and then asked the butler, "I presume she gave a name."

"Yes. Brunhilde Messer."

❧ NINE ❧

"BRUNHILDE MESSER!"

"That's the name she gave me, Miss Dietrich."

"Oh, that is indeed her name. Tall, stunning figure, strong features, and the inevitable monocle in her left eye." Anna May envisioned a very striking-looking woman. Marlene asked the butler, "Where is she waiting?"

"In the drawing room."

"Good. Bring my coffee and a cup for my guest and more toast and whatever cook has handy to impress a girlfriend from the old country. By the way, have the newspapers been delivered?"

"They're on the table in the drawing room."

"They'll give Brunhilde an eyeful. Anna May, my darling, I'll see you at two. You'll probably be gone before I'm through with Brunhilde."

"Brunhilde! How Wagnerian!"

"You're right on the nose. Brunhilde is a trained soprano, as were her mother and grandmother before her. Very strict and disciplined Junkers. I wonder what brings Brunhilde to Hollywood, and I can't wait to find out. See you later!"

Brunhilde Messer was indeed a very striking-looking woman, probably a few years older than Dietrich. She sat on a sofa reading the front page of the *L.A. Times*, which featured photos of Dietrich, Anna May, and Mai Mai. There was a photo of the body being wheeled out of Dietrich's mansion and a larger photo of a cross section of Marlene's guests, which was bound to annoy a number of stars caught in various stages of inebriation.

"Brunhilde!" Marlene entered with arms outstretched. Brunhilde dropped the newspaper and with a Wagnerian yodel of "Yo Ho Te Ho!" hurried to Marlene, and they hugged each other with joy. Brunhilde stepped back, adjusted her monocle, and said, "The camera doesn't lie. You are more gorgeous than ever."

"What brings you to Hollywood?" They sat next to each other on a sofa as the butler wheeled in a cart on which was laid out a carafe of coffee, toast, breakfast cakes, china, and cutlery. In a tiny Tiffany vase, there was a fresh carnation.

"Such a long story," said Brunhilde, and Marlene remembered to her regret that long stories were the soprano's specialty. "Most importantly, I'm here to see you. But first you must tell me about the murder! Have you seen the newspapers?"

"Not yet, not on an empty stomach." The butler placed the newspapers on the cart and Marlene picked up the one Brunhilde had been perusing. "Always the same damn picture with me displaying my legs. Wait until they find out I'm knock-kneed. Oh God, I suppose this will be going on for weeks." She put the newspaper aside and poured the coffee.

"Who would want to murder Mai Mai Chu? She was such a dumpling!"

"You knew her?"

"Knew her? When she was in Berlin last year she did my chart. She was introduced to me by my friend Adolph Hitler."

Dietrich was spooning honey into her cup of coffee, but

now both hands were frozen in midair. "Hitler's your friend?"

"Thank God. A very powerful friend. His star is very much in the ascendency in Germany. He has the president right here." She indicated the palm of her hand. "The president is almost senile. He will have to be deposed in the very near future, and when he is, mark my words, Adolph will become chancellor of Germany."

The butler was busy fussing about the room. Marlene said, "Just a moment, Brunhilde." She raised her voice so the butler would know she was addressing him. "That will be all, thank you."

"Yes, Miss Dietrich." He left the room hurriedly.

Brunhilde asked, "He eavesdrops?"

"Every domestic in Hollywood eavesdrops. It's a popular pastime, and frequently profitable if there's some gossip to sell to the columnists. So it was Hitler who introduced you to Mai Mai. I wonder if she ever did his chart."

"Of course she did. He's a fanatic about astrology. He doesn't make a move without having the stars consulted. You certainly remember I share the same enthusiasm. It's the stars that brought me to Hollywood."

"So you're looking for a career here."

"Not at all! I'm doing superbly back home. Haven't you heard? I'm producing and directing films. Leni Riefenstahl and I are now arch rivals. Leni isn't acting anymore."

"How foolish of her. She's Germany's biggest star."

"Not foolish at all." She held up a pastry. "What is this?"

"A Danish pastry."

Brunhilde was impressed. "All the way from Denmark?"

"No, all the way from Levy's bakery."

Brunhilde bit into the pastry. "Mmmm. Very nice. Prunes."

"There's also cheese and raisins and whatever. Tell me more about Leni."

"She's been winding up all her acting commitments to

102

make more of those mountain pictures she loves to do. You know, skiing, climbing, and all that physical activity I abhor."

"What sort of films have you been making?"

"*Power*. Films about power. Political power, financial power, the power of men over women and the power of women over men. I just finished one with Willy Forst and Hans Albers."

Dietrich laughed. "I had affairs with both of them. I did a film with Willy in Vienna, *Café Electric*, That's when Igo Sym taught me how to play the electrical saw. Believe me, my dear, that was one period when I was all charged up. Willy got mad at me when I returned to Berlin to do a musical with Margo Lion, *It's in the Air*."

"I remember that one. You and Margo played lesbians."

"Yes. The lesbians lost."

"Adolph intends the German film industry to be the biggest in the world. He has a tremendous amount of financial backing."

"Amazing. I heard him talk once. He was so nondescript looking, but I must admit his effect on the audience was hypnotic. And now he is becoming powerful." She thought for a moment. "Power can be very dangerous in the wrong hands. Very very dangerous. I wonder if Mai Mai accurately predicted his rise."

"Oh, yes. Indeed she did."

"You saw his chart?"

"No, but he read some of it at a dinner several months ago. She predicted truly astonishing things for him. Your friend Ivar Tensha was there."

"Tensha is not my friend. I dislike him intensely."

"But I see in the paper he was at your party last night."

"The Countess di Frasso brought him. I met him last night for the first time."

"Monte Trevor was here too. Isn't he a friend?"

"He came with Dorothy di Frasso and Tensha. Same story. I met him last night for the first time. You know him?"

"Oh, yes. He spends a lot of time in Berlin. He's looking to get a foot in the door of the movie industry. I'm sure he's still badgering Tensha to invest in films."

"Yes, I'm told that's going on."

"And everyone was here last night witnessing Mai Mai's murder! Oh, why didn't I try to reach you yesterday. I could have been here and seen all the fun!"

"Fun! Since when is murder fun?"

"You know what I mean! I should have called Raymond too."

Marlene was fascinated. Tensha, Trevor, and Raymond Souvir? "You know Raymond Souvir?"

"Yes, the darling boy. I brought him to Berlin to test for a film I'm thinking of doing about the flying war ace, the Red Baron. I saw Raymond in a play in Paris and thought he had the right boyish good looks. The Red Baron was only twenty when he was brought down in flames." She shrugged. "Talk about a misspent youth." She was lighting a cigarette. Marlene lit one too, while deep in thought.

Marlene said, "The three are suspects in Mai Mai's murder." She told Brunhilde about the seven suspects, which was interspersed from Brunhilde with "No!" and "You don't say!" and lots of tongue clucking. Finally Marlene said, "Souvir and Dong See are quite close."

"I'm glad to hear Dong See has recovered."

"Was he ill?"

"Automobile accident about half a year ago. He was badly smashed up."

"There was nothing in the newspapers about it here. At least not that I recall."

"Because it was kept out of the papers. His manager canceled his tour and Dong See was hidden in a sanatorium in the Swiss Alps. The accident occurred in Italy, where they are perfectly dreadful drivers. They drive their cars as if they were riding bicycles. Italians are children. They're lucky to have Benito Mussolini to direct their destiny. Well, at least Dong's recovered. I hope the accident hasn't affected his playing."

"He's in no rush to return to concertizing. He's rented a house here in the hills above Sunset Boulevard. He says he's going to spend the next three months composing a violin concerto."

"How ambitious of him. I had no idea he composed too."

"Many musicians give it a try."

"I must get in touch with Dong. And with the others too." Marlene looked at her wristwatch. "Am I keeping you from anything?"

"There's still time. I have a date at two with Herb Villon, the detective investigating Mai Mai's murder. Anna May Wong is joining us."

"I see her picture's on the front page. You've just done one together for von Sternberg, I read somewhere."

"Always for von Sternberg. How I ache to do something with Ernst Lubitsch or Rouben Mamoulian. A cheeky piece of froth in which I can show my audiences how funny I can be. But no, they keep me chained to von Sternberg, and he continues to trap me into one piece of exotica after another. In my next I'm exiled to the tropics. The tropics, for crying out loud."

Brunhilde adjusted her monocle and said firmly, "Fate has brought me to you. Marlene, I want you to come back to Germany and become the Fatherland's greatest star. Don't argue. Hear me out! You will do comedy with Oskar Karlweis, operettas with your Willy Forst. . . ."

"Hardly *my* Willy Forst."

". . . or another erotic drama with Emil Jannings, another *Blue Angel*."

"Work with that monster again? That mountain of *dreck*? Never!" She was on her feet and pacing, nostrils flaring. "Jennings is garbage! *Garbage!*"

"*Achtung!*" cried Brunhilde, flabbergasted by this sudden outbreak of invective.

Marlene swept her hair back and with hands on hips, towered over the seated Brunhilde and said, "I'll thank you to keep a civil *Achtung* in your mouth."

"Beloved Marlene. Come back to us. Come back to your roots."

"I have new roots, Brunhilde. They are here. In this country."

"In this house? Where a woman was murdered while your child slept under the very same roof?"

"Brunhilde, your monocle is slipping. It might fall to the floor and break."

"No matter," said Brunhilde, screwing the monocle back into place, "I have dozens of others." Marlene sat, and Brunhilde took her hand and pressed it gently between hers. "Marlene." The voice was now grave, dramatic. Marlene recognized something momentous was about to issue from her friend's mouth. "I have a personal message for you from Adolph. I committed it to memory." Now she was Adolph Hitler. All that was missing to complete the picture was his Charlie Chaplin mustache. " 'Fräulein Dietrich. I speak from my heart, a heart that is yours for the asking.' "

Marlene hastily lit a cigarette to keep from emitting an embarrassing guffaw. " 'I implore you to return. When I come to power as the Emperor of Germany, possibly the Emperor of Europe, possibly the emperor of the world, I will build you a palace. The walls and the ceilings will be imbedded with precious jewels. The fixtures will be of pure gold and platinum. I will build a movie studio especially for you. It will be the most magnificent in the world, the ninth wonder of the world. The world's greatest scientists will discover the formula for eternal youth, and it shall be yours. While Garbo and Crawford and Shearer and Harlow grow old and wrinkled and turn to dust, you shall be forever young.' "

Dietrich couldn't contain herself any longer. She howled with laughter while clapping her hands together. Her cigarette fell to the floor, and with a look of undisguised annoyance Brunhilde retrieved the cigarette and consigned it to her coffee cup. Dietrich's laughter soon subsided into a cough, and exhausted, she leaned back gasping for breath. "Brunhilde, you tell your beloved Adolph that I am flattered to know he thinks so highly of me. . . ."

"He worships you." She almost sang the words in high C.

"He mustn't worship a false god. Look what happened to the Israelites when they put too much faith in Baal. They ended up with Baal in the wrong court. No, Brunhilde Messer, no, no a thousand times no."

"That is your final word? You won't reconsider?"

"You've known me a long time, Brunhilde, and you remember, when I say *No*, it's *No*."

Brunhilde was polishing the monocle with a handkerchief. "How Adolph suffers. Just a few months ago he was shattered by Geli Raubel's suicide."

"And who was Geli Raubel?"

"His niece. The great love of his life."

"Good heavens!" Marlene feigned shock. "He was *shtooping* his own niece? That's incest!" She thought for a moment. "Isn't it?"

"If Adolph indulges in incest, it is on a rarified plain."

"*Liebchen*, incest is incest even if it's kept in the family."

"Now he has Eva Braun."

"Another niece?"

"No relation. She is madly in love with him."

"Good. Tell him to build the palace for her."

"Marlene." The voice was grave again. "You are taking this much too lightly. Adolph Hitler is not to be mocked or scoffed at. Soon, very soon, his voice will resonate through the world and . . ."

"Enough of this nonsense, Brunhilde. You didn't come seven thousand miles to bring me his offer. You could have mailed me a postcard."

"Well," Brunhilde sighed, "then I must have a talk with Garbo."

"You'll grow hoarse shouting."

"She's deaf?"

"No, she's in Sweden. Had you known, you could have

saved on the carfare. Tell me, Brunhilde, the Ivanovs, the Russians, Natalia and Gregory, did they ever take an excursion to Berlin?"

"He served in their Berlin embassy briefly before being assigned to Los Angeles."

"I presume you met them."

"They are peasants."

"Don't make sport of peasants. Without them there would be no crops."

"Gregory is very boring. He used to do card tricks."

"Oh yes? He has nimble fingers?"

"Very nimble fingers. I slapped them away twice."

"Where are you staying, Brunhilde?"

"You want to be rid of me. I am annoying you."

"On the contrary, you have been amusing me, but then you always did have a delightful sense of humor. Remember a performance of *Götterdämmerung* when Beniamino Gigli bowed to the audience and you pushed him into the orchestra pit and he fell headfirst into a tuba?"

"It wasn't Gigli. It was Lauritz Melchior. Gigli couldn't sing Wagner. He excelled at Puccini and Verdi. I'm keeping you from your appointment."

"I still have time. Would you like to see Maria? She's growing up into a very beautiful child."

"I'd love to see her."

"Now, don't be annoyed with me, Brunhilde. You descend on me unannounced . . ."

"I'm sorry. I was so eager . . ."

"It doesn't matter. I'm delighted you're here. And if you'll take the time to think about your Adolph Hitler's very amusing offer . . . yes . . . amusing . . . nothing more and nothing less . . . you will realize in the long run it's ridiculous and inappropriate, and wait until I tell von Sternberg. Ha! He could use a good laugh right now. Come!"

"Morton? Morton?" The landlady banged on the door with her fist. "There are a couple of flatfoots out here! They want

108

to talk to you!" Her name was Bertha Gull and she looked familiar to Herb Villon and Jim Mallory, and Villon told her so. "You probably seen me in pitchers," she said with what she was sure was a beguiling smile. "I do a lot of extra work. So does Morton."

"I took a guess at that," said Villon, "That's how I tracked down his address."

"Morton also works as a waiter. He worked for Miss Dietrich last night. Morton doesn't do as much extra work as I do. I'm what they call a 'dress extra.' That's because I own some exquisite ball gowns, which I lifted from . . . which I bought at Magnin's with my savings. I get paid more then Morton does. I run this rooming house in case the movie industry suddenly collapses and disappears."

"No chance of that, I'm sure."

"Oh, no? Do you read *Popular Mechanics*? Well, it's my favorite read next to *Liberty* magazine. Well, *Popular Mechanics* had this here article on television, which is a combination of radio and movies, and they predict in another twenty or thirty years television will wipe out *both* movies and radio. *Morton!*" She was banging hard on the door again. "This isn't like him. I know he didn't go out because I sit by the downstairs window all the time, especially on a holiday like today, just to check the comings and goings of my tenants, y'know, if they snuck somebody in for the night, which I do not permit. I run a clean house. You want hanky-panky, sit in the top rows of the Hollywood Bowl. Morton has the best apartment. The Presidential Suite. It has its own kitchen. *Morton!*"

Villon was growing impatient. "Use your passkey."

"Well, all right, if you insist. This isn't like him. Maybe he's taking a shower and can't hear me. I don't want to frighten him."

"Please open the door, Mrs. Dull."

"*Gull.*"

"Sorry. New Year's Day whammies." He'd had very little sleep, and Hazel had hogged most of the bed and the blanket. Too much wine had taken its toll and his performance was way below par, and Hazel didn't hesitate to tell him as she stumbled to the kitchen to make herself a salami and provolone sandwich. The door was open and the detectives trailed the landlady into the seedy room.

"Well! He didn't sleep here last night at all! The bed's still made. Morton? Are you in the bathroom?" She looked inside the bathroom, but Morton remained elusive.

Villon shouted from the kitchen. "He's in here. But if you have a weak stomach, stay where you are. Jim, call for the coroner and some of the boys."

Bertha Gull screamed. She was standing in the doorway, with her hands on her cheeks.

"I told you to stay where you were," Villon reminded her.

She said in a tear-stained voice, "He owes me two weeks rent."

"Well now, why don't you look on it as a farewell gift."

"This is no time for levity, officer. Poor Morton. I recognize the hilt. That's his best carving knife. Stainless steel. He bought it at the Broadway. I was with him. We'd just come from a day on Connie Bennett's *Common Clay* at Fox. We each had a line, as a matter of fact." Jim Mallory was delighted to leave Bertha Gull to Villon as he went out to the unmarked squad car to radio headquarters. "I said, 'It was a delightful evening,' and I think Morton said, 'Charmed, I'm sure.' No chance he might still be alive?"

"Only if you believe in miracles." He was hunkered down examining the space between the body and the sink. He got to his feet and saw the broken glass in the sink. "Must have been getting himself a glass of water when the knife hit."

Bertha Gull said quite logically. "He wouldn't be getting himself a glass of water if someone was breaking into the place, would he?"

"You're right. Nice thinking, Mrs. Hull."

"*Gull.* Just think of flapping wings and splashes when they dive into the water for a fish."

"Sorry. I didn't expect to find him dead. Maybe a little shaken, but not dead."

"I read the paper this morning. I read about this here Chinese lady being murdered at Miss Dietrich's. Morton worked there last night, like I told you. You think Morton had something to do with it?"

"Now I'm positive Morton had something to do with it. Enough to get himself killed to shut him up."

"The boys are on their way," said Mallory as he came back into the apartment.

Bertha Gull asked, "Why would somebody want to shut him up?"

"To keep him from talking."

"Talking about what?"

Was she truly this innocent, Villon wondered, or was she slightly retarded? Mallory was smiling, the Bertha Gulls of the world would never cease to be a source of constant amusement to him. Mallory was also an innocent and therein lay his charm. Marlene Dietrich had recognized this, and as a congenital protector of innocents, took to him immediately at the party. Villon saw no harm in giving Bertha Gull information, unless it might turn out in a surprising switch that she was Ivar Tensha's mistress. "We think Mr. Duncan might have had something to do with the murder last night."

"Oh, don't be silly. Go away!" She dismissed the information with a disdainful wave of a hand. "Morton and murder, they both begin with 'm' but that's about as close as they'll get. Morton was a gentle soul. He attended Mass religiously, and he never went to confession because he had nothing to confess. Believe me, gentlemen, Morton Duncan was just about the dullest and most tiresome man I ever met, and I suppose I'll never see that back rent he owes me." They had abandoned Morton Duncan and were in the bedroom–sitting room searching in drawers. "Believe my word, you won't find a thing."

The bottom drawer of the dresser was filled with pornographic material. Villon and Mallory feasted as they flipped through magazines, postcards, and obscene comic strips featuring such old favorites as Tillie the Toiler, The Katzenjammer Kids, and Moon Mullins in acts that were eloquently filthy. "What have you got there?" demanded Bertha Gull. She was at Villon's elbow and could clearly see what was causing him to smirk. Her cheeks reddened and she backed away, looked at the corpse on the kitchen floor, and then said in a very small, sad voice, "Still waters certainly do run deep. Well, it's no wonder he met such a violent death. It was God's punishment for never confessing his guilt and taking his dose of Hail Mary's."

"Could you possibly spare a shopping bag?" Villon asked her. "These will have to be confiscated and taken to the station house."

"Oh sure," she said with a cynical sneer and left to find a shopping bag.

Villon leaned against a wall while Mallory settled into a chair. Mallory said, "Well, your hunch was right."

"That was no hunch, that was detective work. It had to be him who dropped the pill in the champagne because his explanation of not seeing a hand pass over the glass was too damned elaborate, too well thought out. He was paid to drop the pill, but I don't think he knew it was lethal. He was conned into thinking it was a joke, something like that. Probably slipped him a ten or a twenty, but when he realized she was dead, the price went up and who's to blame him? A smart prosecutor could have nailed him good. So at the party he said more money or else. They met here and again the price went up, probably from, say, a hundred to maybe five or more. So his visitor, who is no dummy, knows Morton Duncan is now dangerous and therefore expendable. So he asks for a glass of water, follows Morton into the kitchen, and good-bye Morton and don't forget to write."

"Poor Morton. I was so positive we'd get the name of who supplied the pill out of him. He looked like the type who frightened easily."

"Not movie extras. They're a tough bunch."

They heard sirens. "They made good time. We have to pick up Marlene and Anna May in half an hour and it's going to take that long to get to Marlene's place. Hello there, Irving, top of the morning to you."

The coroner threw him a filthy look. "I suppose this one's been poisoned too." He had performed the autopsy on Mai Mai Chu a few hours earlier and confirmed the poison was strychnine.

"No, Irving, this was a straightforward plunge of a carving knife into a back, leaving the stiff very stiff."

"Anyone we know?"

"You might recognize him if you saw a movie called *Common Clay.*"

The coroner, a movie buff, moved Morton's head for a better look at his face. "Oh, of course! He's the extra who said, 'Charmed, I'm sure.' " Villon's jaw dropped.

ᎤᏢ TEN ᎤᏢ

"STABBED IN THE back!" Anna May Wong was genuinely shocked.

"That's nothing new in this town," commented Marlene cynically. "So it was he who poisoned the champagne. Damn, just when I was going to cast suspicion on Gregory Ivanov." She caught Villon's questioning look and explained what she had learned from Brunhilde Messer. "He does card tricks. Very clever with his hands, very nimble fingers. But alas, he's in the clear."

Villon said, "Brunhilde Messer." He screwed up his face, prodding his memory. "Opera. Tall broad. Built like a wrestler."

Marlene elaborated on Brunhilde's visit and Adolph Hitler's bizarre offer, saving the best of her information for last.

Anna May said seriously, "If you became the queen of the German film industry, you could make them write good parts for me."

"Oh Anna May, how desperate you sound. Would you want me to betray my principles and accept Hitler's ridiculous offer?" She was enchanted by the way Mallory's lips moved as he read one of the newspapers. She sighed. "My countrymen will follow him like sheep. He offers them hope and a future and they are desperate for both. The country is sinking under a cruel recession. Bread is ten dollars a loaf! Can you imagine that? Bread! Thank God my mother and sister have me to send them enough money to survive. How the others manage I do not know." Her hands were clasped together as she shook her head from side to side. Then she laughed, a laugh tinged with bitterness and irony. "How the hell did I manage when I lived there? But together, Rudy and I were able to earn enough to live better than most. How often you have told me I'm too cynical, Anna May. But Germany breeds cynicism. Germany lost the war and now Hitler promises to lead them to financial recovery. He promises those poor humiliated people that soon they will raise their heads again with pride and take their rightful place again as a powerful nation. Who knows? Who am I to condemn him? I'm here in the United States. I make money. I live better than I deserve. And for crying out loud, why am I bemoaning the lot of Germany when right here in my adopted country there's a frightening depression and armies of homeless roaming the country, living in Hoovervilles of shacks with newspapers for blankets when they sleep. Men selling apples on the street, banks failing, and what the hell am I carrying on about? Anybody want a drink? We're not leaving for Mai Mai's just yet. I have lots more to tell you. Brunhilde Messer was a geyser of information." She paused. "Geyser, or geezer?"

"Geyser," said Villon, thinking she ought to know, having been erupting for the past couple of minutes.

Nobody wanted a drink. Marlene lit a cigarette and sat on a straight-backed chair next to an end table and an ashtray stolen from the Brown Derby restaurant. "My friends, all of our suspects are liars."

Mallory folded his newspaper and placed it aside while hearing Villon saying, "Aw, Marlene, you don't really think that?"

"Oh, all right, all right, Herb, don't be such a smart aleck.

Brunhilde knew them all in Berlin, where they all knew each other. And their center of gravity was Hitler. Monte Trevor was there trying to weasel his way into the film industry. The Ivanovs were with the Russian Embassy before being transferred here. Raymond Souvir was brought to Berlin by Brunhilde to test for a movie she's planning to produce and direct. Tensha was there and is possibly one of Hitler's financiers. Stands to reason for a munitions maker. Hitler wants power and you need an army to wrest power for yourself."

"Mai Mai's prediction." Anna May's voice was ghostly. "The second world war."

Marlene felt a chill. "I wonder if Nostradamus had any Chinese blood in him?"

"Nostra Who?" asked Jim Mallory.

"Nostradamus lived hundreds of years ago. He was a seer and he made some pretty knockout predictions for the future." Villon's hands were in his pants pockets as he slowly paced the room. "What about Dong See? Wasn't he in Berlin too?"

"Apparently not then. It seems he'd been in a terrible automobile accident in Italy and was so severely injured that he had to be sequestered in a Swiss clinic for six months."

Anna May said, "You'd never guess from the way he looked last night. Anyway, they say Swiss doctors and surgeons can work miracles. I've heard there's a new clinic that has perfected a serum that prolongs life. How do the Swiss find the time when they're so preoccupied with chocolate and cheese?"

"Did Miss Messer mention di Frasso?" asked Villon.

"No, but Dorothy is a butterfly. She flits from capital to capital as the whim strikes her. Last March she was on a safari in Africa. Before that she was found at an archaeological dig in Egypt. She also collects important people like other women collect charms for a bracelet." She did a scathing impersonation of di Frasso. " 'I just *adooooorrrre* Benny Mussolini. He makes the trains run on time.' " She crushed her cigarette in an ashtray. "She's a charmer, I have to hand her that."

Villon was now sitting and contemplating the view from the picture window. Marlene's daughter and the chauffeur were on the lawn throwing a beach ball back and forth. "Mai Mai Chu was in Berlin too?"

"*Ach Gott.*" Marlene slapped her forehead. "How could I forget *this*? She was not only there, but she read Hitler's chart!"

"Some girls have all the luck," said Villon. "I hope she kept a copy of that one." He chuckled.

"What's so funny?" asked Dietrich.

"I was thinking about what Hazel's missing. She's so busy doing the New Year's Day party circuit. From Marie Dressler to the Wesley Ruggles and then on to Ramon Novarro, even though she's heard Metro may not be renewing his contract."

"Ramon is so sweet, poor darling. Bi-lingual, bi-sexual, and now by-passed." She winked at Mallory and hoped he wouldn't faint. He had a very silly expression on his face, which reminded her of the comedian Stan Laurel, whom she considered funnier than Chaplin. "Well, my friends, what are we waiting for? There's nothing we can do here, and I say we get going downtown to Mai Mai's place." She was on her feet, and Mallory admired her slacks and jacket. Women wearing pants, what's the world coming to? "Well Herb, this is turning into quite a case, isn't it. Mai Mai murdered last night, the waiter murdered in his kitchen early this morning, and we have ten hours ahead of us for further interesting developments. Shouldn't we go in one car?"

Villon agreed. The ladies would travel with him and Mallory. Dietrich spoke on the intercom, advising Maria's nurse that she and her guests were leaving. Since her chauffeur would be free, she suggested an excursion to the Venice Beach amusement park. It was Maria's favorite place. It was the nurse's too. She especially loved the Tunnel of Love and especially with the chauffeur's arms around her.

"Maria's nurse thinks she's kidding me," said Marlene as she led the way out of the house. "She thinks I don't know she sneaks out to the chauffeur's room above the garage when the household is supposed to be asleep."

117

"Why not?" asked Anna May, who long ago had drawn a protective veil around her own private life. "As the title used to say in silent pictures, 'Youth calls to youth.'"

"In this case," said Marlene, "youth howls to youth." She added mournfully, "Ah, to be in the first flush of youth again." She laughed, "Although I was never all that innocent. How about you, Jim Mallory? Are you still a virgin?" His knees began to wobble. He held tight to the rear car door he was holding open for the ladies. Marlene patted his cheek and then settled back on the seat.

Anna May said to her as she sat, "Must you torture him?"

"Don't be silly, he loves it." Mallory was at the wheel of the car. Villon was speaking into the car radio, telling the precinct they were leaving Dietrich's house and heading south to Mai Mai's loft. The dispatcher gave him a message from Hazel demanding he join her later at one of the parties. The coroner left word that the knife that had sent Morton Duncan to his unjust reward had gone clean through his heart, causing instant death. *Charmed, I'm sure,* thought Villon. What a world. What a life. What a death.

Marlene spoke suddenly. "It can't be Hitler."

"You've lost me," said Anna May. "It can't be Hitler what?"

"Just because all the suspects were in Berlin and know Hitler doesn't mean he's in any way the reason why Mai Mai was murdered. It has to be something deeper, something more malignant. An abscess that needs to be lanced." She had their attention while cautioning Mallory to keep his hands firmly on the wheel and his eyes on the road ahead of them. New Year's Day meant New Year's Day drunks, and at the wheel of a car drunks could be lethal. "Why should anyone fear Mai Mai because she had seen them in Berlin at the same time? They were there legitimately to all intents and purposes. One for a screen test, another looking for a wedge in the film industry, two of them were gainfully employed in their country's embassy; and Tensha makes no bones about how he earns his money, and Hitler has a professional eye for finding financial backing. So what if Mai Mai *did* recognize them en masse? But . . .'"—and now her voice darkened—"if Mai Mai knew there was something else involving these people, possibly also involving Hitler, something more awful than the rise of a would-be dictator, something, for want of a better expression, earth-shattering."

"Sounds reasonable to me," said Villon.

"It has to be reasonable. Why else murder Mai Mai? It's in the horoscopes. It has to be. Their gathering at my party was a tragic coincidence. Mai Mai was a last-minute inspiration on Anna May's part, so the plot to kill Mai Mai didn't exist until one of the seven phoned her to . . . wait a minute, wait a minute! The plot to kill Mai Mai *very much existed*. She'd been marked for murder for months. But finding out she'd be at my party was for them a blessing in disguise, they could try eliminating her that night. And what better setting? A crowded ballroom, an orchestra, lots of noise, a cacophony of voices and a strychnine pill that had been kept in reserve if other means of killing her were not propitious. Oh, poor Anna May, I'm upsetting you."

"No. It's not what you're saying. That's logic. But murder is insanity. I've read about it, I've played killers, but it has never come this close to me. You read about a murder in the papers, and reading about murder has its own fascination. Then you shrug it off and turn to the funnies. But now I realize people are reading about Mai Mai then shrugging her off and turning to the funnies. Now I know how terrible murder really is. Mai Mai was a real person, warm, loving, always laughing. But so were all the other victims we've read about. But one has to be cold about it, doesn't one, Herb? You can't sentimentalize murder because there's the killer to apprehend, and if you go soft then the mind grows lazy and logic evanesces."

"Herb will catch the son of a bitch," Marlene assured Anna May, not also realizing she was assuring Villon, who frequently had his doubts about nailing a murderer. "And Jim Mallory will be invaluable to Herb, as he has already proven

to be, and watch out for that bastard coming up on your left!"
Jim swerved in time to avoid a collision. "Well! We came
within a hair of making headlines tomorrow!"

"You'd get top billing," said Anna May sullenly.

"Oh, Anna May." Marlene did not fear death; she frequently contemplated her own mortality. It was Maria she
worried about. What would become of her? She doesn't
know about Rudy's mistress. If Marlene died, would Rudy
marry the woman? Would she and Maria like each other?
Would she be the right person to raise Maria? Marlene
groaned and Anna May shot her a look but didn't question
her. Am *I* the right person to raise Maria? She has a nurse and
a maid, and there are butlers and a chauffeur and there are
bodyguards, and I am at the studio sometimes as long as
twelve hours a day when I'm filming, and I'm away on trips
and I can't always take her with me. Oh, what the hell, how
many children in the world wish they could trade places with
Maria, so there.

Marlene's thoughts sidetracked to the actors she'd hired to
be Father Time and the New Year's Baby. How pathetic their
distress to realize they'd passed out and never got to do their
act. Father Time wouldn't take the money the butler pressed
on him, and the butler had to fetch Marlene, who held the
actor by his arms, insisting he take the money. The poor
bastard. Washed up. Washed out. No hope for him. Maybe
she could find a way to wangle him onto Paramount's talent
roster. All the studios maintained a company of stock players
contracted at a minimal weekly salary to be on tap to do bits
and walk-ons. Metro had several silent favorites who had
fallen on hard times on stock contracts. Aileen Pringle, May
McAvoy, Marie Prevost, to name three. How often at a
screening had Marlene heard a buzz from the audience when
a former favorite flashed by and was recognized. Maybe a few
years from now that would be her. Like hell, not Marlene.
Marlene is a survivor.

"That's the building on the northwest corner. The one with
the grocery store on the ground floor." The streets were

almost deserted. This was the commercial area that abutted Chinatown, where they would find hustle and bustle if they were in search of it. But in this neighborhood on a holiday afternoon, all was quiescent. Villon knew that behind some of the façades there were illegal factories paying coolie wages to illegal immigrants. There were illegal fan-tan parlors where the Chinese who were compulsive gamblers played mah-jongg and fan-tan and blackjack and rarely escaped the bondage and thrall in which the gamblers held them because of their constant indebtedness. Some traded their daughters and their sons for their freedom, some even offered wives and sisters. They defied the tongs, who frowned on the practice. The tongs were family societies who looked after each other, benevolent societies who financed business ventures for their relatives. They arranged marriages and made sure their dead were given funerals befitting a respected member. The movies libeled and slandered tongs, depicting them as gangs of cutthroats and thieves constantly warring with each other. They did on occasion feud, but differences were usually settled over a pot of tea and honey cakes.

Jim Mallory parked at the entrance to the hallway leading to a small elevator that rose to Mai Mai's loft. Marlene was astonished by the lack of security. "She could have been killed *here!*" cried Marlene. "The door is unbolted. Anyone can get in."

"Marlene, many eyes watched this doorway, as many eyes are watching us now. Here Mai Mai was safe. This was her fortress, secluded and impenetrable. I never told you this before, I had no reason to, but Mai Mai was a princess. Yes, she was of royal blood. Her ancestry goes back so many generations. Tragically, she is the last of her line. She had no brothers. Let me lead the way."

Two of the pairs of eyes watching Anna May leading the others into the building couldn't believe what they were seeing. One spoke softly, "Honorable Fong Shen Un, do my miserable eyes deceive. Is that not Marlene 'Legs' Dietrich I see?"

121

The second pair of eyes replied, "I do not deserve to look upon her. She is too far above for this humble and unworthy nobody. It would be an honor to grovel before her and have her humble me with her feet in my face. Oh Gut Tsu Donk, how often I have dreamed of screwing her."

The hallway was beautifully papered with decorative designs. Anna May explained they were the work of a young muralist whose work Mai Mai had seen and admired in Hong Kong. Mai Mai had arranged to bring him to the United States, and when last heard of, Anna May said, he was laboring in a vineyard in the Napa Valley.

"How sad," commented Marlene.

"Not sad at all," countered Anna May. "He owns the vineyard."

The four squeezed into the elevator, which made its way slowly and laboriously to the top floor. It came to rest with an agonizing grinding of the brake. When the door opened, the four stepped into a paradise, a shrine to the zodiac, a magnificently appointed room with high ceilings and many windows draped with multicolored materials imported from the Orient. The twelve signs of the zodiac covered the walls. The furniture was lovely in its simplicity. There were sofas and easy chairs, and oversized pillows dominated the floor. At the furthest end of the room, away from the elevator, was a hallway, the entrance to which was camouflaged by a curtain of stringed bamboo beads. Anna May explained that beyond the curtain was Mai Mai's bedroom and bath, and a kitchen.

"This room was the center of Mai Mai's life. Here she entertained and here she did her charts. She worked at this desk." It was built into a wall next to a huge chart of the zodiac signs. Past the chart was a row of steel cabinets and behind their doors Herb Villon was positive they would find the copies of the charts they were seeking. From her handbag Anna May extracted a ring of keys. "These will open the cabinets. The honorable Mr. Gai Ah Veck, the leader of Mai Mai's tong, entrusted them to me. I saw him before returning to your house, Marlene, and he was glad to learn there would

be no rest until Mai Mai's murderer is brought to justice."
She gave the keys to Villon.

He chose the cabinet closest to the desk. After several tries a key fit and he opened the door. He was faced with a filing cabinet. "Mai Mai certainly believed in security." He pulled open a drawer and Anna May smiled at the perplexed look on his face. "I told you everything would be in Chinese. Let me have a look."

Marlene wandered about the room, studying the portraits of relatives and ancestors with which the tables were heavily populated. The family, thought Marlene, the all-important family. The Chinese worshipped their ancestors. Respected them and revered them. It was an honor to be elderly in the Chinese world. The elderly had a vast store of knowledge and shared it with the young. The elderly were not shunted off to nursing homes or abandoned to a miserable lot. The family took care of the elderly and honored them. Not like us, thought Marlene, to whom the elderly are a nuisance. The Eskimos used to set them out on an ice floe to freeze to death. My mother is lucky. Her apartment is steam heated, and there aren't many of *those* in Germany.

Jim Mallory dogged Marlene's trail. They exchanged comments on some of the paintings that hung on the walls. Mai Mai had good taste, not too eclectic, and some of the pieces Marlene judged to be very valuable. She recognized an Ingres and a Picasso of a period unfamiliar to her. The bookcases contained what would prove to be many valuable first editions. There were volumes on astrology that Marlene was sure were priceless. She examined several, the pages yellowed with age. She told Jim Mallory they were priceless. He wanted to tell her so was she, but that took the kind of courage he had yet to develop.

Anna May was dismayed. "This may take forever. These files must contain thousands of charts!"

Marlene and Jim joined Villon and Anna May. Marlene took a chart from Anna May. "How delicate a design."

"Those aren't designs. Those are Chinese words. Our alphabet is very complicated. No A to Z for us. Oh dear, oh dear, oh dear. I may have to spend weeks translating these."

"We haven't got weeks," said Villon. "It's not going to be easy holding on to the suspects. And I've no reason to place them in custody. Tensha's arm probably reaches into high places in Washington, and I can't touch the Ivanovs or they'll claim diplomatic immunity. Don't you know any people who can help you?"

Marlene had a thought and crossed the room to the bamboo curtain. The beads tinkled a strange tune as she passed through them, or perhaps it was Mai Mai singing a song of encouragement. The kitchen was on the left and her epicurean curiosity got the better of her, delaying briefly the continuation of her mission. It was well furnished with cutlery and beautiful glassware and plates and dishes and bowls of excellent manufacture. There were numerous woks and a shelf of cookbooks of international origins. An herb chest almost brought tears to Marlene's eyes. There were jars of every exotic herb one might bring to mind. The pantry was small but contained cans and boxes of provisions, most of which were imported.

Finally Marlene stood in front of the refrigerator. It was the latest model, with the engine jutting out from the top and encased in white aluminum. Marlene rubbed her fingers together like a burglar about to attack a safe. She pulled the door open and almost collapsed with laughter. There was a half-eaten ham sandwich on a small dish, a box of chocolate-covered marshmallow cookies, a bowl of what looked like cream of mushroom soup, a half-filled bottle of milk, some jars of jam and peanut butter, and finally, wrapped in wax paper, a potato knish. Sighed Marlene, ah the enigmatic Chinese.

She crossed the hall to what had to be the bedroom. She opened the door and felt as though she was about to enter a shrine. The room was also colorfully decorated, as Marlene had expected it would be, but it was completely feminine. The double bed was covered with a knitted throw, which featured a green dragon, undoubtedly a symbol of protection. Half a dozen pillows were artfully arranged against the headboard and Marlene could tell they were handsewn. Astonishingly enough, they were not emblazoned with the signs of the zodiac. The dressing table was much like one Marlene had in her dressing room. It was a theatrical model with dozens of small bulbs ringing the mirror. There were perfumes from France, from Italy, from Spain, from India, and, of course, from China. Her hairbrush and comb and hand mirror were antique, decorated in pearl. Her closet was a large walk-in with dozens of shoes, magnificent dresses for all occasions, and, surprisingly enough, hats. Oriental women rarely wore hats. Only the peasant women wore the straw hats that tied under the chin to protect them from the brutal sun when working in the rice fields. Next to the bed was a table, which held a night lamp and a telephone extension and a stack of books. The table's twin was on the other side of the bed. On it was a stack of folders and atop the folders rested what were apparently Mai Mai's reading glasses. Marlene placed the glasses aside. She opened the top folder. As she expected, it was written in Chinese. Marlene counted eight folders and felt her heartbeat accelerating.

Horoscopes. Eight horoscopes. The seven suspects? Could the eighth be Hitler's? She lifted the folders and held them as though they were sacred. Before leaving the room, she took one last look, drinking heavily of the atmosphere in which a very great lady had reigned as the royal she deserved to be. Then quietly, as though walking down a church aisle, she went to rejoin the others.

This isn't chutzpah, thought Monte Trevor, as he guided his rented coupe toward Marlene Dietrich's estate. This is my European upbringing rising to the surface. In Europe when you have been royally entertained the previous evening, you call on your host or hostess the next day to thank them in person. The hangover that had hammered in his head all morning had blissfully abated, though the memory lingered on. He didn't remember too much of what had happened to him once he entered the hotel bar, but he did remember phoning the Countess di Frasso and telling her he hungered to nibble on her nipples. This did not sit well with the lady, if he remembered correctly, and damned if that isn't her coming out of Marlene's front door. He drove up and managed a small smile as she recognized him. He got out of the car and before he could greet her she snapped, "There's nothing to nibble around here, Monte, Marlene's not receiving."

"Oh? Still recovering from last night?"

"She's not in. She went out several hours ago. With Anna May Wong and the two detectives who entertained us in the study last night. So you'll have to go peddle your papers elsewhere." She walked to her Hispano-Suiza, which to Trevor's surprise she was driving herself.

Trevor followed her to the car, looking as forlorn as an abandoned lapdog. "The detectives? Were Marlene and Anna May taken into custody?"

She got in behind the wheel. "Don't be an idiot, though it's too late for you. From what the butler surmised, and he seems pretty astute at surmising, they were off to investigate Mai Mai's loft. Searching for horoscope charts is my guess. And don't tail me, Monte! I loathe being pursued in general, especially by nibblers!"

Monte Trevor stood solemnly in the cloud of dust made by the expensive foreign car as the Countess sped off, undoubtedly to the adventure of somebody's cocktail party.

Charts! He hurried back to his car and sped off in the direction from which he had just come. A telephone was what he needed, but a telephone in the privacy of his hotel room. Oh Mai Mai, he was thinking, why didn't you take my advice and destroy those copies? But no, you were adamant, you told me to go do the physically impossible, and now you have suffered the consequences I predicted you would suffer. Now you are officially an ancestor.

* * *

126

Marlene came through the beaded curtain carrying the folders. "Could these possibly be what we're looking for? I found them in Mai Mai's room along with her glasses. It occurred to me that, like so many ladies of a certain age, Mai Mai preferred to work in the comfort of her bed at night." She placed the folders on a table. "Come on, Anna May. Have a look. Maybe I've struck pay dirt. Ah, Jim! What a sweet expression on your face! You must have been a beautiful baby."

◖◗ ELEVEN ◖◗

ANNA MAY EXAMINED the contents of one of the folders. "This is very complicated. It is not easy to decipher. I will need time with them, but they're positively the charts we want. This one is Monte Trevor's. I'll take them home and start working on them at once."

"Just for the hell of it," Marlene asked eagerly, "see if the eighth folder contains Hitler's chart."

Anna May examined the title page of each folder. "Bingo. This one's Hitler's."

"I thought one of them would be. Ha! Now I know how a prospector feels when he strikes gold!" Marlene's eyes sparkled and her cheeks glowed; her enthusiasm was infectious. "Have I the makings of a good detective, Herb?"

"That was a damned good deduction thinking the folders would be in Mai Mai's bedroom."

"Mai Mai and I were sisters under the skin. I also do my best work in the bedroom."

Monte Trevor made his phone calls but did not connect with Dong See or Raymond Souvir. Ivar Tensha was surprisingly undisturbed by Trevor's information. "It was inevitable the police would look for the charts and find them. They are quite innocent. Mine reveals very little that isn't already public information. It sounded a bit simpleminded when Mai Mai read it to me."

"Mai Mai was a very complex and a very brilliant woman. She could be very devious, surely you knew that. It's what she *didn't* read to you that's dangerous."

"She has been silenced. She can no longer chart, she can no longer read, and, most importantly, she can no longer speak. She had her opportunity and she rejected it. I thought the long period of inactivity before we all met here in Los Angeles might have led her to believe the plot was abandoned. But unfortunately, Fate played a trick. Mai Mai saw us at the party. So her suspicions were restored and deepened. There's nothing more to say. We'll speak later, Monte."

Monte Trevor wasn't satisfied, but there was nothing he could do. He would have to wait for the police to make the next move. He glanced at his wristwatch. Ramon Novarro's party must have started by now. No use sitting around a hotel room and stewing. I may as well go there, continue playing the role of an independent film producer on the make. Tomorrow, with the holidays out of the way, business would resume. He had appointments with several of the most powerful men in Hollywood. At least one of would have to be interested in what he had to offer. The studios were badly hit by the Depression. Paramount and Universal were on the brink of bankruptcy. MGM was demanding salary cuts from all employees, especially their stars. The country was in chaos. Jack Warner was banking on his friend Franklin Delano Roosevelt to win the Democratic nomination and the election. Roosevelt had confided in him his planned financial reforms to stabilize the economy and reward his future constituents with a New Deal that promised new prosperity was "Just Around the Corner."

Herb Villon was hoping the solution to the murders was 'Just Around the Corner.' Back at Marlene's place, Anna May retrieved her car and with the folders resting on the passenger seat dutifully eschewed all New Year's Day party-going to head for home and get to work translating the charts. Marlene planned to spend some time with her daughter before changing into something stunning for Ramon Novarro's party. Villon and Jim Mallory were headed back to the precinct. A police team had been left at Morton Duncan's apartment to dust for fingerprints and the usual routine search for clues. Villon doubted they would turn up anything valuable. He told Marlene he'd probably see her at the Novarro party, which he would attend to keep the peace with Hazel, the quilt hog. Marlene sang to herself as she made her way up the stairs to her boudoir. She rarely used the small elevator the owner of the house had installed at great expense. Climbing stairs was good for the hips, she'd been told by Madam Sylvia, filmdom's illustrious masseuse, and so Marlene took every opportunity to climb stairs. She went to her room first to select a dress and remembered she had given her maid the day off. No problem. Marlene knew how to look after herself; she'd done it for years before American stardom helped her afford servants. She looked in on the nursery, but Maria and the nurse had not yet returned from Venice Beach. Returning to her suite, she met the butler in the hallway and startled him.

"I didn't know you were back, Miss Dietrich. The Countess di Frasso stopped in while you were out. And when she left, I saw her encounter Mr. Trevor. She obviously told him you were out and so he promptly left."

"Did the Countess leave a message?"

"No, madam. She said she'd probably run into you at a party this afternoon."

"More than likely. I'm not sure if I'll be in for dinner tonight, but tell the cook not to worry. I enjoy raiding the refrigerator."

Within a few minutes, Dietrich wore a negligee and sat at her dressing table, brushing her hair. There they were reflected in the mirror, Mai Mai Chu and Morton Duncan.

130

How glibly he had lied to her and Villon last night. The fool. He might still be alive today had he told the truth. But no, it was not to be. Greed was his undoing. In these terrible times, could you blame the man for wanting to earn some extra cash? He wasn't even around to blame himself.

And you, delicate Mai Mai Chu. How could so tiny a woman emerge as so huge a threat? What was the link in those eight charts that triggered your suspicion these people were creating a dangerous situation? What an eclectic group. What in the world could bring them together? The Ivanovs aren't in the same league as the others. She gave that further thought. She replaced the brush with an emery board and went to work on her nails. The Ivanovs. Maybe they are not what we think they are. Maybe they are secret agents. She brushed that thought aside as insignificant. Russian spies were a glut on the market; the whole world knows that and jokes about it. But they're here and involved in this plot, whatever this plot turns out to be. They are therefore much more important than we think.

Raymond Souvir? From Rouen. His father's a shopkeeper. Aspires to American stardom. He *must* be something else, and if he is, he's giving one hell of a good performance. The fear the studio might cancel his test if Mai Mai's murder led to scandal was convincingly played by him. Tomorrow I test with him. There will be plenty of time to spend with him and perhaps learn a few things he will inadvertently let slip. That should be amusing if not fruitful.

Monte Trevor. Well, what do I know about him? He *has* produced films, several of them quite good I've been told, so those credentials are credible. He fawns on Tensha, but then, so does everyone else. Tensha is a brilliant financial tactician. She had learned long ago in Europe that people like Tensha used their business organizations as a front. One cannot easily dismiss his role as a foremost munitions dealer, but that is the tip of the iceberg. He's known to have a network of financial and political interests that spread around the world like one vast spider's web. What is he doing in this hornet's nest of seemingly minor characters? And Dorothy di Frasso? Is she involved? She hungers for a share of Tensha's financial life, and I wouldn't put it past her to permit herself to become his tool if the rewards were ample and dazzling.

Dong See. Automobile crash. Six months in a Swiss clinic. What was it that Dorothy di Frasso had said when seeing him for the first time in ages? Marlene worried her memory and then it came to her. *He's changed some since then.* How changed? wondered Marlene. What a jigsaw puzzle. Was Brunhilde Messer another piece that could fit in here somewhere? Hitler's errand girl. Hitler. Well, he needs all the help he can get, and he will get it, because he knows how to get it. World domination, a very understandable ambition. It didn't pan out for Napoléon Bonaparte, but that doesn't mean another contestant can't take a stab at it. There's an awful lot of world out there to dominate. Wasn't there possibly someone skulking in the wings with an ambition to only rule *half* the world? Don't they say 'The Sun Never Sets on the British Kingdom'? Why aren't we bellyaching about them? They're all over the place. Africa, India, the Bahamas, Canada, for Pete's sake. That's a lot of domination.

This is all too complex for me. I must give my brain a rest or it will explode. She went to her wardrobe, selected a dress, took a quick shower, and was sure a cocktail party was what she needed to revive her spirits. Why do they need reviving? You found the charts in Mai Mai's bedroom. You struck gold. You could tell Herb Villon and that adorable Jim Mallory were quite impressed with your deduction. Deduction my eye. Feminine intuition is more like it. Ah, the water feels wonderful and it's deliciously warm, but why am I feeling a chill?

Ramon Novarro's house in Beverly Hills was beautiful in its simplicity of design. A bachelor, Novarro looked after his mother and his many sisters and brothers. He was shrewd with money and owned property in Malibu Beach and downtown Los Angeles. If his star was descending, he would not lack for the wherewithal to continue living in the style to which he was accustomed. His New Year's Day parties were legendary. Here the biggest stars mingled with those no longer too much in demand. Ramon was loyal to his old friends. Loyal to director Rex Ingram, who gave him his first break and to Ingram's stunning actress wife, Alice Terry, who wisely turned a deaf ear to the rumor her husband and Novarro were lovers. She liked her marriage; it was comfortable and for years they luxuriated in living and making films in the south of France. Their suns had set in Hollywood, but they, like Novarro, were financially secure. And they, like Novarro, were busy gossiping about the murder at Marlene's party. In fact, everybody was gossiping about the murder, and Hazel Dickson flitted from group to group like a moth in a closet full of appetizing clothes.

Ramon Novarro was with a group that included Basil Rathbone and his wife, Ouida Bergere, and Lionel Barrymore, who was standing and bravely enduring the arthritic pain that would soon paralyze his body. "To think she was murdered right there before our eyes," said Ramon. "And how ironic, she had earlier predicted some of us at the party would be murder victims."

"Did she name names?" asked Lionel Barrymore.

"Oh no, she was much to discreet for that. Imagine if she had pointed a finger at me and said, 'Ramon Novarro, you are going to be murdered.' Ha ha ha. I'm sure if she'd had, I'd have sued her for causing me mental distress."

Ouida Bergere said to Hazel, "Isn't detective Villon your heartthrob of the moment, Hazel?"

"Not if he doesn't show up soon." Hazel was working up to her third gin and orange juice.

Ouida continued, "Raymond Souvir told us you and Marlene sat in on his interrogations. Isn't that a bit unorthodox?"

"Oh, phooey. Everybody in town knows Herb gives me preferential treatment. It's no different than Irving Thalberg

making sure Norma gets the best scripts at Metro. And Marlene sat in because the murder took place in her house and
Herb felt she had every right to sit in."

"Well, come on," prompted Rathbone, "let's hear what
went on."

"You can read it tomorrow in Louella's column."

"Hazel," said Rathbone, "start talking or you'll never get
another item out of me or Ouida." Hazel was one of the few
news hens invited to the Rathbone's frequent parties. She
told them almost as much as she could remember while mini-
mizing the importance of Mai Mai's charts. Lionel Barrymore
wandered away in search of something to sit on and was
grateful when Ruth Chatterton indicated she would love his
company beside her on a sofa.

"I see Hazel's probably been filling you in on the murder,
and don't ask *what* murder; today it's our only murder."

"No, as a matter of fact, it isn't."

"Oh?"

"Seems a man was found dead this morning, stabbed in the
back with a carving knife. It was on the radio. It turns out he
was a waiter at last night's party."

"Isn't that fascinating! Do you suppose there's a connection between the two?"

"Well, Ruth, I don't have much of a deductive mind, so it
didn't interest me if there's a connection or not. There's a
good man on the case, Herb Villon, and if there's a connection then he knows about it. I'm sure the authorities aren't
too eager to release too much information about the murders,
but sooner or later we'll have all the facts and if they're sordid
enough, all Hollywood will wallow in them. Where's your
husband?"

"You mean Ralph?" She was married to actor Ralph
Forbes.

"As I recall that's his name."

"He's staying at his mother's."

"Is she ill?"

"No. I told Ralphie I wanted a divorce and he was so angry with me he packed his bags and went home to mother. Which made a great deal of sense as I couldn't very well pack my bags and go home to mother as mother's been dead for years and you don't pack your bags and go to a cemetery."

"I'm sorry to hear this. Ralph's a nice man."

"Oh, terribly nice. They don't come any nicer. Or more tiresome. I think Ralph will always be remembered for having passed through life without giving offense. How's the composing going?"

"Still slogging away at it. I don't get much time the way Metro schedules me in one picture after another."

"Have you met Dong See?"

"The violinist? Is he here?"

"Yes, he's over there by the buffet. I'll see if I can catch his eye."

"Oh, don't bother. He's with that Monte Trevor, and he had me cornered for ten minutes convincing me I should play Herod in his *Salome* movie."

"It looks like a pretty heated conversation. I wish I could read lips."

Monte Trevor had told Dong See about the group going to Mai Mai Shu's loft and his fears that the charts would reveal something incriminating. Dong See was telling him, "There was nothing that I found worrisome when Mai Mai read my chart to me."

"Did she let you read any of it yourself?"

"Of course not. I couldn't anyway. I caught a glimpse of it and it was written in a script I don't understand. Probably Mandarin."

"But don't you see, I suspect Mai Mai told us only what she wanted us to know. I tell you, there's going to be trouble if we don't do something about those charts."

"What can we do? If the police have them, forget it. It's out of our hands."

"If the charts are in Chinese, doesn't it stand to reason they may have asked Anna May Wong to help translate them and they're in her possession?"

"I suppose you've told all this to Raymond? Look at him. Now he's got Dorothy di Frasso all worked up."

The Countess di Frasso was wearing a dress with floral patterns and a matching hat and handbag. Ouida Rathbone had commented that she looked like a float in a holiday parade. At the moment, di Frasso's language was as colorful as her outfit. "Don't be an ass, Raymond. The earth won't open up and swallow us. When Mai Mai read me she didn't tell me anything I didn't already know. I mean, to tell me I'd be involved in a long series of love affairs is like telling a pickpocket he'd have his hand in a lot of things."

"I should not have let myself be seduced into the promise of a glorious future," said Souvir.

"Hogwash. You've been on the make ever since I met you. You're a very ambitious little twit, and while you may never admit it, I know you'll let nothing stand in your way. Do you think I'm blind to the way you're sucking up to Marlene? Getting her to do the screen test with you and no less than von Sternberg to direct it."

"I didn't get her to do anything," he stormed. "She volunteered."

"Lower your voice. People are looking at us."

"Let them look, and let them listen."

"Oh, the hell with you!" Di Frasso went in search of more pleasurable—and wealthier—company.

Dong See replaced her at Raymond's side. "You're behaving very foolishly, Raymond."

"I'm worried, and you should be too."

"There's nothing to be done. It's out of our hands. We have to wait and see what develops. And look, there's detective Villon."

"Oh my God."

"Leave God alone. He has too much to occupy his attention these days. Have a look. Villon is with his lady, the Hazel Dickson person. And she seems to be giving him a hard time."

Villon warned Hazel, "You make a scene and I'll walk out."

"Don't you dare. Did you find the charts?"

"Not now, Hazel."

"Why not now? Herb!"

"Because this is no time or place to discuss them."

"Are you kidding? That's all they're talking about here! It's Mai Mai this and Mai Mai that. I'm thinking it might be profitable opening a restaurant and calling it Mai Mai's."

"Good idea. It might take your mind off trivialities."

"Oh, so now I deal in trivialities." He walked away from her. "Where are you going!"

"To get myself a drink." She hurried after him. When she was after information, she was relentless. Villon was hoping Marlene would arrive. He had sad news for her and he wanted to tell her before she was seen by the other guests. Luck was on his side. Through a window near the bar he saw her car drive up and the chauffeur getting out to open the back door. Herb hurried outside while Hazel, seeing it was Dietrich he was joining, was wise enough to keep her distance. Marlene saw him and smiled.

"Herb! You look so handsome. Did you know Morton Duncan's murder was on the news today?"

"Yes, I heard it at the precinct. Listen Marlene, before you go into the party, take a walk in the garden with me."

"You'll make Hazel jealous. She's standing on the veranda watching us." She had a wicked notion and waved at Hazel. "Hazel, darling, I'll be with you in a minute." Then Marlene took Herb's arm while serving him one of her most dazzling smiles.

Hazel went to the bar for another gin and orange juice, her face grim, her request made through clenched teeth.

Novarro's garden was one of the most beautiful ones in Beverly Hills. It was dotted with a series of fountains designed and built for him in Italy. The centerpiece of one fountain was *Venus de Milo*, and the centerpiece of another was an Egyptian houri. Marlene saw Adonis in one fountain and Apollo in another. They were unusually well endowed, especially for statues.

"You look so serious, Herb. You certainly couldn't have heard from Anna May this soon."

"No, it's nothing to do with the case. At least I don't think it does. Last night you hired two actors to play Father Time and the New Year Baby."

"How do you know? They never made their appearance. They had passed out in a room where I had them waiting. They drank an awful lot of gin and it was good stuff too."

"The midget told one of my men. He and the actor who was Father Time were living in the same boarding house. Father Time was Lewis Tate. He'd been a big name in silents once."

"Yes, I know that. A mutual friend implored me to hire him and his friend. Tate's in very desperate straits. Oh dear. Has he done something terrible?"

"Very terrible. He hung himself."

Marlene said nothing. She walked away from Herb and stared into a bed of jack-in-the-pulpits. It took her a minute before she could compose herself. Then she came back to Villon. "When Mai Mai generalized that there would be murder victims and suicide victims, do you suppose she knew her predictions had traveled upstairs and embraced a tired old man who probably knew then that this would be the last New Year he'd welcome? Well, welcome is hardly the appropriate word." She took his arm and headed him back to the house.

"I want to pay for his funeral," said Marlene.

"That's very kind, but we've made arrangements with the county."

"You mean bury him in a pauper's grave?"

"We can't trace a family. He's been living on welfare for the past couple of years."

Marlene was firm. "He will not have a pauper's grave. He

138

is Lewis Tate. He is a star. And he shall have a proper place in Forest Lawn and I shall order a stone to mark his grave, and on it will be his name and a reminder that he starred in films. Yes, that's what I shall do. His final billing. Come, I need a drink."

⟪⟨ TWELVE ⟩⟫

FROM THE MOMENT she swept into the house, Marlene Dietrich took center stage and held it. The room rang with many varieties of "Hello Marlene" and "Darling" in various octaves and "Loved your party" and "Wasn't it awful about Mai Mai Chu" and "Is it true you're working with the police" and "Are you sure you're not in danger yourself," and Marlene batted answers to the infield and the outfield until confronted by Ouida Bergere.

"What's wrong, Marlene? Why weren't Basil and I invited to your party?"

"But you were, darling. I'm positive my secretary sent you an invitation."

"Are you sure?"

"Would you like me to repeat the sentence in the presence of a notary public?" Dietrich, like so many women in Hollywood, didn't like Ouida Bergere. She was pushy and pretentious and a climber who kept her husband constantly in debt with her expensive parties and gift-giving and other extravagances.

Ouida realized she was behaving foolishly. "Well, communications are always being snarled up in this town. I see Basil needs me. I'll phone you tomorrow."

"What's with the human icicle?" Marlene turned and was happy to see her good friend Adela Rogers St. John. Adela was just about the best chronicler of life in Hollywood, and magazines across the world paid handsomely for her services. Her father had been the notorious and sadly alcoholic criminal lawyer Earl Rogers. But when sober, he was a genius in the courtroom. *A Free Soul*, which starred Norma Shearer and Lionel Barrymore, was based on Adela and her father and made a star of Clark Gable as the sadistic gangster who slapped Miss Shearer around.

"Very upset she wasn't invited to my blowout last night."

"And what a blowout, from what I read in the papers and heard on the radio."

"Why didn't you show up? You could have had it all first-hand."

"There were so many parties to attend, I took in the one closest to me and then promptly at midnight fled home without leaving a glass slipper behind. I'd like to talk to you about the murder; I could use a good story."

"The good story is what Herb Villon is looking for. He's the detective on the case. He's over at the bar with Hazel Dickson, his sweetheart, and she's very jealous of me."

"I'm very jealous of Hazel. Isn't Mr. Villon something?"

"He has an adorable assistant who's smitten with me."

"Every male I know is smitten with you. Be a good gal and introduce me to Mr. Villon."

"No problem. But I'm warning you, there's not much to tell you that you haven't already read about or heard."

"I knew Mai Mai. She was a great gal. If she was murdered, I deduce it had something to do with astrology and those weird predictions of hers."

"That's what we think."

"We? Have you joined the police force?"

"Let's just say Mr. Villon thinks I'm just about the best amateur detective he's ever met." She told St. John about the incident of finding the folders in Mai Mai's bedroom."

"Good thinking indeed," said St. John with sincerity. "Who are these suspects and why?"

"I can't tell you why because that information has yet to be unearthed. I can tell you who because you'll be happy to know some of them are here." She pointed out Monte Trevor, Raymond Souvir, Dong See, and the Countess di Frasso."

"Di Frasso doesn't murder women. She's a man killer," said St. John wryly. "Who's among the missing?"

"Ivar Tensha and a couple with the Russian Embassy, Gregory and Natalia Ivanov."

"Well, they're a mixed bag and I've seen lots of mixed bags in my lifetime. What about this waiter who was stabbed to death?"

Marlene didn't dare reveal the truth about his administering the strychnine pill.

She said matter-of-factly, "Villon has him under investigation now. I don't think he's learned anything yet."

Adela Rogers St. John was nobody's fool. She chucked Dietrich under the chin playfully. "I think he's learned plenty and you're just playing possum."

Marlene smiled. "Come, I'll introduce you to Mr. Villon. I assume you and Hazel have already crossed paths."

"And swords."

Herb Villon had read many of St. John's articles and pleased her when he praised her fine writing. Hazel kept a stiff smile on her face while the bartender poured champagne for Marlene. While Adela carefully and cleverly questioned Herb about the murders, Marlene decided it would be politic to engage Hazel in conversation.

"Hazel, I know so little about you." Hazel suppressed a hiccup. "As a child, did your parents urge you to do anything specific?"

"Run away."

Dietrich wasn't fazed. "And so you did and here you are."

"It took longer than that to get here. There was once a husband. I can't tell you much about him because his face, like his brain, is a blank. But he was Dickson and I kept his name because it was easier to deal with than the one I was born with, which has too many syllables and ends with a *ski*. All I remember is we lived with his parents and they treated me like one of the family. Miserably. Barkeep! Another gin and orange."

Marlene's and Herb's eyes met and they told each other Hazel had had too much. Marlene hoped Herb hadn't told her too much, if anything, about the afternoon's excursion to Mai Mai's loft. Alcohol loosens tongues and Hazel's tongue was rarely tied. Gently, Herb put his arm around Hazel while signaling the bartender to go easy with the gin. Hazel shrugged the arm away and leaned against the bar, drink in hand, looking like a "B" girl in a sleazy bar waiting for some sleazy company. "I don't like this party," she slurred.

"Let's go. I'll take you home," said Villon.

"I don't want to go home."

Adela suggested to Villon, "There's a guest bedroom on this floor. It's through that door at the end. Down the hallway the last door on the left. It'll be quiet and you can reclaim her when you're ready to leave. You don't want to go now, do you? The party's just warming up."

"Okay, Hazel baby, we're going for a little walk." He had a firm grip on her arm. Adela relieved Hazel of her drink and placed it on the bar.

"I know where we're going. This is the Last Mile. And there's going to be no last-minute reprieve from the governor. I'm innocent, I tell you, I'm innocent!"

"Demand a retrial, dahling," growled Tallulah Bankhead, holding a glass of bourbon with a little ice. "Some women drink much too much, dahlings," she said over her shoulder to Marlene and Adela. "As for myself, I can never get enough of it. Do you mind if I leave my group in the lurch, which is where I found them in the first place, and join you two dahlings? Murder becomes you, Marlene. You should be framed and hung in the Louvre."

"I can take the compliment two ways." She smiled at Adela. "Framed and hung."

Tallulah roared with laughter. "Of course! Of course! Ha ha ha ha! But I truly meant it as a compliment, dahling. By the way, now that I've got you, why won't von Sternberg direct my next picture?"

"I don't know, Tallulah, maybe because he's already set to direct mine."

"It's really a terrific script. The *Devil and the Deep*. Gary Cooper's opposite me and there's a dishy newcomer, Cary Grant, in the brief role of one of my lovers, which is too true to life. All of my lovers have been brief, and most of them not brief enough. And for my husband they're giving me something from England called Charles Laughton. Talk about England, do you believe Winston Churchill once made a pass at Ethel Barrymore? Ethel claims he did, but she also claims she's the first lady of the theater, and where does that leave Lynn Fontanne and Helen Hayes? Although there are those who insist Lynnie's husband, Mr. Alfred Lunt, is the first lady of the theater. Talk about first ladies, how do you think Eleanor Roosevelt will shape up? I adore her myself and I'm exhausted campaigning for him, but I think she has a tendency to fade into the background. Come clean, Marlene, who murdered Mai Mai Chu?"

There was at that moment a sudden lull in conversation so that her baritone broke the sonic boon and all eyes were on the three women. Adela suggested they link arms and do a time step, while Tallulah suggested to Marlene, "Here's an opportunity to make a brief speech on behalf of the United Jewish Appeal." Most of the guests upon seeing Tallulah resumed talking to each other or whatever they were doing, assuming Tallulah was once again in her cups, not the ones keeping her breasts firm. "You'll have to forgive me, dahlings, but it seems I'm always prone to commanding attention when I least desire it. Now *there's* something I could desire."

144

Herb Villon returned and Marlene introduced him to Tallulah. Tallulah persisted. "All right, dahling. Who murdered that poor unfortunate?"

"I don't know."

"I hope you're not as simple as your answers!"

"Herb Villon is much more complicated than you think," said Marlene, coming to his rescue. "He's a brilliant detective and you must take my word for it; I've been working shoulder to shoulder with him the past twenty-four hours and I have nothing but respect and admiration for this man."

Tallulah said to Adela, "I suppose that's what drove his girlfriend to drink."

Monte Trevor descended on them. "Tallulah Bankhead and Marlene Dietrich under the same roof!"

"Why not, dahling? We were invited." Dietrich introduced them.

"How I would love to see you both in the same film," enthused Trevor.

"Why not *Uncle Tom's Cabin?* I'll do Topsy and Marlene would be a divine Eva. Or better still, why not round up Greta Garbo and Jean Harlow and we could do *Little Women.*"

"You're pulling my leg," said Monte Trevor.

"Don't hold your breath. And who's this dear little chap?" Dong See had quietly entered the scene. "You seem to resemble that violinist I heard in Carnegie Hall a few years ago."

"Permit me to introduce myself. I am Dong See, the violinist."

"Well dahling, you were nothing short of miraculous."

Marlene stepped in swiftly. "Miracles seem to favor Dong See. He was almost killed in an automobile accident." There was no expression on Dong See's face, and no lack of expression in Marlene's voice. "Why wasn't it international news at the time, darling?" She continued to the others. "He was so badly crippled, they feared for his life."

"Who is 'they,' dahling?" asked Tallulah, who was running low on bourbon.

" 'They' in general," said Marlene airily. "They hid him away in a Swiss clinic for six months. How did you endure it, Dong?"

"Where did you learn all this?" asked Dong See, not looking particularly pleased.

"A mutual friend is here in Hollywood. She probably hasn't been able to get in touch with you. She arrived last night. Brunhilde Messer."

"Oh. Brunhilde is here in Hollywood?" He might have been giving a stock market quotation, his voice was so dull and lifeless.

Marlene couldn't resist. She repeated Hitler's invitation by way of Brunhilde. Bankhead was impressed.

"I never ever get any invitations like that," said Tallulah mournfully. "Nobody ever puts me on a pedestal unless it's to measure me for a dress."

Marlene said to Dong See, "You don't sound terribly enthusiastic."

"Perhaps she gave you the mistaken impression that she and I are close friends. We met a few times in Berlin, but it was never more than that."

"How strange." Marlene handed Villon her glass and he went in search of more champagne. "She seemed so surprised that you were at my party. Even more surprised that you had completely recovered. Was there a rumor that you had been killed?"

"There are always rumors about me. They seem to favor me much the same as these miracles you attribute to me."

Our suspects are liars.

"Well, Brunhilde seemed genuinely delighted to hear you had completely recovered."

Herb Villon returned with Raymond Souvir in tow. Marlene accepted the champagne gratefully while Bankhead wandered off for more bourbon. Adela Rogers St. John was like a sponge, absorbing information and innuendos, and when the opportunity presented itself she introduced herself to Dong See. She had met Monte Trevor on another occasion and Novarro had introduced her to Souvir earlier at the party. She knew Marlene was up to something, and whatever it was Marlene had it in complete control.

Marlene said to Souvir, "Raymond, did you know Brunhilde Messer is in town?"

"Brunhilde Messer?" Dong See shot him a look that did not escape Dietrich. "Oh, of course. Brunhilde. It's been so, long!"

"Not all that long," corrected Marlene. "She said she recently brought you to Berlin to test for the part of *The Red Baron*."

"Yes, she did, but so much has happened to me since then, I guess I forgot." He cleared his throat. "Did she mention if she has abandoned the project?"

"No. I wasn't that interested. I would doubt that she has. I've known Brunhilde since I was a kid starting in show business. Brunhilde never abandons anything. Adela, do you remember her?"

"And how. Years ago she sang in San Francisco. I was there. Terrific voice. Has she given it up?"

"She is now a film producer and director."

"Aha! Following in Leni Riefenstahl's footsteps."

"Nobody follows in Leni's footsteps. She never leaves tracks."

Adela smiled at the group in general. "With so many international notables in town, sounds to me like there might be some kind of conspiracy brewing."

Marlene said grandly. "Adela is so wise. She doesn't miss a thing. You're one smart woman, Adela."

"That's a compliment I like, especially coming from another smart woman."

Villon finally spoke. "What kind of conspiracy, Adela? You have anything particular in mind?"

"Nothing really special. There are so many varieties and assortments. They're the kind of stories I try to specialize in. It brings in a wonderful cross section of scoundrels, rogues, and vagabonds."

"And murderers," added Villon.

"Oh, thank heaven for murderers," said Adela. "My father, who, if you didn't know, was the great criminal lawyer Earl Rogers . . ."

"I must do a movie about him!" cried Trevor.

He was ignored as Adela continued, ". . . and as a girl, I sat in on most of his trials. Trials that made his fortune, which as everyone knows he largely drank and squandered away. Murderers always fascinate me. But our American murderers don't hold a candle to your European ones. They're so much more colorful, so much more bloodthirsty, so much more imaginative." She indicated Raymond. "You French have one of the greatest mass murderers, Bluebeard." She zeroed in on Trevor. "And the British have so many, I've lost count. And you, Marlene, who can hold a candle to the Dusseldorf killer?" Dong See stood with his arms folded. "China has had more than its share of brutal murders. I can't say too much on behalf of Italy and the Iberian countries. They may be hotblooded but apparently they're coolheaded. And what have we got to show for it here in the good old U.S. of A.? Ruth Snyder and Judd Grey, two colorless drabs who kill her husband for his insurance. Why don't you do a movie about that, Mr. Trevor?"

"Oh, no. As you say, much too colorless and much too drab."

"Have you heard, Adela," Marlene was saying, "Raymond is screen-testing tomorrow."

"Good luck to you, Raymond." Adela's good wishes were genuine.

"My luck is with Marlene. She's doing it with me, and von Sternberg is directing."

"No kidding! Which one are you sleeping with?"

"Adela, behave yourself," Marlene remonstrated. Raymond was extremely uncomfortable, and Villon was enjoying himself immensely and glad that Hazel was out of the picture while sleeping it off.

"How I envy Raymond," said Dong See.

Marlene had that familiar wicked look in her eye again. "You know, *you* should be screen-tested too." Dong See was startled. "You're young, you're handsome, a violin virtuoso. That's what films are really lacking today, good, serious music. I'm going to talk to Ben Schulberg at Paramount. He must whip together a script for you and Anna May Wong. I noticed last night how much you complement each other in looks."

"I'm not an actor, Marlene," Dong See demurred.

"Oh, I think you are."

Careful, Marlene, careful, thought Herb Villon.

There was no stopping Dietrich. "Everybody's an actor. We professionals are in a class apart because we study, we train, we work hard to find a foothold in our profession, and once we've arrived we fight hard to hold on to our positions. But to the layman, whom we refer to as civilians, every day requires acting. It's all a world of make-believe out there. Husbands and wives have to act as though they love each other long after the dew is off the rose. Shopkeepers have to act all day as though they care about every customer with whom they do business. Professional men are constantly acting! The doctor telling a patient there's little hope. The dentist assuring a patient there will be no pain. A lawyer or a prosecuting attorney trying to convince a jury of someone's guilt or innocence. Children are the greatest natural actors in the world. You see, Dong, acting is lying. Just as writing novels and short stories is lying. Am I right, Adela?"

She concurred. "Everybody lives a lie. Look at Tallulah. She's making believe she's having a terrific time. She's hanging in because she probably has nowhere else to go except home. Look at the Countess di Frasso," and they all looked because it was the first that they were aware she had arrived. And she was heading straight toward them. ". . . Dorothy di Frasso kids herself into thinking she's one of the most desirable women in the world."

"I heard that Adela, and I don't kid myself about anything. Have I interrupted anything important?"

"We were discussing acting and lying," said Marlene. "I claim both are the same."

Di Frasso took a glass of champagne from a passing waiter carrying a tray. "And what brought on so profound a discussion?"

"I suggested Dong See should do a screen test," said Marlene, "and he protests he is not an actor. And I say he is, everyone is."

"Even me?" asked the Countess in the process of raising the glass to her lips.

"Especially you," said Adela, who took every opportunity to needle the woman she considered an opportunistic parasite.

"You're so brave drinking from that glass," said Marlene. "You don't know where it's been."

Di Frasso's eyes narrowed. "What about *your* glass?"

"Mr. Villon fetched it for me. He wouldn't want to poison me."

"You're sure?" joked Villon.

"Quite sure," replied Marlene.

Di Frasso found a smile. "I don't think my number is quite up . . . yet." She sipped the champagne. "And anyway, there were several glasses on the waiter's tray. They couldn't all be poisoned."

"Just one," said Dietrich, "sort of Russian roulette. Oh, drink your drink, you silly girl. I doubt if anybody is marked for death tonight."

Di Frasso's eyes widened as she asked, "Where's Anna May? I don't see her. Wasn't she invited?"

Marlene said, "She decided not to come. As you know, having dropped in at my house and just missing us, we spent a very tiring afternoon."

Liar. That was Villon's thought. But beautifully done.

Marlene continued, "So she went home to rest and to contemplate. She deeply mourns Mai Mai Chu. They were very very close."

"Why do I suspect Anna May is at home studying some astrological charts she found in Mai Mai's apartment?"

Marlene laughed. "Dorothy, there were *thousands* in Mai Mai's filing cabinets. If we were looking for any specific ones, it would have taken ages to locate them."

"My money's on you, Marlene. You found what you were looking for."

"You're so sure."

"If you hadn't, you and detective Villon wouldn't be here. You'd still be downtown searching. You don't give up easily, Marlene; I know that."

"Quite right. But also quite wrong. Herb, shouldn't you look in on Hazel? I'm not leaving just yet. Raymond, you should be at home studying your lines."

"I've already memorized them. I was hoping we could meet earlier at the studio tomorrow and go over the script together, rehearse a bit. I would so appreciate it."

"No need to worry about that, my dear. Von Sternberg is a martinet where rehearsals are concerned. Of course, he's a martinet where everything else is concerned, but that's another story that bores me. Dong See, why don't you come to the studio tomorrow and give Raymond some immoral support," Adela bit her lip.

Monte Trevor said jovially, "Well, it looks like we'll all be on the lot tomorrow. I've got a meeting with Cecil B. De-Mille."

Making his way through the crowded room, Villon was thinking, Marlene Dietrich, you are a very dangerous lady and you could just be asking for some trouble you don't want.

"Cecil B. DeMille. How impressive," said Marlene flatly. "Adela, could I talk to you privately for a few minutes?" They excused themselves and walked out to the veranda.

Making sure that no other guests were within earshot, Marlene took Adela's arm and guided her down the stairs onto the lawn. "Adela, did you know Lewis Tate?"

"Good grief, I haven't heard that name in ages."

"Today he hung himself."

"Oh dear, the poor bastard."

Marlene told Adela of the circumstances leading up to Tate's suicide. "I think passing out at my party was the last straw."

"No, the last straw made its appearance a long time ago. But he kept hanging on, hoping for a comeback, a chance to prove he could make it in talkies. He even failed at a chance in radio, and that wasn't worth a hill of has-beens. You taking up a collection for his burial? I've got a spare twenty on me."

"No, I'm taking care of everything. I've arranged for a service in the chapel at Forest Lawn. The day after tomorrow at ten in the morning. Could you try to round up some people?"

"I'll do my damndest. I'll try to round up some of his ex-wives. There's enough of them to form a small crowd. Lewis Tate. Hung himself. Made a pass at me a couple of times. I'm sorry I didn't take him up on it, well, at least once. He was quite a guy in his day." They headed back to the house. "Marlene, what were you up to back there?"

"Up to? Up to what?"

"You know better than to try and kid me. All that stuff about everybody's a liar. You made an impression, honey; I could tell by the looks on their faces. And somebody especially didn't like the inference that he's a liar."

"That's good. That's very very good."

"It more than likely could be bad, very very bad."

"I don't think so. Anyway, Adela, I have a very special God who looks over me and protects me. Haven't you suspected that by now?"

"Oh, I knew a long time ago you stepped into a lot of that certain something that's supposed to mean good luck. But murder is something else. You're dealing with a steel-hearted killer."

"A conspirator?"

"It seems to be pointing in that direction."

"You make me feel more confident. I'm glad you're my friend, Adela Rogers St. John."

"I wouldn't have it any other way, sweetie." They rejoined the party in time to see Tallulah Bankhead attempting a high kick and falling heavily on her backside.

"Okay, you sons of bitches," she growled from the floor, "which one of you bastards pushed me?"

⟪ THIRTEEN ⟫

HERB VILLON, HAVING returned from looking in on Hazel Dickson, helped Tallulah to her feet. "Thank you, dahling, it's comforting to know chivalry isn't dead." She now realized it was Herb who had come to her rescue. "Oh, it's you, dahling,"—her voice was now a seductive purr— "have you any plans for Passover? But let me finish my story," as though there was any stopping her, thought Adela. Tallulah said, for the benefit of Marlene, Adela, and Herb, while the three were being scrutinized by Dong See, Monte Trevor, and Raymond Souvir: "I was telling them about my sister getting rid of her girlfriend with a swift boot out the door. Well, dahlings, she had gotten to be a bit too much. An absolutely slovenly slattern. She always left the toilet seat up. What have you two been up to?" This was directed at Marlene and Adela.

Villon was holding a match to the cigarette Marlene had in her mouth. Adela told Tallulah, "We were talking about Lewis Tate's funeral."

"Tate is *tod?*"

"Very dead," said Marlene, "he hung himself."

"Oh, dear God. His agent must be shattered."

"He hasn't had an agent in years," said Adela. "The funeral's the day after tomorrow in Forest Lawn Chapel, ten in the morning. He was alone, Tallulah, absolutely alone. Abandoned by everyone. Friends, family, everyone."

"How dreadful. I shall be there. He was very nice to me years ago in New York when I was just getting started. I shall certainly be at the services. Who's catering?"

Marlene addressed the group surrounding them. "It would be nice if some of you could attend. He gave a lot to the industry; it is so little to ask that the industry give this in return." A few people assured Marlene they'd be there. Ramon Novarro promised to round up a group. Adela said she'd get a notice to all the newspapers, where her persuasion was very powerful. Marlene was pleased with herself and feeling very beatific. She didn't dare admit to anyone in the immediate vicinity that she loathed funerals.

Monte Trevor said to Marlene, "Lewis Tate. Dead. How tragic."

Marlene blew a perfect smoke ring and said, "For some people death isn't the tragedy. It's life that's the tragedy."

Trevor asked, "Nietzsche?"

"Dietrich." She moved away in search of a telephone and found one in the adjoining study.

Anna May Wong, wearing a traditional Chinese kimono, sat at a desk sipping tea, studying the eight charts that were spread out before her. She and the kimono were two of the few Oriental items in the apartment. Outside of family portraits and mementos scattered about on tables and shelves and sideboards, the apartment itself was predominantly art deco. Much of the furnishings the actress had acquired when traveling and working abroad. She had filmed in England, Germany, and France, where she was a great favorite. There she was an interesting exotic, whereas in her own country, although the only Chinese actress ever to attain recognition, she was relegated to playing mysterious women in thrillers or cold-blooded killers. She had worked steadily until the past year, and through thrift and excellent financial advice was comfortably well off. She longed to get back before the camera, but at the moment she had no prospects. So she welcomed the opportunity to decipher Mai Mai's charts. She was working on Dorothy di Frasso's horoscope when the phone rang. It was Marlene.

"Why don't you take a break and come to Ramon's party?"

"I'm sure I'm not missing a thing."

"You're missing Tallulah Bankhead."

"I'm not missing a thing."

Marlene laughed. "Actually, she's outrageous, but less than usual. In fact, she's rather subdued, like the aftermath of a hurricane. How's it coming?"

"I've got Dorothy di Frasso's in front of me."

"Anything revealing?"

"Listen to this prediction Mai Mai made. 'You will never be in want. The Lord will provide. And if he doesn't, your ex-husband will.'" Mai Mai specialized in giving care and comfort to abandoned wives, ex-lovers, and stray cats. Actually, though, there's something I think a bit out of the ordinary. Here and there certain words are underlined, but for the life of me I can't see why Mai Mai thought them significant. I checked the other horoscopes and they too have underlined words, but they tell me nothing."

Marlene was thinking. "Tell me some of the words."

"Believe me, Marlene, they are nothing special."

"Name a few."

"There's 'forever' and here's 'worship' and 'states' and 'squad.'"

"'Squad'? You're sure it isn't 'squid.' Mai Mai adored cooking."

"I know that. No. It's 'squad.' But I'll double-check. Chinese is so complicated it might turn out to be 'squash.' Where can I find you tomorrow if I need you?"

"I'm at Paramount most of the day. Raymond's test. With

Joe directing, it's bound to be an all-day session. In fact, I'm positive it will be and he'll work me until I'm ready to drop. He's furious I didn't dance attendance on him at my party."

"Wasn't he aware there was a murder?"

"Yes and he'll never forgive Mai Mai for stealing the spotlight. Don't stay up late."

"If I can't reach you tomorrow, what about Wednesday?"

Marlene told her about Lewis Tate's suicide and the funeral. Anna May had worked with him in an adventure story, *Bound East for Shanghai*. "I'm coming to the funeral. I want to pay my respects. Hanging. He deserved better then that."

"Amen to that. Good night, darling."

Anna May arose and turned on the radio. She fiddled with the dial until she found a program of symphonic music. She entered her bedroom. In one of its three closets she found a cardboard box that contained photographs and stills representative of her career. She rummaged about and found what she was looking for. Lewis Tate holding her in his arms unaware of an Oriental villain lurking behind them. Written in ink at the bottom, she read, 'Why doesn't he mind his own damn business. I hope I go on ravishing your lovely self into eternity. I adore you. Lewis.' He had indeed ravished her, but not into eternity. A lovely redheaded ingenue had diverted his attention and she became his seventh wife. Anna May tried to remember her name. Minnie? Miriam? Melissa? Not important anymore. It had been important once and she brought her broken heart to Mai Mai in search of one of her miraculous cures. And Mai Mai waved the redhead aside with the prediction she would die of a social disease in a Honolulu brothel. Lewis Tate. Dead by hanging. She carried the photo back to the desk and placed it in a bottom drawer, where from time to time she would look at it and remind herself she'd been very much loved, if only briefly.

Margaret Dumont, who had won instant recognition in films as the tall, dignified, and majestic foil to the Marx Brothers, was inconsolable about something and Tallulah was trying to offer her sympathy and bourbon.

"Anything I can do, Tallulah?" asked Marlene.

"I don't think so, dahling. Margaret's come to Hollywood and found religion. One of those sects that seem to proliferate in this deadly climate. But now her group's been set adrift with the sudden death of their spiritual teacher, and dahling, a religious sect without a leader is a non-prophet organization. There there, Maggie dahling, don't take it so hard, have a sip of bourbon."

"Nothing to drink, Tallulah, I'll be all right. If only Mai Mai Chu hadn't been killed. Whenever I was under stress, she was always such a comfort." She was suddenly and mercurially no longer feeling distressed. "Marlene, is the gossip true?"

"Which gossip?"

"That you and Anna May Wong know who killed Mai Mai but you're not naming the killer until you have concrete evidence?" Marlene wondered if there was anyone in the room who hadn't heard her. Hers was a voice that could penetrate lead. Herb Villon rode to Marlene's assistance on an invisible white steed with an invincible lance in his hand prepared to joust an adversary.

"Forgive me, Miss Dumont, but Marlene and Anna May are as much in the dark to the killer's identity as I am."

"Indeed?" She drew herself up to her full height and produced a lorgnette, through which she studied Herb Villon and quite obviously liked what she saw. "And who are you?"

"Herbert Villon, the detective in charge of the case."

"How thrilling," she gurgled, "you're my first detective and it's such a pleasant experience. Do you know my friend Hazel Dickson?"

Villon said affably, "We've been introduced."

"Then you must be her inside dope."

"Oh, God," groaned Tallulah to Marlene, who now held a much-needed glass of champagne.

Dumont charged onward like a locomotive out of control. "Hazel says she's positive you think Marlene and Anna May know the killer's identity and it's all in some of Mai Mai's horoscope charts. And didn't the waiter who was stabbed in the back have something to do with it?"

"I don't really know," said Villon. "He was dead when I found his body so there wasn't much he could contribute to the case other than some added mystery."

"But Hazel told me you and Marlene questioned him in her kitchen. You must have learned something then."

"Yes, we did," said Villon, treasuring the look of expectancy on the face of the actress who was about to be deeply disappointed. "We learned he didn't know anything about the killing, or so he professed. At the time, I believed him when he said he didn't know the glass of champagne he was bringing to Madam Chu contained the poison."

"You have to be very careful with waiters," warned Miss Dumont. "Waiters can be terribly two-faced, on one hand recommending the *shrimps rémoulade* and on the other pushing the *moules marinières*, which I loathe."

Marlene said to Villon, "Herb, here comes Hazel. She's escaped."

Villon excused himself and went to Hazel's aid.

"She looks a bit done in," commented Miss Dumont, "as though she herself's been poisoned."

"If she hasn't," said Marlene, "she may soon be."

"I feel terrible," moaned Hazel as Villon led her to the veranda for some fresh air.

"What can I get you?" asked Herb. "You've already got a big mouth."

"Don't be mean. I feel awful. Why is everybody looking at me?"

"Your old buddy Margaret Dumont just got through telling the whole room that you told her Marlene and Anna May know the killer's identity."

"I did no such thing. You don't believe me. I can see it in your face. A puritan father ready to smack Hester Prynne with the Scarlet A. Let go of my arm. I don't want to go outside. I want a drink."

"I don't think that's a very good idea."

"I don't give a damn what you think. And Dumont isn't my old buddy. I don't have any old buddies. I don't have any young buddies either, come to think of it. If Dietrich doesn't wipe that smile off her face I'm going to wipe it off for her."

Adela Rogers St. John said to Marlene, "Our Hazel now resembles a basilisk."

"A what?"

"A basilisk, a fabulous creature with death-dealing eyes and horrible breath."

"Why Adela, dahling," interjected Tallulah, "I didn't know you knew Jeanette MacDonald."

Monte Trevor's impending departure had put Ramon Novarro in mind of one of the late Sarah Bernhardt's interminable farewell tours. Trevor was insisting, "But Ramon, you must seriously consider doing films on your native soil. You could become the emperor of Mexican film production. And wouldn't Dolores Del Rio complement you regally as the empress? I will be traveling to Mexico soon to visit some friends in high places and I wish I had your permission to tell them you're interested in returning there."

Marlene and Adela, standing nearby with Raymond Souvir and Dong See, exchanged glances.

Ramon was telling Monte Trevor, "Despite the rumors circulating that I'm about to be professionally beheaded by MGM, I have an ironclad contract that has another three years to go, so unless they pay me off with hundreds of thousands of dollars, I will not be available in the near future. And Metro does not part with huge sums of cash, even in an emergency. It was so nice of you to come to my party. *Goodbye.*" Novarro left Trevor in the isolation of his extended farewell, and somewhat embarrassed, Trevor waved at Marlene and the others and beat a hasty retreat.

Tallulah was saying to Raymond Souvir, "If you like, dahling, I can coach you in your lines tonight. I've got no immediate plans and I'd just adore coaching you, dahling."

Souvir's eyes beseeched Dong See's help but the violinist's

mind was elsewhere. Dong See saw the Countess di Frasso materialize at the other end of the room, after what seemed like a prolonged absence. With her was Brunhilde Messer.

Marlene said, "I didn't see her come in."

"See who?" asked Adela.

"The tall woman with di Frasso." She explained Brunhilde Messer.

"She looks like a national monument," said Adela.

"She intends to be. I didn't know she knew Ramon."

"In this town you don't have to know the host to crash a party," said Adela. "When I was first beginning as a reporter, I'd go to some shindig at Harold Lloyd's and just say I was joining Charlie Chaplin. Since I was only sixteen at the time and you know Chaplin's reputation for leching after girls fresh in their teens, it looked obvious that Charlie was somewhere in the house panting for my presence. Dong See's beaten you to Brunhilde."

"I don't want to get to her."

"She has Herb Villon fascinated. He's over there at the bar with Hazel Dickson, who's staring daggers at us. What could be eating her?"

"Me. She's jealous. She thinks I'm of special interest to her boyfriend."

"Well, aren't you?"

"Not the way she thinks. Poor Raymond Souvir. He looks as though he wishes the floor would open and swallow him. Aha! Brunhilde is waving him over. I don't believe she hasn't seen me."

"She has," said Adela, "about the time you first saw her. She was looking at us then. Very slyly, mind you, but I caught it."

"Let's join Herb and Hazel," suggested Marlene.

"Is it safe?"

"Adela, there's a special God who looks after me. I will always be safe."

"Such self-confidence in the face of Margaret Dumont

161

practically declaring you and Anna May the most likely targets for murder by the killer. After all, declaring that you might know his identity!"

"Why not *her* identity?"

"Of course. Di Frasso and the Russian lady."

"Natalia Ivanov."

"That's it. Ivanov."

"And Brunhilde Messer."

"She told you she got in late yesterday, too late to know about your party."

"That's what she said, but it doesn't have to be so."

"Marlene, if she had been at your house last night, you would have seen her."

"Not necessarily. I didn't join my guests until almost eleven o'clock. . . ."

"Of course. Outfoxing Connie Bennett."

"By the time I came downstairs, there was such a crush of party guests, it was impossible to know who was there unless they sought me out. When Mai Mai Chu got on the bandstand, the crush was even worse because those who were in the other rooms and on the other floors or outside in the garden came hurrying in to see Mai Mai do her bit. After Mai Mai's murder, I must admit most everyone was well behaved, but there were many who just went right on partying whether or not they realized they'd witnessed a murder."

"That's my Hollywood," said Adela. "The natives are always restless and self-occupied."

"Then I was with Herb and Anna and that adorable Mallory boy in the study for quite some time, and although for most of that period my guests were forbidden to leave, Herb soon relaxed the security and I'm sure several left almost immediately. In fact, I saw very few of them."

"Didn't you get to sing?"

"No, I left that to the suspects."

They had reached Herb and Hazel. Adela asked solicitously, "Feeling better, Hazel?"

"I'm just dandy. Who's the big broad with di Frasso. She's staring at us right now."

Marlene kept her eyes on Herb and Hazel and explained Brunhilde Messer for Hazel's edification. Hazel rejoindered with, "That ought to be worth a couple of items. So Hitler wants you to be his Queen of the May. I'm going to use that."

"I wish you wouldn't," said Marlene. "I do not wish to be connected with Hitler even in a joke."

"It's too good a story for me to pass up."

Adela said quietly and pointedly. "I'm passing it up. And when I speak to Louella, I'm sure she'll pass it up. And don't try leaking it to Skolsky or Jimmy Fidler or the international press or it'll be the last item you peddle to any of them."

"I'm not afraid of you." Hazel's voice was weak, the timbre unusually thin.

"There's no need for you to be. I'm just trying to let you know that there's a time in every business to practice ethics and understanding. To deliberately try to hurt Marlene's career . . ."

"That's baloney! I think it's a big laugh!"

"Then go have a chuckle somewhere and keep it out of print. You know this town as well as I do. An item like that can be turned against Marlene, especially if Hitler becomes all powerful and a person to be feared."

Villon said softly but forcefully. "Hazel's going to forget she heard what Marlene told her in what Marlene and the rest of us assumed was the strictest confidence, or I'm going to paste her one in the face."

"Oh dahlings, who's the lucky recipient of that paste in the face." She looked closely at Hazel as the bartender replenished her bourbon. "You, darling? You look as though you've already been pasted. Oops! Forgive me! I thought you were someone else. I'm not wearing my glasses." She turned on Villon. "You brute, dahling. You wouldn't strike a defenseless woman, would you? Not with a surname like Villon. Surely you've heard of François Villon, the poet. Dennis King played him in *The Vagabond King*. The way he swishbuckled around, it should have been *The Vagabond Queen*. Now I know who that is with di Frasso. Brunhilde Messer. I heard her sing in London at Covent Garden. She woke me from a deep sleep with her "Yo Ho Te Hos." The opera's a perfect place for an insomniac." She paused, took stock of her somber-looking companions, and then said knowledgeably, "I'm sure one of you is grateful for my rude interruption. Marlene, are you well? You seem very strange."

"I'm tired. I've had little rest since the party. I'll have one for the road and then be on my way."

On the other side of the room, Brunhilde Messer was telling her group, "There is much to be done, despite the police investigation. They'll find out nothing. I'm sure I can rely on you all to befuddle them."

Di Frasso asked, "Supposing it's true; supposing Marlene and Anna May are on the right track."

"I don't believe it," said Brunhilde.

"Anna May has the astrological charts, *our* astrological charts. Monte Trevor insists they will be incriminating."

"Perhaps, perhaps not." She chose that moment to wave at Marlene, who acknowledged her with a flutter of her right hand. "Something's troubling Marlene. I can tell. I've seen that look before, many times."

Dong See interrupted. "I'm tired. I'm going home."

"I'll give you a lift." Dorothy di Frasso had a lot on her mind, and Dong See was the person she wanted to discuss it with.

Souvir said to the violinist, "I thought I was driving you home."

Dong See said affably, "You stay and enjoy yourself. Lots of pretty little starlets are starting to arrive. It looks as though Mr. Novarro's party is going to progress well into the late hours."

Brunhilde trilled at Souvir. "Raymond, darling. Why don't we join Marlene's group. I do so wish to meet Mr. Villon."

Adela said to Marlene, "She's headed this way with your French actor. Try a smile for a change. You look like Sylvia Sidney in anything, and she's always on the verge of tears."

Tallulah Bankhead said to no one in particular, "That young man is really beautiful. I wonder if that's all there is to him."

Marlene suddenly brightened; catching her second wind had brought with it a dynamite shift in her mood. "Brunhilde, I thought you'd never join us." She introduced Messer to everyone. Tallulah roared, "You woke me up in London!"

Brunhilde took a few steps backward, startled, expecting to be attacked, but Tallulah's face was wreathed in one of her most enchanting smiles. "And I'll be eternally grateful to you because I awoke to one of the most exquisite voices in the history of opera."

Brunhilde also wore a phony smile. "You are too kind."

"Not too often."

"So, Mr. Villon," said Brunhilde, "I hear you are up to your waist in murder. I knew Mai Mai. We were good friends. She did not deserve to die, at least not this way. And the waiter, obviously murdered to silence him. But he probably wasn't aware the pill was poisoned."

"Oh, so that's it!" blurted Hazel.

"Be quiet." Villon might have hit her with a whip. "Where did you get your information, Madam Messer?"

"What information?" Her voice was husky. Marlene had a tight grip on her handbag and Adela's instinctive nose for news told her there might be a story brewing here.

"About the waiter."

Brunhilde was cool and self-contained. "My friends just explained to me what they told you when you questioned them last night. That, and what I read in the papers and heard on the radio gave me enough hints to come to my conclusion. So, obviously I am correct and it annoys you. Why are you so upset?"

"I'm not upset. I'm delighted with what you said. Very delighted. Hazel, you should be very delighted. Here's an item

for you, in fact, a bit of a delicacy like broiled pig's snout."
Hazel said nothing and just glared at him. "Adela? What does
what you heard from Madam Messer imply to you?"

"That somebody should have kept their mouth shut, but
blissfully didn't."

Marlene was thinking, somebody thought the information
was safe with Brunhilde. It was Brunhilde who should have
kept her mouth shut, but she was so busy being charming and
enchanting with Herb Villon that she inadvertently supplied
him with the break he so desperately needed. He was right.
One of the suspects was Morton Duncan's contact. He killed
Morton Duncan because Duncan might tell who supplied
him with the pill if his blackmail demands weren't satisfied.

Hazel said, "You'll have to excuse me."

Marlene said, "There's a phone in the alcove under the
staircase in the hall. You can't miss it. There's a lovely paint-
ing of the Madonna and Child hanging near it." Hazel shot
her an unpleasant look and left.

Souvir had been chatting affably with Tallulah until he
heard Brunhilde's gaffe and was now dabbing at his brow with
a handkerchief. Marlene and Villon recognized his discom-
fort. Tallulah asked Souvir, "Are you warm, dahling? It is a
bit close in here, isn't it."

"Delightfully so," said Adela, who was making a mental
note to consider the possibility of a very long article about
this case for the *Saturday Evening Post.*

Brunhilde deftly changed the subject. "So, Marlene, you
are helping Raymond with his screen test. You are always so
generous."

"Just like you, Brunhilde," said Marlene with a sly smile.
"We are birds of a feather. I see the Countess and Dong See
left together."

"She offered him a lift home and he accepted."

"Did she really? But Raymond, I thought *you* were his
favorite chauffeur."

Adela asked, "Doesn't Dong See drive?"

Raymond said, "Not since his near fatal car accident last year."

Adela looked amazed. "But you can't exist in this town without driving a car. The public transportation is a myth and there were more covered wagons crossing the country than there are taxis to be found here. He'd better hire himself a car and driver. There are lots of those available." She paused. "I think Tallulah's lost interest in us. She's wandered away."

Souvir said nervously. "She wants very much to coach me."

"Is that how they put it these days?" asked Adela.

Marlene said to Herb, "I'm sure you're thinking what I'm thinking. And isn't it delightful. I'm going to phone Anna May and tell her when I get home." She remembered something and drew Villon away from Adela and Souvir. Adela was a good sport about it and engaged Souvir in a conversation about acting techniques, of which his knowledge was sadly negligible.

Herb was repeating what Marlene had just told him. "Certain words are underlined?"

"In all the charts."

"When we put them all together, I'm sure they'll spell 'murder.' "

"Aha!" said Marlene very eagerly, "you think they are a clue."

"Marlene, everything I look at, everything I touch and smell, is a clue. And believe me, it's not an easy thing to deal with. Do you suppose the soprano's aware she blew it?"

"Oh yes, but she covered beautifully. Well, at least we know the murderer is definitely one of them and not somebody we hadn't thought of, such as my chauffeur or my very boring butler. Oh dear, Adela is struggling to converse with Raymond. Let's rescue her."

Villon said, "Brunhilde just stands there staring at Raymond. Do you suppose she sees something we don't see?"

Marlene said, "More than likely, she knows something we don't know."

Villon stayed Marlene with a touch of his hand on her wrist. "Do you suppose Messer knew exactly what she was doing when she dropped her clanger?"

"It's possible. But somehow I don't think so. You see, it completely unnerved Raymond. You can't feign perspiration. If you haven't observed it for yourself, then let me tell you in very plain English, Raymond Souvir is a very frightened young man, and from the way Brunhilde is staring at him, I think his fear is contagious. Ah, you three! Forgive us for being so exclusive for a few minutes, but Herb wanted some advice on a birthday gift for his delightful young assistant and I made a suggestion. Did I make sense, Herb?"

"Marlene, you most certainly did make sense."

Brunhilde Messer was lighting a cigarette. She took a deep drag and exhaled a frightening cloud of smoke. Adela was reminded of a volcano in eruption, not realizing the analogy was right on the nose.

⊄Q FOURTEEN ⊅⟩

DOROTHY DI FRASSO drove like royalty. She demanded the road to herself, an impossible exclusivity. Her impatience with other drivers was nerve jangling, bearing down on the horn as often as she bore down on the gas pedal. Dong See was as uncomfortable with her driving as he was with Raymond Souvir's, but he said nothing. Her mouth had also accelerated and she was now busily grinding Brunhilde Messer into pulp.

"The big cow. They should never have sent her here. Using that preposterous offer for Marlene from Adolph as an excuse. Why are the Germans so unimaginative?"

"They only seem so," said Dong See. "Don't discredit them so rashly. There are some very impressive imaginations at work there. You'll soon be witnessing a rebirth of that country that will astonish the world."

"That cow would have to give the game away."

"She gave nothing away."

"Don't be dense. She confirmed for Villon the fact that one of us convinced the waiter to drop the pill into the champagne. He could have been kept floundering in the dark for ages."

"You mustn't underestimate him while overestimating yourself. The man's smart and he's smart enough to let Dietrich and Wong contribute. They're very smart ladies. I'm amazed at the large population of clever women in this town. Properly used, they could be very helpful. Adela Rogers St. Johns has a mind like a steel trap."

"She's a bitch."

"I like her. She's forthright and convincing. I can see where she can be a very dangerous enemy. I'm sure you're aware she doesn't like you."

"Very few women like me. I've been aware of that ever since I set out in the world to make my fortune. My family was dirt poor and I made up my mind at the age of seven, when I seduced the son of a candy store proprietor, that I was going to be a somebody and be in a position of purchasing candy instead of bartering for it."

"You've been bartering ever since."

"It becomes a pleasant habit after a while." She shouted out the window to a jalopy she finally managed to pass. "Hire a horse, you nitwit!" This won her an obscene gesture. "Marlene intensely dislikes me. We've been rivals in love."

"Dietrich doesn't strike me as a woman who will suffer the indignity of being the third point in a triangle. She accepts her husband's affair with Tamara Matul. Her bisexuality is an open secret; I can't imagine you two having been rivals for a woman."

"Of *course* not."

"I can't believe this offer of Adolph's was a sincere one. Doesn't he know her maternal grandfather was a Jew? Conrad Felsing. He sold jewelry. Hitler loathes Jews. You should read his book; it tells you everything you could want to know about him."

"I tried. I found it unreadable." She was bearing down on the horn again, and a little old lady pulled over and let her pass. She recognized character actress Beryl Mercer. "Those charts are beginning to worry me. I'm beginning to think they contain something that can be very injurious. Anna May was

Mai Mai's pet. She could have told her things or hinted at things that could add up to trouble. Like you said, Anna May's a very clever woman."

Dong See said, "I have a yen for her."

"It'll take more then a yen to get her. I've learned she's unattainable."

"Doesn't she like men?"

"Oh, very much. What little one knows of her involvements, they are of brief duration. She's the kind of woman Virginia Woolf champions in her essay *A Room of One's Own*. Anna May's a rebel who at an early age was determined to have her own space. Now that she's got it, she's holding on to it. What's this about Monte Trevor planning to go to Mexico?"

"Someone's needed there. Monte's the logical one."

"Villon will never let any of us leave town. Not while he suspects one of us is the murderer."

"Dorothy, it won't be too hard to slip out of here when it becomes necessary."

"What about Raymond?"

"What about him?"

"His test. Supposing it's a success."

"Good for Raymond. He goes under contract to Paramount, a major studio. This leads to major contacts. He could become even more important in the scheme of things."

"He's a pussywillow bending in the wind."

"Raymond has greater strength than you give him credit for."

"I can only judge by what I see. We have an expression in this country, 'weak sister.' Raymond strikes me as a 'weak sister.' He perspires a lot."

"At the wheel of a car he has nerves of steel. Christ! Must you use that bloody horn so often?"

"I have no tolerance for anything that gets in my way."

"Take the next right. That's my road. It's a dead end. My house is at the top."

"Raymond has me worried."

"There's nothing to worry about. Watch out for that rabbit!"

"Let it watch out for itself. It should look both ways before crossing the road!"

Ivar Tensha wished he found Brunhilde Messer sexually attractive. It had been days since he'd been favored with a woman's favors and if he didn't have one soon, he was afraid he'd break out in a rash. They were sipping brandies, having finished the dinner he'd ordered from room service. Ivar stared at Brunhilde as she lit a cigarette. The thought of bedding down a woman her size repulsed him. He had to remind himself she wasn't here for a romantic rendezvous.

"Why do you look at me that way? Is it the unfortunate slip I made before Villon?"

"You must learn to think before you speak, Brunhilde. You treat every place like it is the extension of a stage in an opera house. Everything you do is large, as though you're trying to be heard at the top of the second balcony. I must admit you're in the right place. Everything in Hollywood is larger than life, like you are. This Villon is no fool. He's no hick cop in a hick town. I have done a check on his past record and it is formidable. He is a favorite son of the movie industry. His superiors are never less than supportive. He has not been known to make a false move. His only apparent lapse in taste is this Hazel Dickson."

"He's a magnet for women. Tallulah Bankhead salivated at the sight of him. And I suspect Marlene is keeping him in reserve once she's had enough of Chevalier and Herbert Marshall. I don't know how she does it. She juggles lovers like she's center stage in a music hall. Well, why not, she began in music halls."

Tensha was lighting one of his torpedo-style cigars, and Brunhilde was finding it hard to mask her distaste. "I don't understand Mai Mai's foolishness last night."

"How so?"

"A few of her predictions were too close to the bone. Too

close to what she had learned in Europe. She was told too much." He sighed. "But we were so desperate to have her. She would have been such a valuable asset. It was Trevor's idea to go after her and I seconded it. She could have disseminated so much false information, she would have been invaluable. But no. She was a woman drowning in ethics and morals and was shocked that we would think she would even consider betraying her great gifts." He shook his head from side to side. "When will people learn that loyalty is much too expensive. Did Dietrich believe you when you said you only just arrived last night?"

"I'm sure she did. One thing I know you admire in me is how convincing I can be when I have to be. I'm a much better actress than Marlene."

"Marlene doesn't have to act. She has a face."

"I had the devil's own time keeping out of her way at the party last night. I'm positive Mai Mai saw me. She was on the bandstand and could see over everyone's head. Still, she might not have recognized me immediately in my red wig."

"You looked like Harpo Marx."

"That's terribly unkind."

"I'm too rich to be kind."

She sipped her brandy. "Something may have to be done about Raymond."

"I like Raymond."

"I think he's frightened. He perspires more than usual."

"It's the little boy in him. Try mothering him. He'll respond."

"He doesn't interest me that way. I like big boys. Very big boys. Is there no way to kill this investigation?"

"There is, but I prefer to see it expire a slow death. Villon won't rest until he's caught the guilty party."

"That means you could be trapped here indefinitely!"

"If necessary, we'll give him a murderer."

"Who do you have in mind?"

"At the moment, no one in particular." His smile was crooked and ugly. "There is no dearth of candidates. On the

173

other hand, if Villon solves the case quickly, we'll be spared any unpleasantness among us."

"If Villon succeeds, there could be another kind of unpleasantness. An explosive one."

"Silence can be induced. I wonder how Miss Wong is faring with those charts? Mine sounded amusingly simple when Mai Mai read it to me. Of course, I now suspect strongly she was guilty of the sins of omission." He was on his feet and pacing, cigar in mouth and hands clasped behind his back. "Damn her for her fidelity to herself. She even quoted Shakespeare at the time. Shakespeare! That hack!" He boomed the quote, " 'This above all, to thine own self be true.' Polonius in *Hamlet*."

Brunhilde made a face as she helped herself to more brandy. "I never liked the character of Hamlet. He had terrible taste in women. Ophelia and his mother."

"Unfortunately, my dear Brunhilde, Hamlet had to suffer the manipulations of his creator."

"What happens now?"

"My dear, we continue to follow the blueprint. I haven't too much time to spare. I must get back to Romania. There's a new gas we're developing that will soon be tested in northern Tibet. It's safe to test there. Nobody cares if entire villages are destroyed in outlands like northern Tibet. I considered an Eskimo community in the North Pole, but you can't be sure there's not some party of explorers in the vicinity who might survive and report the infamy. You know, Mai Mai predicted I would be involved with a tragedy in an outlying territory. I wonder if she meant Tibet or the Moon." He sat and folded his hands in his lap. "I have some interesting plans for the Moon. But they'll have to wait. Pour me some brandy, Brunhilde, this one should give me the glow I desire."

After leaving the party, Marlene and Herb made a detour to Anna May's apartment house. Hazel had been condemned to coventry by Herb for her miserable behavior at the party, much to Marlene's displeasure.

"You can't let her drive in the condition she's in," insisted Marlene. "Get one of Ramon's hired help to take her home."

"Marlene, Hazel's car knows the way back. Don't worry about Hazel. I'll follow you to Anna May's, and don't go too fast. In this darkness I might lose you."

"Herb, when I don't want to be lost, it's not easy to lose me."

When they arrived at her apartment, Anna May led them to the living room, where there was champagne cooling alongside a hot plate of egg rolls and spare ribs.

"I thought you'd like a little nosh," said Anna May. Marlene was no advocate of art deco but had to admit Anna May's apartment seemed more comfortable than bizarre. Anna May had the horoscope charts laid out on a dining table, and while sipping champagne and nibbling at egg rolls Marlene and Herb examined them. Anna May translated more of the underlined words for them but they could make no sense of them.

"This isn't going to be easy," despaired Villon. "If they form some kind of cryptogram, then I'm finished. They had me working in decoding when I first joined the army, but they soon shifted me elsewhere. What do you make of it, Anna May?"

"I haven't given it that much thought. I've been too busy interpreting the Chinese characters. For a woman with a very orderly mind, Mai Mai wrote very disorderly charts."

"Perhaps disorderly to you, but they obviously made a great deal of sense to Mai Mai. All of us have a shorthand all our own. Mine is terribly complicated to everyone in my household when I write them notes. The cook did guess that 'en em liv' meant no more chopped liver appetizer for a while, for crying out loud, but she's a wiz at things like crossword puzzles." Marlene was at the cooler helping herself to more champagne. "We haven't told Anna May about Brunhilde Messer."

Anna May looked surprised. "Was she at the party?"

Marlene said, "Was she ever." She had Anna May's complete attention.

Having absorbed Marlene's information, Anna May said, "She's no fool, and on the other hand she's never been known to be a mental giant. Still, here she is and I think you're right, Marlene. I have a feeling that silly offer from Hitler is a smokescreen."

"And where there's smoke," said Marlene, "to use a boring but appropriate cliché, there's fire."

Anna May refilled Villon's glass and then attended to her own. "I've been having a lot of thoughts about Mai Mai and the charts. The deeper I get into translating them, the more I'm growing suspicious there's more to them than the innocence of having their astrological charts mapped. I think Mai Mai was offered some kind of involvement with these people, and Mai Mai offered to read their charts not for their edification, but as protection for herself."

Villon said, "Christ, I hate that word."

Marlene was bemused. "Which word. You've spoken five."

"I'm speaking it now. Conspiracy. I hate that goddamned word. I think I prefer 'plot.' " He said to Anna May. "You think Mai Mai was offered the opportunity to become a member of whatever this bunch is up to?"

"It stands to reason," said Anna May. "She was very much a part of their circle in Europe. She was highly respected. I'm sure her psychic gifts were seriously considered of paramount importance to them. Coupled with her brilliance at charting the future, Mai Mai would have been invaluable. But she refused them, obviously." She leaned forward. "Before refusing, she learned a great deal. She learned too much. And now she had to be eliminated. It must have taken them some time to realize she must have consigned what she knew to the charts, not just as protection for herself, but as information to be deciphered after her death. I'm positive Mai Mai knew she was to be murdered."

Marlene was aghast. "And she didn't go to the police? She didn't seek protection?"

"She didn't need the police. She had the tong. You'll forgive me, Herb, but the police are no match for the tong."

"They were nowhere to be seen this afternoon."

"In which lies their genius."

"Why didn't they protect her at my party?" Marlene was more indignant than confused. "If she knew she was in danger, why did Mai Mai consent to attend the party? It was a last-minute invitation. She could have given you any number of excuses why not to attend. Aren't I logical, Herb?"

"Very logical, Marlene. I wasn't going to, but I'm going to tell you what I omitted from the coroner's report." Marlene had a feeling she knew what was coming. "Mai Mai was terminally ill." Tears formed in Anna May's eyes. Marlene had guessed right. She handed Anna May her handkerchief. "She would have been dead within a few months."

Anna May needed a few moments to compose herself, after which she said, "I'll tell you something ironic. Mai Mai swore if she ever became fatally ill, she would kill herself. She couldn't see herself consigned to a hospital at the mercy of the medical profession. She didn't wish to end her days as a burden, as she put it to me, with her family and friends wishing she would die and be out of not only her misery but their misery." She dabbed at her eyes. "Mai Mai had poison pills. They were given to her by the tong's apothecary with the tong's approval. They were strychnine."

Marlene slammed her fist on an arm of the chair. "Irony or no irony, murder is a heinous crime. The other one, Morton Duncan, he wasn't terminal, was he Herb?"

"I haven't read his report yet. The coroner delayed it. He had tickets to a football game. But I doubt if Duncan had a serious illness."

"He looked and sounded awfully healthy when you questioned him. *Ach Gott*, I'm so weary, I can't think clearly. What to make of the underlined words, what?" She returned to the dining room table and stared at the charts. She transferred her attention to the few pages Anna May had translated, with their underlined words.

" 'Forever.'

'Worship.'

'States.'

'Squad.' "

Those were the words Anna May told her on the phone. Now there were others.

" 'World.'

'Future.'

'Clouds.'

'Monsters.' "

She repeated them aloud.

"Anna May, do you have a piece of paper?" Herb Villon had his fountain pen ready. On the slip of paper Anna May gave him, he jotted down the words, which Marlene repeated for him. She read them slowly and with what Villon considered was a great deal of unnecessary feeling.

Anna May asked Marlene, "Do you want a copy for yourself?"

"Not necessary, darling. I've committed them to memory." Marlene was known to be a fast study. She took great pride in the fact that she could commit a script to memory in just one day of concentrated study. This was a gift generally attributed to child actors, who usually memorized not only their own lines but everybody else's so they could provide them with the dialogue they couldn't remember. Child actress Mitzi Green had made an art of it, and there was a collective sigh of relief at Paramount when they dropped her option. "And when I get home," said Marlene, "I must commit to memory the dialogue for the scenes I'm doing tomorrow with Monsieur Souvir. What's worse, I have to be up at the crack of dawn. But oh well, at least I will have breakfast with Maria." A thought struck her. "Anna May. The tong."

"What about it?"

"Does it protect you?"

"I could ask them to. Do you think because of Brunhilde, our lives are in danger?"

"Herb? You're the authority. Do you think we're marked women?"

He thought for a moment. "It's a possibility. But still, if they tried to score a hit on either one of you, they know I'd put them all behind bars and throw the keys away."

Marlene asked, "Isn't that unconstitutional?"

"Probably," said Herb, "but who among us can recite the Constitution?"

"Herb Villon, within you there breathes a rogue and a knave. Are you off to make peace with Miss Dickson?"

"I've had enough of Miss Dickson for one day. Anna May, just for the hell of it, bolt your door after we leave."

"Herb, I'll do that, but trust me, it's not necessary. All the other apartments are occupied by relatives and friends. One yell out of me and they'll be up here like a swarm of killer bees."

Marlene reminded them she employed bodyguards. "I also have a handgun and I'm a deadly shot." Villon believed her. "Come Herb, and thank you, Anna May. The food was delicious. Herb, do you really think I might be in danger?" He reassured her he didn't think so. He didn't tell her he had two detectives tailing her and two tailing Anna May. In the elevator, Marlene stifled a yawn and asked him, "Herb, is detective work always this exhausting?"

"It is when you're drinking champagne."

"But Tallulah, please! That's not in the script!" Raymond Souvir was backing away from the formidable Bankhead, who, having enticed him to her rented house for some coaching, had changed into a flimsy negligee and was now setting about enticing him into bed.

"Of course it isn't, dahling, it's an improvisation. The sort of thing that Russian person Stanislavsky is so fond of. Have you never seen the Russian Art Theater?"

"You mean the Moscow Art Theater?" He was perspiring profusely. Tallulah was dabbing at his face with a dish towel, which she was grateful to find protruding from under the couch, where she had kicked it several nights earlier while trying to cause an effect with a studio electrician she'd invited up to inspect her wiring.

"The Moscow Art Theater. Of course. They're always improvising. In fact, they're known to rehearse a play for a year before exhibiting it before the public. Now come over here, Raymond. You may have done some films and some theater, but what little I've heard from you tonight tells me you're still wet behind the ears and I'm determined to dry them. Now then, in the film you're Marlene's protector, she having sold herself to you to get the money she needs for her husband, who has one of those deadly diseases you'll never find in a medical dictionary but is attributable to the highly underworked mind of a Hollywood scriptwriter. So she gives herself to you and rightly so, as you're absolutely divine. And I haven't seen anyone so beautiful since I tried to coach Lew Ayres. Oh, do sit down, Raymond. The way you're flitting about the room you're making me think of Lillian Gish trapped in that damned closet in *Broken Blossoms*, and believe you me the last thing I want to think about at a time like this is Lillian Gish. You poor boy, you're still perspiring buckets, you're a nervous wreck; I know just what you need to calm you down." There was a dish of white powder on a table with a spoon at the side. She scooped up the powder and advanced on Raymond with a devastating smile. "Sniff this, dahling. It'll calm you down. It's the best cocaine this side of the Mexican border. Come on, dahling, *Sniff!*"

Herb Villon sat in his underwear in his favorite easy chair, positioned so that he could look out the window at the lights of Hollywood, a twinkling carpet spread below his apartment at the top of a building in the Hollywood Hills. He had much to think about. The two murder victims, the seven suspects, incredible women like Marlene and Anna May, the astrologi-

cal charts with their underlined words, Lewis Tate's suicide—
which he knew had no connection to the murders, but the
tragedy gnawed at his gut. Brunhilde Messer. A kettle of fish
he could do without, but there was the possibility proposed
by Marlene that she could have been at the party New Year's
Eve. He thought more about Brunhilde and Marlene's party.
It wasn't a masquerade ball, so she couldn't have been there
in disguise. Getting out of the party might have posed a problem until Herb decided to relax the security, but how did she
get away with Marlene not recognizing her? He prodded his
brain mercilessly until a thought came to him that caused him
to snap his finger. He looked at his wristwatch. Not yet midnight. Marlene couldn't be asleep yet. She's probably at her
dressing table meticulously removing her makeup with cold
cream and then sponging her face with alcohol. He'd read
somewhere that was her nightly ritual. He gave her number to
the operator and hoped he wouldn't meet with a blockade
known as the butler.

Marlene answered on the third ring. "Oh, Herb! This is
extrasensory perception. I've been thinking of you and wishing I had your home number. Listen. I have a thought. How
Brunhilde wasn't easily recognizable at my party. Herb, she
could have been wearing some kind of a wig."

He smiled. How he loved her. "Marlene, that's why I called
you. I got the same idea."

"Darling," said Marlene, her voice seductive and exciting
as it caressed his ear, "what's that they say about two great
minds?"

◖◗ FIFTEEN ◖◗

THE COFFEE IN Herb Villon's cardboard container looked as though it had been drawn from a Louisiana bayou. Jim Mallory's container of coffee had long been drained of its contents and Jim finally got around to dumping it into the wastepaper basket. Both detectives had arrived early at the precinct and immediately closeted themselves in Herb's office. Brunhilde Messer as a fresh entrant in the suspects sweepstakes displeased Herb. Last night's phone conversation with Marlene lasted almost an hour. Brunhilde's wig stoked their adrenalin and it led to a discussion of a great many facets of the case, which Herb had shared with Mallory over the better part of an hour. Brunhilde, Herb and Marlene had agreed, was probably a red herring. As Marlene succinctly put it, Brunhilde could bore you to death, but she'd never use a weapon. Yet they were not too quick to dismiss her. She most certainly had to know about the plot to kill Mai Mai and, as she had put it to Marlene the previous morning, she didn't want to miss the fun. A very strange woman, Marlene explained to Herb, a very ambitious woman, a very jealous woman, she couldn't bear not to be in on things. And that's probably what her presence in Hollywood was all about, she didn't want to be left out of the action. Marlene concluded that Brunhilde had messages to deliver of such importance that they needed to be conveyed in person by someone who could be trusted. Power, that's what Brunhilde's films were to be about, power. Murder is power.

"Murderers are like rapists," Herb said to Marlene. "They're cowards." And he repeated this to Jim Mallory, who was entertaining a vision of Marlene Dietrich spoon-feeding him apple pie.

Herb had been writing on a yellow-paged legal pad, and he sat back in his swivel chair to survey his work. "Okay, let's start at the top again and see what we've got. Come on, Jim, get that dumb look off your face and concentrate. Seven suspects and the Messer broad we keep in reserve to one side. First we have Ivar Tensha. He'd never have stabbed Morton Duncan in the back. That's dirty work and Tensha hires people to do his dirty work for him. The Countess di Frasso. I don't see her meeting up with Duncan in that dump of his, especially in that part of town. Also, I don't see her plunging the knife."

"Not even in a fit of anger?" Mallory remembered his mother flinging a pot of boiling coffee at his father, and then her thankfulness that she had missed.

"No knives for di Frasso," said Herb. "Her tongue would be more lethal. So, to continue. Dong See. Yeah, he could kill. Musicians are very temperamental. They're worse than hairdressers. He was out of action for six months. Badly smashed up in the car accident. I wonder if he was driving. He doesn't drive now. Or I assume he doesn't. Souvir's been chauffeuring him around, and last night the Countess took over the job, driving him home from Novarro's party. At least I assume she drove him home. That brings us to Souvir. Could he murder?"

"The manual says everybody's capable of committing murder." Jim lived by the detective's manual.

"Souvir's a devil behind the steering wheel, but does he have enough of an evil streak to commit murder?"

"He could have stabbed Duncan."

"Now we come to my personal favorite, Monte Trevor. He's not only a producer, but I suspect he's a damned good actor. The way he goes about trying to convince actors they're right for his movie. When you've got the cash with which to pay them, actors don't need too much convincing to accept a job. He's been trying to get money out of Tensha for his movie. Why should he have to? They've known each other a long time, I'm sure of that. Why not just say, 'Hey, Ivar baby, I need half a million for a new movie.' So maybe Ivar doesn't like movies, ah, who the hell knows. And back to Souvir, where's he getting the money to live the way he does? Marlene says he couldn't have earned all that much in Europe, and I believe Marlene."

"You're right. She's so believable."

Mallory was lucky Herb liked him tremendously. Herb was beginning to have his doubts about putting up with much more of Mallory's schoolboy-like infatuation with Dietrich.

"Natalia and Gregory Ivanov. They could use a knife. That Natalia could penetrate an elephant's hide with a salad fork. That's one powerful lady. Gregory would do as he's told. He was born to take orders and carry them out." He scratched his chin while staring at the revolving ceiling fan. The fan was of little use; all it did was rearrange the warm air so it wouldn't grow tired of remaining in the same position. "So what have we got? We've got a gang of people who we know are up to no good, but what that no good is we'll never dig out of them, so we have to wait and see what Anna May comes up with. Got any other ideas?"

"I was thinking why haven't we tried to find out where the suspects were when Morton Duncan was murdered."

Herb laughed. "You really want to bother? You want to listen to and file some more double-talk? Take it from me, they've composed perfect alibis. I've played this scene before. I'll wait for someone to slip up. Jim, we're going to have to enter through the back door of these crimes to find the killer.

Somebody's going to slip up the way Brunhilde did last night."

"I thought you and Marlene thought she blabbed deliberately."

"As of my phone conversation with Marlene last night, she's rewritten that theory. Brunhilde was never one, in Marlene's experience, to think before she spoke. Marlene said something funny about her. Brunhilde Messer needs to hear cues." He arose and looked out the window. Palm trees. Nothing but effing palm trees. Rats nest in them. Who needs sterile palm trees? They don't flower. They don't bear fruit. It costs the city a small fortune to keep the fronds trimmed. He hated palm trees. "I wonder how the screen test's going? And why do I give a damn?"

There wasn't an unoccupied soundstage on the Paramount lot. The studio had to grind out fifty-two films a year to keep its chain of theaters supplied. Contract stars were expected to film a minimum of four films a year. One actress remembered shooting three films at the same time. She worked for one director from eight in the morning until lunchtime. She had time to grab a sandwich and coffee while having her hair restyled to work for another director all afternoon. After a hasty dinner of soup and a hamburger, she was driven to another soundstage to do pickup shots for a film she'd completed a month earlier. She feared there'd be no continuity with her performance in this one because she'd forgotten her interpretation of her character.

Most features took from two to five weeks to complete. An occasional epic such as one directed by Cecil B. DeMille usually took ten to fifteen weeks to complete. The westerns were shot on the back lot or on a rented ranch in the valley. These were filmed in five days. Marlene's films were the most expensive, and that was because Josef von Sternberg was painstakingly meticulous and demanded sets that were elaborate and expensive. For *Shanghai Express*, an entire village and miles of railroad track leading into it took months to construct. The sets were never to be used again.

Expenses could also mount with screen tests, especially if they were personally directed by any of the studio's "A" directors (so called because their films carried the heaviest budgets and topped the bill when double featured). "A" directors included DeMille, von Sternberg, and Ernst Lubitsch.

Raymond Souvir's test was definitely going to cost more than the studio planned to spend. Von Sternberg was the martinet to Raymond Souvir's martyr. Marlene stood by helplessly as von Sternberg shouted and raged and struck furniture with his riding crop to emphasize his unreasonable dissatisfaction. Earlier that morning Marlene could no longer contain her equanimity and exploded.

"This is not my screen test! It is Raymond's! I'm already under contract! Stop bullying us!"

Von Sternberg shouted back at her, and while the two roared and snarled at each other like kings of the jungle battling over the carcass of a fallen wapiti, Raymond Souvir's already frayed nerves further unraveled until a makeup woman, on constant call for facial repairs, feared the young actor would fall victim to a nervous breakdown. The front office had already received a communiqué from a spy that things were not going well with the Souvir test and the suspicion was hinted that von Sternberg was deliberately sabotaging Souvir's chances as a means of satisfying his current vendetta against Dietrich. He had been told that morning that after his next film with Marlene, *Blonde Venus,* she would do *Song of Songs* with Rouben Mamoulian directing. ("Marlene is mine," he screamed at studio head B. P. Schulberg, "I am the only one who directs her! I discovered her! I created her! Without me she is nothing!")

The makeup woman busied herself wiping Souvir's perspiration away and hoping he'd stay dry enough for her to apply a fresh layer of makeup. There were an unusual number of visitors on the set, which aroused the interest of the technical staff. Perhaps Souvir was more important than they thought.

After all, von Sternberg is directing and Dietrich, a big star, is playing opposite Souvir. Marlene was also surprised. She was even more surprised that von Sternberg hadn't ordered all visitors off the set. He was probably too busy being troublesome to notice.

What in God's name are the Ivanovs doing here? And who are those three people with them, two men and a woman who looked as though they had just returned from fighting a campaign in Afghanistan. Marlene had to satisfy her curiosity. "What brings you to the studio?" The very fact that a great star chose to mingle with them made the Ivanovs bristle with self-importance for the benefit of their friends.

Gregory explained, "We are entertaining these very important visitors from our country. Please to meet them as I'm sure they'll be very thrilled."

"I'd be delighted," said Marlene while smiling at Monte Trevor, who was there killing time before his meeting with DeMille.

Gregory pointed to the woman. "This is Masha Smetana, chairman of the Tractor Committee of the province of Georgia. And here I am pleased to introduce Bronislaw Gerbernya, who manages the largest collective farm in the Ukraine. This trip is his reward for having produced over half a million dozen eggs, three quarters of a million bales of hay, a million bushels of corn, and cultivated thousands of acres of alfalfa and garlic. And last but surely not the least, Vladimir Gehoggurt of our secret police and the conductor of numerous successful purges."

"So," said Marlene to Gehoggurt, "you are the conductor of numerous successful purges. How do you sleep?"

Natalia explained, "He has no English."

"He also has no humanity," said Marlene.

Gregory said quickly, "Your studio was very kind to give us permission to visit today. We are so surprised to find so many acquaintances are also here."

Marlene wasn't surprised at all. Countess di Frasso had arrived a few minutes earlier on the arm of the studio's newest hopeful, Cary Grant. He was surprised Souvir was testing for the part of Marlene's protector in *Blonde Venus*. He'd been told the previous week the part was his. He'd have to have a word with B.P. about it. Dietrich wasn't in the least bit surprised to see Brunhilde Messer with Ivar Tensha. Marlene had an assistant director apprise Tensha that smoking was not permitted on this soundstage. His foul cigar offended her.

"Marlene, *liebchen*. Raymond asked me to give him moral support so here I am with Ivar, who was curious to see how the studio operates," simpered Brunhilde.

"It is not unlike a munitions factory. The films that are produced here are the ammunition needed for huge profits. Of course, because of the Depression the studio is hurting badly, the whole world is hurting badly, but the people need films to take their minds off the bad situation. Some films explode into fantastic successes. Appropriately enough, they are known as blockbusters."

"I find the analogy most interesting," said Tensha, having ground the life out of his cigar under the heel of a shoe. "When I think of filmmaking in those terms, I'm almost interested in thinking of investing in the cinema."

"Ah!" cried Marlene. "The person I've been waiting for! Dong See, where have you been? Poor Raymond is being put through hell by that beast with the riding crop. I want you to meet him."

"I don't think there's much I can do to help."

She took his hand and led him to von Sternberg, who—remembering they had met at Marlene's party—was suddenly a picture of charm and good manners.

"Here he is, one of the world's leading musicians. He belongs in *Blonde Venus*. Joe, you must test him. Look at his wonderful features. That bone structure. Where's that violin I asked for? Ah! Thank you, darling." The assistant director brought the violin to Marlene. Dong See's face was a mask. Marlene fingered the strings and brought forth a melody. "You don't know I'm a trained violinist," said Marlene off-

handedly, "Mother made me study very hard. I've even mas-
tered the musical saw. I don't play anymore. This looks like
a very fine instrument. It's not an Amati, but I know the
magic of your fingers will make it sound like one."

"No."

"No? Then perhaps you will enrapture us with what might
sound like a Stradivarius."

Dong See backed away a few feet.

"Why, Dong See. You look absolutely terrified! The instrument won't bite you! The violin is your friend; it is your
life's blood. Here . . ."—she held it out to him—"take it,
make love to it." She signaled the cameraman and the sound
engineer. "Boys! This is a take!" Von Sternberg stood with
the cameraman, eyes blazing. Again she was usurping his
position. Again she was sticking a finger in his eye. How she
will suffer for this. What's wrong with this Chinese fiddler?
Why does he shy away from the violin? I recognize that expression on Marlene's face. I've seen it often enough. It's that
look she gets when she's proven something to herself. What
is she up to now?

"Does this violin displease you? Now, don't disappoint me,
darling. I promised myself I'd get some film of you and you
mustn't let me down."

Raymond Souvir watched the scene taking place in front of
the motionless camera amidst an embarrassing silence. Dong
See was on the spot, and Souvir knew him well, knew and
feared his temper.

"I cannot play," said Dong See.

"You mean you won't play here, for the camera." Marlene
smiled. "You're not prepared. I should have realized that."

"I can't play because my fingers were shattered in the accident. They will never be the same again."

"How terrible." Marlene placed the violin on a table.
"That's why your tour was canceled."

"That's right. I'm finished as a musician." He walked away
from her.

Von Sternberg shouted, "Can we now get on with the business of making a screen test?" The set buzzed and hummed again.

Marlene brightened on seeing Herb Villon and Jim Mallory standing near the soundstage door. She hurried to them. "Did you see the scene I just played with Dong See?"

"I wish I had it on film," said Villon.

"So do I. Very heartbreaking. I'd burst into tears but I mustn't ruin my makeup."

"Why, Marlene Dietrich, you're a heartless beast."

"Not where this person who says he can't play the violin any longer is concerned. At my party, Dorothy di Frasso said something about this Dong See that I can't get out of my mind. She said something about not having seen him for quite some time, but that he'd changed some since then. Last night because I could not sleep, our talk, you darling man, was so exciting and stimulating"—Herb restrained from preening while Jim Mallory's eyes were green with jealousy—"I got to thinking about everyone involved in the case. My mind was a motion-picture projector and the film unreeled them, and when I thought it necessary I stopped this film and studied my subjects carefully; I dissected them. Dong See worried me the most. I kept coming back to him over and over again. There's so much goddamned noise, let's go over there behind the backdrops." They followed the leader.

"Won't they be looking for you?" asked Herb.

"They'll find me. Von Sternberg's on my back. He's poking around wasting time and money and I'm afraid poor Raymond isn't coming across at all. A robot has more animation."

"Let's get back to Dong See," Villon prompted.

"I studied his face hard. A thought kept coming to me. He was in an automobile crash so terrible that it caused him to be confined to a clinic for six months. Now think, what had the crash done to him?"

"Shattered his fingers for starters," said Jim Mallory.

"While he told us this, I had a good look at his hands. There are no scars."

"There was probably plastic surgery," said Villon.

"Those fingers had no plastic surgery. His face has had no plastic surgery. The process is not all that infallible. It leaves scars. Have you noticed Carole Lombard's left cheek? She too was in a terrible automobile accident and had extensive surgery for months before being given any hope she would be able to work in front of a camera again. She still has a scar on her left cheek. It's barely noticeable because our makeup men here are magicians."

"She's gorgeous," said Jim Mallory, then feeling like a traitor.

"Of course, darling, that's because her makeup is borrowed from mine. I shave my eyebrows and use a pencil; so does Carole. My makeup emphasizes hollows in my cheeks; so does Carole's. But so what, our personalities are totally dissimilar. Listen to me, boys. It is not easy to reconstruct shattered bodies and shattered faces. There are hospitals in Europe where tragedies are quartered. Men whose faces were so badly destroyed and deformed that they are kept hidden away from the public eye."

"Dong See was one of the lucky ones." Jim Mallory looked innocent enough to betray, thought Marlene, and hoped the future would be kind to him.

"This Dong See has had no plastic surgery, Herb. Trust me. Believe me."

"But six months in a Swiss clinic. What was that all about?"

"What's it all about? It's a trumped-up story, that's what it's all about. There was no six months in a clinic. This person is perfectly healthy. Don't you get it? Why do you think I planned this scene? And if I must say so myself, I pulled it off brilliantly. Boys, I had to see and hear him play the violin. I had to trump up getting him here and putting him on the spot. This man can't play the violin. He is not Dong See."

"Are you thinking of confronting him with that suspicion?"

"Of course not. He'll just continue playing his act as beautifully as he did just now, when he weaseled out of a tight spot. You mark my words, gentlemen. The real Dong See is probably dead. There probably was an accident and it killed him. Why wasn't it in the newspapers? Dong See was world famous. News of his terrible accident should have spread around the world. This man is not Dong See. He's an imposter. He's an agent. He's an instrument. Impersonating Dong See opens doors for him that would be shut to any ordinary Oriental. And these people are seeking to have doors opened.

"Herb, are you allowing Monte Trevor to leave the city?"

"Like hell I am."

"Ramon Novarro told me Trevor is planning a trip to Mexico. He tried to convince Ramon to consider returning there and helping resuscitate Mexico's film industry. I phoned Dolores del Rio and Lupe Velez and they confirmed that Monte Trevor made the same pitch to them. Herb, Monte Trevor acts the pushy pest, but it's an act. He's a very clever man, I'm positive. He must be. Why else does he have Tensha's ear? Check him out and you'll see he's not had a money-making film in years. He stays in an expensive suite. Who's paying for it? Raymond Souvir lives and spends like an emperor. Who's paying for it? How did the Ivanovs move to such important embassies as Berlin and Los Angeles if they are the bourgeois dolts they appear to be? And Dorothy di Frasso. She flaunts wealth as though she really has it. That mansion she lives in. That expensive car she drives."

"I thought she got a big settlement from her ex-husband."

"Yes, it was a handsome settlement that soon began to lose its looks, the way she spends. Gary Cooper told me she tried to borrow money from him and at a time when Gary wasn't making the kind of dollars he earns today. Who supports this Dong See effigy? Herb, these people are *subsidized*."

"Tensha?" Herb knew as he spoke the name it was a waste of breath.

"No, darling, I doubt that very strongly. Oh I suspect Ten-

192

sha is heavily involved financially in whatever is going on. Herb, if you haven't been thinking about it, then I urge you to contact Interpol about these people."

Jim Mallory smiled as Villon told her, "What was that about two great minds?"

Marlene laughed, threw her arms around Villon, and kissed his cheek. After which she decided to give Jim Mallory equal time, not realizing he'd be days recovering from the shock. "Let's see what's going on out there. God, we'll never finish this bloody test."

Von Sternberg was supervising a fresh camera setup at the top of his lungs. Hazel Dickson, chatting with Monte Trevor, saw Marlene, Herb, and Mallory out of the corner of an eye and abruptly left Trevor. "Well, well, well, the unholy three," said Hazel.

Marlene oozed charm and concern. "I'm so glad to see you got home safely last night, Hazel."

"I didn't know I was in any danger. I suppose you've seen the papers."

"I haven't had the time, darling. Von Sternberg has kept us hopping, the sadistic bastard."

"Lewis Tate's made headlines. I mean, forgotten by the press and the public and the powers that be all these years, and so he goes and hangs himself and all of a sudden he's big news. The poor slob, if he were alive somebody would probably offer him a contract."

God bless you, Adela Rogers St. John, thought Marlene; God bless you. Lewis Tate may be dead, but today he lives, more alive than he has ever been.

Hazel was speaking directly to Marlene. "I hear I missed a hearts and flowers episode between you and Dong See. What was it all about?"

"Let Herb tell you."

"Herb can't tell me anything." Villon winced as each word struck him like a pellet shot from a BB gun. "I got a hot item out of Monte Trevor. He's been asked to come to Mexico to help pump some new life into their dying film industry. God, they make lousy pictures. Oh oh, di Frasso's got her tentacles around Cary Grant. He'd better be careful."

"I'm told he can take care of himself," Marlene reassured Hazel. "I don't see Raymond. I should go over some lines with him. Poor baby, I'm sure he's learning to his sorrow that working in Hollywood is a far cry from working in Europe. I'll see what I can do to pump some energy into this test. Ah! There's Dong See with Brunhilde and Tensha. I must apologize to him."

Von Sternberg was shouting. "I am ready! Marlene Dietrich!" She kept walking toward Dong See without missing a beat. "Where is Mr. Souvir? Are we making a test here or is this some kind of tea party?"

Herb Villon thought, If it's a tea party, it's more the Mad Hatter's than one given by his Aunt Hattie. He watched Marlene as she spoke to Dong See. Smooth as silk. What a woman.

"I do understand," said Dong See with charm. "I know you didn't mean to embarrass me."

"Still, no longer being able to play. What a loss. What a tragedy. I'll never forget your "Flight of the Bumble Bee." That bee was so real, I remember looking around for a flyswatter."

Von Sternberg shouted her name again. Marlene shut her eyes, clenched her fists, and took a deep breath. Brunhilde whispered something to Tensha about expecting fireworks, while Marlene opened her eyes and past Brunhilde and Tensha she saw Raymond Souvir holding a paper cup, clutching his stomach and staggering forward. Marlene shouted for Villon, and he and Mallory hurried to her on a trot. She rushed to Souvir's side and Villon and Mallory were too late to catch him. He fell face down, crushing the paper cup beneath him. Villon and Mallory turned him on his back and Marlene knelt and shouted Souvir's name over and over again. He didn't respond. His eyes were half-open and from what she could see of them, Dietrich told Villon they reflected no life.

"He's dead. Look, those beads of perspiration. Poor soul. Poor Raymond. He's perspired his last."

◖◉ SIXTEEN ◉◗

"WHAT FOUL FIEND destroyed this beautiful youth! Who did this to Raymond! Oh my poor child, cut down in the prime of life!" Tallulah Bankhead beseeched God to strike the unknown killer with lightning and thunderbolts. Word of the murder had spread through the studio like brushfire, and Tallulah's anguished cry in the fitting room caused the walls to tremble. Her secretary drove her to the soundstage where the test was supposed to be shot and Tallulah swept into it like Medea satisfied at her success in polishing off her two brats. With fingers intertwined and a loosely tied dressing gown showing two incredibly well shaped legs, she stood staring down at the corpse, which had been covered with a blanket.

Marlene wisely stood aside with Herb Villon and Jim Mallory and let Tallulah take the spotlight. Outwardly Marlene looked unaffected by Souvir's murder; inwardly there gnawed at her stomach the fear that Souvir's murder would trigger others. She had shared this intuition with the detectives while Villon retrieved the crushed paper cup and entrusted it to Mallory for safekeeping until it could be gotten to the lab for tests.

"Oh, how I coached him last night and oh, how he adored my coaching, once he relaxed, dahlings. I saw his potential and I promise you it was large, very very large. Didn't you see it too, Marlene?"

"No darling, it hadn't shown itself." The coroner arrived with his assistants, followed by several plainclothes men. The coroner flung the blanket back. Very businesslike, he pulled an eyelid back. Then he pried open the mouth and studied the tongue. Next he went south to the fingernails. In between he made little grunting noises, difficult to discern whether they were of dismay or pleasure. Marlene recognized him as the same man who had attended Mai Mai's body. She commented to Villon, "He's terribly efficient." The coroner heard her and smiled gratefully. He instructed his assistants to wrap the corpse and take it to the morgue and file it in a refrigerator box.

"Poison," he told Villon and Mallory. Mallory handed him the crushed paper cup and the coroner sniffed it. "Something of the nightshade family, but that's just a guess. Let me take this; I'll turn it over to the lab boys. Well, Miss Dietrich, ha ha, it seems you have a fatal attraction to homicides." He indicated the visitors to the soundstage, who stood about in groups, nervous, worried, anxious, and shocked, "You holding them for questioning?" he asked Villon.

"That would be as useful as applying iodine to a knife wound. I'll have the boys take their names and addresses and then we'll get in touch with them individually."

Marlene was smoking a cigarette. "Of course, there are the old familiar faces who need no further introduction. Look at them. Tensha keeps glancing at his pocket watch; he's anxious to be out of here. Di Frasso is touching up her lips. Dong See looks a bit sad the way he watches the body being wrapped for shipment, perhaps he does mourn his old pal. Monte Trevor and Brunhilde look as though they're waiting for an orchestra to begin the next dance, and from the look of the Ivanovs and their guests I suspect they might be holding a conference on the decadence of Western civilization. Hazel is scribbling away on her pad while Tallulah has von Sternberg cornered, undoubtedly demanding he be her next director. Poor Raymond, he is written off, but perhaps his memory will linger on. After all, he had a great deal of coaching. I look at all of them and it reminds me of a quotation from A *Midsummer Night's Dream*. 'The lunatic, the lover, and the poet are of imagination all compact.' There are many lovers here and I presume one among us is a poet, but the lunatic is yet to be trapped. I must phone Anna May and tell her before she hears it on the radio. Ah! Von Sternberg has escaped. Tallulah is heading our way. I think it's you she's after, Herb.''

"Mr. detective person," she bellowed, "I must have a word with you. You can stay, Marlene, this will interest you too." She paused for effect. "Give me a drag of your cigarette, Marlene." She inhaled and forced the smoke into her lungs and then slowly exhaled. At last she spoke, darkly dramatic. "Raymond Souvir had a presentiment last night. He knew he was going to die soon." She paused to give that line time to sink in. "Between coaching, he did a lot of talking. Occasionally I'm a very good listener, thank God last night was one of those rare occasions." She asked Villon, "Forgive me, dahling, but what's your name again?"

"Villon, and this is my assistant, Jim Mallory."

Her eyes widened as though she was just now seeing Jim Mallory. "Isn't he divine looking. Dear young man, do you want to be an actor? I'd be delighted to coach you."

Jim was tempted to tell her he'd prefer being coached by Marlene, but instead said, "I'm very flattered, Miss Bankhead."

"Tallulah," said Marlene, exerting great patience, "Raymond Souvir."

"Of course. His presentiment. He told me it's in his astrological chart. Mai Mai said there was a break in his lifelines."

"You find lifelines in the palm of the hand, Tallulah." Marlene was lighting another cigarette.

"Well, whatever its equivalent is in the zodiac, she predicted where his life was concerned, he was doomed to be shortchanged. Raymond was involved in something that he intimated would mean his death if he tried to defect. Am I making any kind of sense at all? We both did a lot of heavy drinking last night, not to speak of the heavy breathing, dahlings, so you'll understand I'm telling you as much as I can remember of what he told me."

Marlene stepped in. "See if I've got it right."

"Go ahead, dahling, I'd appreciate some help."

"Mai Mai told him he'd die young. He's involved in . . . for want of a better word . . . some sort of conspiracy. Something big, something very very big."

"Enormous. It covers the world, like the Red Cross."

Marlene continued, "He wanted to get out of it. Am I right in saying this was no sudden decision? He'd been entertaining it for some time now?"

"Exactly!" Tallulah took Marlene's cigarette, which had one last drag left in it, and Bankhead made the most of it. "He was worried what would happen to him if his screen test failed."

Marlene was quizzical as Bankhead crushed the cigarette butt under her shoe. "Are you saying he intimated his life depended on the success of his test?"

"His usefulness." She folded her arms. "Now, what do you make of *that?*

"A great deal," said Marlene.

"Oh really, dahling? You're light-years ahead of me. I thought he was being just another insecure juvenile positive he'd never be offered another job." She smiled at Mallory. "Aren't you glad you didn't let me convince you to be an actor? Anyway dahlings, there was a bit of a show of bravado, not terribly convincing but I think he enjoyed the sound of it. It was something like this. He's not afraid. There's a lot he could tell. And something about Mai Mai had to be silenced even though they knew she was dying. Was she? Oh the poor dahling. Robbed of the chance to put her house in order."

"She left her house in order, Tallulah," reassured Dietrich.

"Oh I'm so glad, dahling. I can foretell mine will be a mess. Have I helped?"

"You've been a great help, Miss Bankhead." Villon thanked her. Tallulah bummed another cigarette from Marlene and then hurried back to the fitting room. She saw Villon's men getting names and addresses, and Bankhead spoke to one who she was sure would want her phone number and gave it to him.

Marlene was saying to Villon, "I'm not much of a writer myself, Herb, but I think together, we could contrive a scenario that would help us in getting the murderer to give himself away. What do you think?"

"I think I'd like to know what progress Anna May has made. But first, I'd like a word with Monte Trevor."

"I'll be in my dressing room. It's that blue caravan at the end of this street. You can't miss it; it's baby blue, like Jim Mallory's eyes."

Mallory didn't realize he was fluttering his eyelashes until Villon brought it to his attention.

When Villon called his name, Monte Trevor excused himself from a group that included Hazel and di Frasso and Ivar Tensha. Di Frasso said, "I think Mr. Villon has heard Monte was thinking of making a bolt to Mexico. Any bets?" She had no takers.

Trevor was huffing with indignation. "But you can't keep me here indefinitely! I have urgent business in Mexico City. It means my livelihood."

"Mr. Trevor, let me remind you that you are a suspect in a murder case. If necessary, and don't force my hand, I can take you into custody."

"Don't threaten me. I have powerful connections."

"So do I. They're called handcuffs. You're forcing me to put a tail on you, Trevor, and that costs money. I'm a penurious son of a bitch and I don't like to spend money unnecessarily."

"You make me very unhappy, Mr. Villon."

"Don't force me to make you unhappier."

He walked away from the producer, with Jim keeping pace. They went in search of Marlene.

Ten minutes later, Dietrich had changed into a smart linen suit and was telling them Anna May needed to see them right away. "She's made tremendous progress but didn't want to tell me on the phone. I promised her we'd be at her place within an hour. But first, Herb, what stupidity prompted the killer to murder Souvir here on the lot, on a soundstage, for crying out loud, in the middle of a screen test?"

"It wasn't stupidity, it was necessity. Look, Souvir's been perspiring buckets ever since I met him. Because of the screen test? Hell no. Because he was afraid for his life. He could have breezed through the test if he hadn't become such a nervous wreck. Where does all that perspiration fit in with the speed demon? On the surface he's tough as nails, even instilling fear in Dong See, whether this guy is or isn't in his passenger seat. What I think, Marlene, is that it was important to this gang to have powerful people in Hollywood allied with them. If they couldn't convert them to their side, then they'd create their own. Don't be so dense, Marlene. Brunhilde positively came here with an offer for you, but it was disguised as one being made by Hitler."

"Supposing I'd fallen for it?"

"You'd be a very powerful lady, but not for very long."

Marlene crossed her legs. "So failing me and Greta and whoever else they were out to conscript, they groomed Raymond in Europe with those three French films and his German screen test. *Gott im Himmel,* who knows how many others like Souvir they may have planted in our midst."

"Who knows?" Villon's hands were outstretched, palms up.

"Herb, do you suppose my confrontation with Dong See had something to do with hastening Raymond's departure?"

Jim Mallory suddenly said, "It might hasten Dong See's departure."

"It's a consideration," agreed Villon.

"I don't know about that," said Marlene. "I think Raymond knew his time was running out." She laughed. "Maybe he was spending too much money. Oh dear, that's a bad joke. The poor thing." She had a new thought. "Nobody cried."

"When?" asked Villon.

"When they saw Raymond was lying there, dead. Nobody cried. There was no sorrow from anyone. Dong See, or whoever he is, did look a bit sad, but the others, there was no sound of sorrow from any of them. I can't wait to hear what Interpol turns up on these people. We better get started to Anna May's. I worry she's alone in the apartment with the charts."

"She's well protected," Villon assured Marlene.

"There were a lot of people on the soundstage, but Raymond was poisoned. Nightshade. Could he have committed suicide? Why not? If what Tallulah told us was indicative of his frame of mind, then from what he was accomplishing in front of the camera, which was pretty disappointing, he may have decided to select his own time of departure and be done with the awful, the awful waiting of knowing you're marked for extermination."

"Marlene, he was murdered. Someone gave him a paper cup of water and there's no point in asking our suspects, because they're hardly about to incriminate themselves. Like I told Jim before, they've got themselves covered. I mean Marlene, if you found a one hundred dollar bill on the floor of a restaurant, you wouldn't ask if somebody lost a one hundred dollar bill."

"I wouldn't ask because I never find anything of value," responded Marlene.

"A common ordinary paper cup," said Mallory.

"Darling, you'd be hard put to find cut crystal around here. You should see how many forms my secretary has to fill out to get a roll of toilet paper. Come on boys, let's get to Anna May's."

*   *   *

"You poor man," Hazel Dickson was saying to Dong See as she gave him a lift to Chinatown, "I heard about that stunt Dietrich pulled on you."

"She didn't know I could no longer finger the strings."

"Still, it must have been terribly embarrassing. How awful to be robbed of your gift. Um, what plans do you have for the future?" Come on baby, give me an item. Any item. Baby needs a new pair of shoes.

"I'm trying my hand at composing a violin concerto."

"That clinic in Switzerland must have put a pretty big hole in your pocket."

"I'm not hurting," he said in a monotone that should have told her she should try minding her own business. But he didn't know that minding other people's businesses was her own business.

"I've heard of that great sanatorium outside Lucerne. Were you there, by any chance?"

"Miss Dickson, could we talk about something else?"

Hazel was never fazed. "Sure. Let's talk about the murders. Who do you suppose did them? What guts it took to kill Raymond Souvir while he was shooting a screen test. You were the best of friends, weren't you?" Dong See said nothing. "You must be terribly broken up, but you're not showing it because you're inscrutable, you know, what they say about you Chinese."

She didn't notice that his hands looked as though he was about to strangle her. He saw Chinatown ahead and his hands relaxed.

"Where do you want to be dropped."

"At the corner would be fine. This is very kind of you."

"I wonder who's next?"

"What?"

"I didn't mean to startle you. Who's next. First Mai Mai Chu, then Morton Duncan, and today poor Raymond Souvir, don't you think there'll be more murders?"

"I don't know. I haven't given it much thought."

202

"Has Souvir's family been notified?"

"I don't know."

"Well, they should be. He may have left some money. He lived as though he had plenty. I'm sure Herb Villon is looking into it. Hey! Good-bye!" Dong See slammed the door shut and disappeared into the crowded street. "What a rude little bastard!"

In the privacy of her home, Anna May Wong wore traditional Chinese dress for comfort. She was pointing to underlined words. "Why none of us noticed it last night, I'll never know. But it came to me this morning. See?" She indicated the words in several charts. "These are underlined in *red*. And they are most significantly underlined in Mai Mai's chart. So I worked on it all morning and I've typed out the most significant sentences."

"But I didn't find Mai Mai's chart," said Marlene.

"We weren't looking for it. I phoned the secretary of the tong and he found it and brought it to me. It occurred to me it might hold greater significance then any of these others, and it does. It's frightening. What I'm about to read to you duplicates in the other charts with the words underlined in red."

"She was taking no chances," said Marlene. "If somehow her chart were to be destroyed by unfriendly hands, there remained her clever duplication."

"Exactly," said Anna May. "Mai Mai's chart is dated six months ago, when she returned from abroad. I'll generalize some things, such as her awareness she would soon be dead. Here she has written: 'At last the doctors and the stars are in agreement. My time is running out. I am ready. I have the pills, though there is every likelihood the Devil's Syndicate, as I choose to call them, will do their utmost to cut my sentence even shorter. I have refused to join them and I know too much. Indeed these are devils. They worship the evil god Molech.' "

To Mallory's perplexed look Marlene explained, "This god demanded the sacrifice of children. He is also known as Mo-

203

loch. He accepted the sacrifices of other people too. He was very democratic about it."

"Notice," said Anna May, "the word 'worship' is underlined elsewhere in red. Let me continue: 'I was clever, probably too clever in retrospect, but I led them to believe I was an excellent prospect. They wanted my mind, they wanted my gift of prescience, my astrological genius. They also want the world. They want to enslave the world. They plan to begin by spreading their poison in the United States. The stock market crash was the beginning. To cripple the country financially is to become a malignancy that will spread across the world. Their disciples are puppets. I know Raymond Souvir, Dorothy di Frasso, Monte Trevor, Adolph Hitler, Ivar Tensha, the Ivanovs, and this Dong See, who is not the musician but a cousin whose resemblance to the original is remarkable. What they have been trained to be are recruiters. Monte Trevor is to recruit the great powers of the world's film industries; Ivar Tensha has a network of his own that controls powerful industries in all corners of the world; Raymond Souvir is a celebrated prostitute and has been to bed with many members of world governments, who will one day rue their brief relationship with him; Dorothy di Frasso is an ambitious climber, and ambitious climbers can wheedle their way into the trusts of the mighty.' " Anna May paused. The look on their faces varied from disbelief to shock to total cynicism. Villon couldn't swallow it, Jim Mallory was horrified, and Marlene was convinced this conspiracy was marked for failure. "You will see 'world' and 'states' are underlined in the other charts in red. Actually, every word I'm reading to you shows up in the other seven charts. How dense we were not to realize it would all be wrapped up in Mai Mai's chart, which, Marlene, was also in her bedroom but in a drawer tucked away under her lingerie. Fortunately, she shared the secret with Tu Low Hung, the tong's secretary."

Anna May continued reading. " 'The Ivanovs represent the Bolsheviks, but I do not think they are fully trusted. Stalin loathes Mussolini, whose interests are represented by his

204

good friend the Countess. These people are but a fraction of their recruits. There are conspirators at work in the Latin Americas and throughout Asia, in Great Britain and Ireland. I have contacted Washington, D.C., and warned them the future president's life is at stake, but their secret service has found no corroboration and they are inadequate fools. An assassination attempt will be made and it will fail. Roosevelt will live to witness the next world war. This will be Adolph Hitler's contribution.' "

Anna May put the paper aside. "The point is, much as I loved and respected Mai Mai, how much of this can we believe? Was her illness affecting her mind? The American secret service are far from fools. What's it really all about?"

"It's all about power," said Marlene, "and as cynical as I am about the chances for this so called conspiracy to succeed, we have seen for ourselves the machinations of these puppets, we have seen Mai Mai and Raymond Souvir murdered because they became threats with the danger of exposure. The point is, my friends, if we show this document to the proper authorities, will they believe us or take us for a group of fools? I think what's most important, Herb, is to trap the murderer. I'm sure we both suspect the same person. And Anna May, again we must turn to you. Darling, I'm offering you what might be the greatest role of your life."

Anna May had lit a cigarette and there was a trace of a smile on her face. "Mai Mai names the most likely candidate to be her murderer. But of course, from her it is pure conjecture. And whoever you and Herb suspect, Marlene, as they say in all the most mediocre cop movies, 'You ain't got the goods on him.' You need the proof to get him and convict him. And the only way is to get a confession out of him."

Marlene said, "You can do it. I could see it in his face he's attracted to you. Are you game?"

"Sure I am. I want to be a recruit. I want to be powerful. I want to be up there with the big boys taking control of the world's finances. I want to make sacrifices to Molech. Who's got Dong See's phone number?"

ᗩ SEVENTEEN ᗡ

VILLON READ MAI MAI'S words for himself. When he was finished, he flipped through some other pages and said to Anna May, "This isn't really her chart, is it? It reads more like a diary."

"I refer to it as her chart for want of a better word. I suppose diary is more to the point. She has pages of comments about everyone, including me. Astrologers don't really chart themselves, but in Mai Mai's case, there was her gift of clairvoyance. This made her special, and she made notes on everything she predicted. You see there's a date on every page, or next to a prediction. This way she could check back on her degrees of accuracy. She was thinking of writing a book about herself and her gift. Several publishers were interested."

Marlene said, "Why don't you finish the book? Well, why not? Don't look so skeptical. I'm sure her heirs would be all for it and it'll give you something to do until an offer finally rears its lovely head."

"It's a thought, isn't it. Meantime, I have a much more important job to do. As you said, Marlene, it might be the greatest acting job of my life."

Villon said, "You're sticking your neck out, Anna May. This could turn nasty and be life threatening."

"You'll rescue me. Believe me, I'm neither worried nor frightened. Well, my friends, we have a lot of preparations to see to, so let's get to work."

Jim Mallory was on the phone talking to the precinct, watching Marlene, Anna May, and Villon hatching the plot with which they planned to snare the killer. When he was finished with the phone, he interrupted them to tell Villon that dispatches from Interpol were awaiting him. Villon was anxious to get back to the precinct.

"I'd like to come with you, if I may," asked Marlene. "I'd like to see what goes on at police headquarters. I have plenty of time. After all, I thought I'd be spending all day with Raymond's test. I wonder who will claim his body."

"The Interpol dispatch on him is bound to name his family and their whereabouts. Otherwise, we'll contact the French Embassy."

"I hope there will be someone to mourn him," said Marlene.

"This is no time to be morbid, Marlene," cautioned Anna May. "This is time for action and I'm all keyed up. Dong See will be here tomorrow at seven. If you three really worry for my safety, then make sure we're fully prepared and pray there'll be no slipup." Marlene had a sly smile on her face. "What's going on behind that smile, Marlene?"

"I was wondering if I shouldn't be playing the scene with Dong See tomorrow. I'm an old hand at dangerous situations."

Villon said, "I'll take the folders with me for safekeeping." Anna May gathered them and gave them to Mallory.

Anna May said to Marlene, "Don't try to rob me of my first good scene in ages."

"And what if nothing comes of it?"

"Something will come of it. I won't let us down."

"Anna May, you'll be brilliant." They embraced.

When she was alone, Anna May phoned her cousin who

occupied the apartment directly below hers. "Lotus Blossom, can you come up for a few minutes? I have something terribly important to discuss with you. Yes dear, I have lots of gin."

Arriving at police headquarters, Marlene parked her car next to Mallory's unmarked squad car. There was a twinkle in her eye as she said, "Herb, I'd like Jim to escort me inside." She took Mallory's arm. He was trembling. "Relax," said Marlene, "I'm not all that special. I'm just a world-famous movie star that millions of men and a certain breed of women dream about. And I'm only flesh and blood."

But *what* flesh and blood, thought Mallory.

Marlene continued, "Stop behaving like a schoolboy and straighten up, shoulders back, head held high. That's it. That's right." Villon thought she could have been one hell of a drill sergeant. "Now forward march. I know this is a big moment for you and you'll never forget it for the rest of your life." She laughed. "And neither will I! Boy, do I have an ego! And if I didn't, I'd still be Louis and Wilhelmina Dietrich's chubby little daughter and probably married to a sausage maker. Okay my friends, let's make an entrance."

It was one of the rare moments in the precinct's history when time seemed to have ground to a halt. Her cheery and sexy "Hello boys!" caused Villon to believe that such a thing as mass hypnosis was entirely possible. The desk sergeant seemed frozen to his chair. Several patrolmen and plain-clothes officers looked with either disbelief or incredulity.

Villon broke the spell with, "Relax, men, it's Marlene herself. She invited herself down to see how we operate, so start operating." She signed autographs, she pinched the desk sergeant's cheek, she chatted amiably and asked intelligent questions about their jobs. Had she been running for office she would have garnered a lot of votes. Finally settled in Villon's office, she lit a cigarette as he sifted through the pages transmitted by Interpol. Occasionally he handed a page to Mallory, whose poker face, Marlene decided, would have made him a great card player.

208

After several minutes of silence, Marlene said impatiently, "Come on, boys, share it with me."

Villon said without taking his eyes from the paper he was reading, "There's nothing all that startling. Mai Mai left most of the same stuff in her log. This is interesting about Raymond Souvir." Marlene leaned forward. "He's not French, he's an Arab. Born in Cairo. And he does come from a lot of wealth. Daddy owns oil wells all over the place. Daddy's also a *gonif*. He has successfully maneuvered the downfall of rival emirates. It seems daddy very much would like to rule the world or be a party to a worthwhile partnership. It doesn't say where to contact him. Maybe we'll ship the body care of American Express."

Marlene grimaced. "That's awful."

Said Villon, "We'll track down daddy. Wait a minute. Maybe we won't have to bother. Di Frasso and Brunhilde should know where to get hold of him. He's had affairs with both of them." He began whistling nothing recognizable as he continued reading. Finally he said, "Nothing new on Tensha except he's a good buddy of Souvir's daddy and they're in business together on a couple of ventures."

"Such as?" asked Marlene.

"Brothels all over the world and Arab slave trading. Christ, does slave trading still exist? I guess it does with the Arabs."

"What about the Ivanovs?" asked Marlene.

"More or less what we got from Mai Mai. Gregory is very thick with Stalin. Natalia was once Stalin's lover. Apparently he rewarded Gregory with Natalia for services rendered. Some girls have all the luck." Suddenly his eyebrows shot up. "Now how about Monte Trevor!"

Marlene was lighting a new cigarette. "Something juicy, I hope."

"Juicy but unproven. It's suspected he engineered the murder of Ivar Krueger."

"The infamous match king?"

"The one and only and never to be forgotten. The suspicion remains unproven, but it seems the match king financed a couple of films for Trevor, who fiddled with the budgets, and most of the money apparently ended up in his pockets and not on the screen."

"A lot of that goes on in pictures," advised Marlene. "What about Dong See?"

"Interesting. Our Dong See, as Mai Mai wrote, is the true Dong See's cousin. Their fathers were brothers. The families lived together. The boys were inseparable until Dong See exhibited his musical talent and was whisked away to be a child prodigy. Our See is named Li Po See and became the protégé of a powerful warlord, another man who ruthlessly pillages and destroys anything in the way of his path to power." He screwed up his face. "What do you do with power? I mean how much power is enough power? You got a theory, Marlene?"

"A very simple one. Power is sought by megalomaniacs. Mussolini, Hitler, Stalin, Napoléon, Alexander, Rasputin, Louis B. Mayer. Sooner or later it destroys them."

Villon set the papers aside. Jim had placed the folders on Villon's desk. Villon stared at them and then looked up. "Now to get the machinery in operation for Anna May's date with Dong See."

"I still wish that was my scene," said Marlene. "I've more strength than Anna May. I could walk into a cage of lions without a whip or a gun."

"Marlene, I think you'll find that beneath Anna May's seemingly fragile exterior, there lies a core of solid steel."

"I hope you're right." She exhaled a smoke ring. "I assume Anna May's cousin will cooperate."

"She'll cooperate, Anna May told me, or she'll get a dispossess notice. You see what I mean by a core of solid steel?"

"Herb, was there a car crash? Was the real Dong See killed?"

"There was a car crash," said Villon. "The brakes were doctored. Dong See refused to be recruited by his cousin. He threatened exposure. The musician was wanted by the organization as an influence on his following and the many important people he knew that could have been of use to them. Dong See survived the crash. And he *was* in a Swiss clinic for six months. It left him shattered in both body and mind. He remembers very little except his music."

"What's become of him?"

Villon handed her a sheet of paper. Marlene read it. "Oh, how sweet. I hope he's happy." She said to Mallory. "He lives in a small village in Palestine near the Dead Sea. He gives violin lessons to yeshiva students."

At ten o'clock the next morning Marlene arrived at the chapel at Forest Lawn cemetery. She had engaged a nondenominational cleric to conduct the services, as there wasn't a clue to Lewis Tate's religion. Anna May decided not to attend but sent a floral wreath, which was prominently displayed near the closed coffin. Marlene was surprised and touched by the attendance, which almost filled the chapel. Marlene wouldn't learn until later that the majority of those present were curiosity seekers who made a profession of attending celebrity funerals. Several former silent greats had volunteered to speak on Tate's behalf. There was Herbert Rawlinson and Mae Marsh, and Bess Flowers spoke a touching eulogy. The background was prerecorded organ music. Marlene was soon lost in her own thoughts, thoughts of the police engineers wiring Anna May's living room and connecting the wires to those in her cousin's apartment. She knew the microphones would be well hidden and that the police technician in Lotus Blossom's apartment would carefully record the conversation between Anna May and the bogus Dong See.

Marlene had phoned Anna May the previous night and told her what the Interpol dispatches contained.

"So he's Li Po See. There was a very famous poet named Li Po, Marlene."

"Yes, I know. Don't trip yourself up and call him Li Po."

"It is Li Po who will trip himself up. Trust me."

"I do, my dear, I do. But I'll be a nervous wreck in your cousin's apartment."

"Don't let her drink too much gin. You'll know she's had enough when she suddenly gets down on one knee and sings 'Mammy.'"

Marlene was shaken from her reverie by the cleric's asking the gathering to join in prayer. Marlene prayed with sincerity. For Lewis Tate she wished a better world for him in the hereafter, and if there really was an afterlife, about which she had serious doubts, she hoped Lewis Tate would find a very good agent. For Anna May Wong she prayed for success and safety, and for herself, she prayed for a thorough rewrite of the script for *Blonde Venus*.

Raymond Souvir's autopsy was completed about the same time as Lewis Tate's coffin was lowered into his final resting place. The coroner was positive it was poison and so went through the motions by the numbers, stifling numerous yawns and anxious to get away to a lunch date in Brentwood.

Hearing that Souvir's body was claimed by Dong See, alias Li Po See, gave Herb Villon cause for speculation. The mortuary attendant who called for the body informed Jim Mallory it was to be cremated and the ashes sent to an emirate in the Near East. All day until it was time to take up his position with his men in Lotus Blossom's apartment, Villon entertained misgivings about the dangerous position Anna May would be in, and the misgivings were far from entertaining. The plan was to rendezvous in the cousin's apartment at six o'clock, one hour before Anna May expected Li Po. Marlene arrived promptly at six with several bottles of champagne. Lotus Blossom, who had been told Marlene would honor her humble abode, greeted her with subdued warmth and was more than glad to chill the champagne for the great star.

"Quite an impressive setup," complimented Marlene as she saw the recording apparatus ready to be manned by the engineer wearing a set of headphones.

"Let us now cross our fingers and pray," said Villon as he glanced at his wristwatch.

"Will we be able to hear what's going on upstairs?" asked Marlene.

"There's bound to be some bugs," explained the engineer. "There always is especially if they're moving around, but Anna May has created a seating arrangement in which the microphone is in a bowl of flowers on a coffee table set equidistant between them. We've tested it and it's working fine."

Marlene thought to herself, the best laid plans of mice and men often go astray. But this isn't mice and men. This is an actress and the police. It has to work. It has to.

"I hope it's dry enough," said Anna May, as Li Po See sipped the martini. She had poured herself a glass of white wine. Now they sat across from each other, the vase between them. Anna May wasn't surprised when he arrived and asked to be shown through her apartment. She knew he must be harboring suspicions and wanted to make sure he and Anna May were alone in the apartment. He told her he liked the decor and asked how long she'd been living there.

"I bought the house five years ago. It was in a terribly run-down condition so I got it very cheap. I've put a lot of money into it." She explained about her relatives and friends and Li Po sympathized. There was a plate of hors d'oeuvres on the table and she offered it to him but he refused. Downstairs, Marlene wondered how long the small talk would continue when suddenly she realized where Anna May was leading the man. Villon looked tense. Jim Mallory had a quizzical expression.

"I'm thinking of selling the house and moving to Europe. I'm not very happy in Hollywood anymore."

"I thought you were very successful."

"I was once, but not anymore. Most of the good parts I can play are given to Occidentals. Don't you realize the prejudice against minorities in this country? In this profession? Black actors are never given parts that have dignity. They're always maids or Pullman porters. Oriental actors are always villains, and the women are servants. I'm sorry, but you see, I'm in a desperate situation."

"Were you hoping I might offer a solution?"

"Perhaps. I've read the charts. I know what you're involved in. What Mai Mai calls 'The Devil's Syndicate.' " He said nothing. He waited. "Why she had to be eliminated. She foresaw her own murder."

He said softly, "She had a truly remarkable gift. Anna May, what are you after?"

"I want to be recruited. I want to join your movement. My name opens the doors of the high and the mighty and I'm fed up being treated like a coolie and scrabbling to make ends meet. I've sold most of the valuable pieces that decorated this room."

"Does Marlene Dietrich know how you feel?"

"Do you think I'm mad?"

"Where are the charts? Are they here?"

"They're back in Mai Mai's apartment." She smiled. "They proved to be useless."

"Useless? Are *you* mad?"

"No, I'm not mad, I'm desperate." There was a cunning smile on her face. "I gave Mr. Villon false translations. I made what Mai Mai wrote sound innocent. Oh, there were certain predictions that were innocent enough, but I did not tell him about the plot to destroy the world's economy. Those charts, in the wrong hands, could be very dangerous and very very incriminating."

"I want them. You must get them for me. I must have them. This man Villon is very clever."

Downstairs, Marlene silently applauded Villon. He didn't like what he was hearing. It wasn't what Anna May had outlined earlier. She was off on a different tack altogether. He suspected what was coming and he dreaded it. Although he didn't share his fears with Marlene, she could see in his face that he felt something was going wrong. *Anna May. Nothing must happen to Anna May.*

"You're very right. He is very clever. He knows who the murderer is."

"Really." His voice was hoarse.

"He lacks the proof but he says he will soon have it. There were fingerprints on the knife that killed Morton Duncan . . ."

"Bullshit!" shouted Li Po. "That hilt was wiped clean and . . ."

Downstairs, Villon said, "That's it!"

Marlene waved him quiet. Anna May was plunging ahead, treading where angels fear.

Anna May spoke softly. "So you killed Morton Duncan. And it was you who paid him to poison Mai Mai. Raymond Souvir could no longer be trusted, so you poisoned him."

Li Po's eyes reflected menace. "Sadly, Anna May, only you and I know this. I don't think I can trust you to keep quiet."

Quietly and unseen, Marlene slipped out of Lotus Blossom's apartment and hurried up the stairs to Anna May's.

"Of course, you can! You're going to help me. You need me."

"Anna May, you're a very good actress. There were no fingerprints on the hilt. Where are the police? On the roof?"

Marlene knocked on Anna May's door and shouted, "Anna May, it's Marlene. Let me in! I'm sorry I'm late."

Anna May picked up her cue. "You're always late." She was staring at the gun Li Po was holding. "What's that for?"

"Let her in."

Anna May persisted. "Why the gun? I don't like guns. Put it away."

Damn Dietrich, thought Villon. "We can't use the stairs. Miss Dietrich had to get into the act! The fire escape! Quick!"

As they hurried out of the room into the bedroom that led to the fire escape, they heard the familiar strains of the Al Jolson favorite. Lotus Blossom was on one knee serenading the recording engineer, "Maaaaaaammmmmmyyyyyyyy!"

In Anna May's living room, Li Po grabbed Anna May's arm and forced her to the door. "Open it," he commanded as he stepped back.

"Anna May, why don't you open the door?" pleaded Marlene.

The door opened. "What kept you?" Marlene remained in the doorway. Anna May faced her, shielding her. Li Po stood directly behind Anna May. Marlene did not see he had a gun aimed at Anna May's back. "Dong See, how good to see you again! Anna May, you look absolutely terrified, what's the matter?"

Anna May said, "You shouldn't be here, Marlene." Villon and Mallory entered stealthily through the window with guns drawn. In the street, the unmarked squad cars instructed to take up positions after Li Po entered the building were in place and waiting. In the apartment underneath, the recording engineer carefully wrapped the incriminating disc and placed it into a container while Lotus Blossom continued her serenade, enthusiastically but sadly off-key.

"Why shouldn't I be here?" asked Marlene. "You invited me for a drink."

Li Po moved swiftly. He grabbed Anna May around the waist, using her as a shield. He said to Villon and Mallory. "I suspected you'd be coming up the fire escape. You're very brave Miss Dietrich to set yourself up as a decoy, but I'm leaving here with Anna May and I don't think you want to be the cause of her death."

"Murder comes so easily to you," said Dietrich.

"I was trained by a master. Get out of the doorway."

Villon commanded, "Come inside, Marlene."

She entered slowly. She and the detectives were of the same mind. The recording engineer was hearing everything that was going on. He was a detective. He had a gun. Li Po was unaware of his existence. He had no idea Villon and Mallory had materialized from the apartment below. He had to assume they climbed up from the street. Marlene was their decoy. A very glamorous one. Marlene was at the table examining the hors d'ouevres.

"Anchovies. I adore anchovies." She popped an hors d'ouevre into her mouth. Villon and Mallory couldn't believe their eyes. The woman was amazing.

Li Po, with Anna May as his shield, backed out into the hallway. Marlene asked him as they went, "I don't know why you had to kill Raymond. He was a nice boy. Of course, we know you didn't like the way he drove."

Her hands flew to her face as she heard the pop of the engineer's service revolver. Li Po cried out and dropped the gun. Anna May moved away as he fell to his knees. Villon and Mallory moved swiftly. The engineer was a crack shot. He'd hit Li Po in the right shoulder.

Anna May said, "All right, Marlene. You can look now."

Marlene looked, was relieved at seeing Mallory handcuffing Li Po, and she and Anna May embraced. "Anna May, you fool!"

Villon said angrily, "Marlene, you fool."

Dietrich said, "Don't be ridiculous. I had to cause a diversion. I knew you'd come up the fire escape behind him. And besides . . ."—she opened her handbag and showed them a handgun—"I borrowed this from one of my bodyguards. And I'm one hell of a shot."

The backup detectives had arrived and two were leading Li Po away. He was cursing them all in a Chinese dialect. "What's he saying?" asked Marlene.

Anna May said wearily, "Marlene, better you shouldn't know."

An hour later, in a booth at the Brown Derby, Marlene asked Villon, "What will you do with the others?"

Anna May and Mallory waited for Villon to answer Marlene. "By me, you mean the police? We do nothing. My job was to catch a murderer, and thanks to you two babies I've made my pinch. As for the others, that's up to the Feds. I'll make some guesses. I'm no Mai Mai Chu, but here's what I predict. The Ivanovs will declare diplomatic immunity, Tensha will envelop himself in the protective cloak of his billions. . . ."

Marlene added, "Of course, Trevor will be permitted to flee to Mexico, where he will be punished with a severe attack of the *turista* and spend much of the time on a different kind of throne than the one he envisioned. Countess di Frasso will have an excellent lawyer who will get her cleared of the charges that she was an accessory to murder. Brunhilde will be deported and will try to sell the film rights to her story, and I'll probably be offered the chance to play Brunhilde, which I will decline with alacrity. And Li Po? I suppose he will be tried and convicted."

"He will die," said Anna May.

"I'll sing no sad songs for him," said Marlene.

"Li Po will never stand trial. *They* will have him killed. It's in his chart, and Mai Mai is rarely wrong."

Villon made a mental note to increase the security guarding Li Po.

"Mai Mai Chu." Marlene spoke the name reverently. "Now there's a part I'd love to play."

"You see," Anna May exploded. "She wants the part of Mai Mai Chu! *I* should play it, not you, Marlene, *I* should play it."

"Calm down, sweetheart. They'll never let me play character roles. They'll make me go on playing the one part I play the best." She raised her glass of champagne in a toast. "And that part is familiar to all of you. It's known as Marlene Dietrich."

She sipped and then winked an eye at Jim Mallory. He winked back and felt wonderful.